# HIVE MONKEY

# HIVE
# MONKEY

## GARETH L. POWELL

SOLARIS

First published 2014 by Solaris
an imprint of Rebellion Publishing Ltd,
Riverside House, Osney Mead,
Oxford, OX2 0ES, UK

*www.solarisbooks.com*

ISBN: 978 1 78108 166 2

10 9 8 7 6 5 4 3 2 1

A CIP catalogue record for this book is available from the
British Library.

Designed & typeset by Rebellion Publishing

Printed in the US

For Mum and Dad, with love.

IN SEPTEMBER 1956, France found herself facing economic difficulties at home and an escalating crisis in Suez. In desperation, the French Prime Minister came to London with an audacious proposition for Sir Anthony Eden: a political and economic union between the United Kingdom and France, with Her Majesty Queen Elizabeth II as the new head of the French state.

Although Eden greeted the idea with scepticism, a resounding Anglo-French victory against Egypt persuaded his successor to accept and, despite disapproving noises from both Washington and Moscow, Harold Macmillan and Charles de Gaulle eventually signed the Declaration of Union on 29th November 1959, thereby laying the foundations for a wider European commonwealth.

And now, one hundred years have passed...

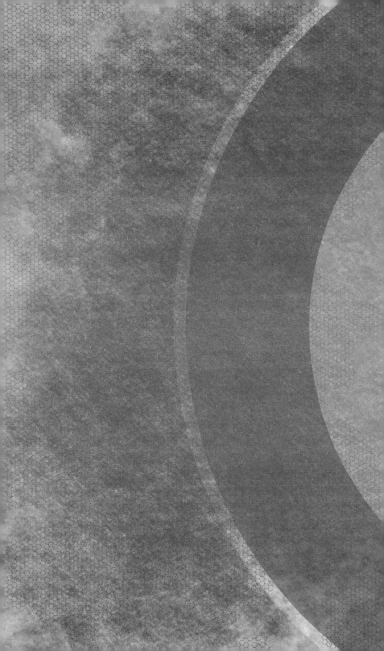

# PART ONE

## BOMBS AND BULLETS

We have met the enemy and he is us.

(Walt Kelly, *Pogo*)

# CHAPTER ONE
## DAZZLE CAMOUFLAGE

IT STARTED WITH a gunshot.

Wrapped in a woollen coat and scarf, his greying hair blown unkempt and wild, William Cole leant against the painted railings at the end of the harbour wall. He looked out over the Severn Estuary. High above the water, against a pale November sky, an airship forged upriver. From where he stood, he could hear the bass thrum of the fifteen nuclear-electric engines that powered its vast, five-hulled bulk, and see the low afternoon sunlight flash against the spinning blades of its impellers, turning them to coin-like discs of bronze.

Unusually, the skyliner's owners had chosen to paint the cigar-shaped hulls with jagged black and white lines. The lines looked unsightly, but William knew the patterns were designed to disguise the airship's exact shape and heading, hindering attacks from ground-based weapons. Allied warships used the same trick, known as 'dazzle camouflage', in World War Two, to confuse German U-boats. The crazy stripes hurt his tired eyes, but he could still read the airship's name, stencilled on its prow in blocky red letters: *Tereshkova*. Named after the cosmonaut, he supposed. Valentina Tereshkova had been the first woman in space, launched into the void two years after Gagarin's pioneering flight. Now though, almost a century later, and long after the collapse of the Soviet Union, how many people remembered her? Humans were still footling around in low Earth orbit, in tin can space stations. The glittering future she represented hadn't come to pass. Some promising early steps had been made, but now no one had been to the Moon in over eighty years. The dreams of the twentieth century were long dead, and space had become little more than a curiosity: a relic of the Cold War, an industrial park on the outskirts of global politics.

He ground his clenched hands into his coat pockets, shivering against the cold.

"Where are you going today, Valentina? And where have you been?" Skyliners like her hardly ever stopped moving, and they never touched down. They spent their lives aloft, being serviced by smaller, more agile craft. This one had probably just crossed the Atlantic from America, en route to London and Europe. Each of its five cigar-shaped hulls had one large gondola slung beneath it, and two or three smaller ones dotted along its length. Yellow lights burned in their windows and portholes. "And why the crazy paint job?"

William closed his eyes. Five years ago, at the age of thirty-nine, he'd crossed the Atlantic himself, on a similar vessel. He'd packed his laptop and manuscripts, and bought a one-way ticket to the European Commonwealth. He'd come to make his fortune as a writer, and marry the love of his life. Her name had been Marie, and she'd been a reviewer for

*The Guardian*. They first met at a book launch in Greenwich Village and dated for a while. It hadn't worked out, but a decade after they split up she came to New York for a conference. They had dinner together and got talking about old times. By that point, they were both divorced and single. She hadn't read any of his books, and he hadn't seen any of her columns; but somehow, buzzed on wine and, in her case, jetlag, they hit it off again. When she went back to England, he followed and, six months later, they were married, at a small registry office in Kensington, with a reception paid for by his publisher.

Ah, Marie.

Marie with the auburn hair and easy smile, snatched away so soon. Had she really been dead two years now? Had a whole *twenty-four months* really passed? He'd crossed an ocean for her, given up his life in America, his friends and family, his ex-wife, only to let her slip away from him, across another ocean, into that undiscovered country from whose bourn no traveller returns.

With his hands gripping the railings, he looked down to the tidal mud at the foot of the harbour wall. He hadn't slept in four days. Below him, the low tide had fallen back to reveal the rounded teeth of a collapsed jetty, its splintered planks protruding from the rippled mudflats like the fossilised remnants of some prehistoric lake village. Gulls bobbed on the sluggish swell; scraps of black seaweed lay strewn and tangled at the high water mark; and a late afternoon breeze ran a comb through the wiry grass. The pain of Marie's loss, so abrupt and unfair, had terrified him. He couldn't face up to it. Not knowing what else to do, and fearing he wasn't strong enough to bear the grief, he'd taken all his hurt and packed it down inside, where he thought it couldn't harm him. He couldn't cope with it, so he buried it. He put it off. Over the following months, he wrapped his grief in protective layers of drug and alcohol abuse. Now, when he tried to remember her, he had difficulty picturing her face with any clarity, or remembering her smell, or the sound of her voice. He'd tried so hard to block out the pain that now he could hardly recall anything about her, and his attempts to spare himself the weight of her loss had only brought him closer to losing her.

The wind blew through him, leaving him empty. For a long time, he simply stood and stared at the water.

Then his SincPhone rang. On the fourth ring, he answered it.

"Hello?"

"Will, it's Max. How are you doing? I'm not interrupting anything, am I?"

"Not really."

William looked back to the black and white airship, and the rippling reflection it cast over the muddy waters of the Severn. He felt set adrift, alone, and left behind. Now Marie was dead, there was nothing permanent in his life. Perhaps, if she'd lived, they might have had a family, maybe put down roots somewhere; but no. Home for him had been a succession of rented rooms, usually above shops of one sort or another; the walls an endless parade of peeling, painted magnolia; the utilitarian furniture pocked with the dents of a thousand small impacts, and pitted with the tiny smallpox circles of ancient cigarette burns.

"Great. Because we need to talk."

William moved the phone from one ear to the other. Max was just about the last person he wanted to hear from.

"This is about the Mendelblatt book, isn't it?" Lincoln Mendelblatt, the Jewish private eye, had been the hero of three of his previous novels.

"I've had Stella on the phone again this afternoon," Max said. "She's very unhappy. You're almost a month overdue."

William groaned inwardly. "Tell her it's coming."

"I did, and I think she bought it, for now. But listen, Will, I need those pages. And I need them, like, yesterday."

A pair of gulls scuffled on the mud, their cries sharp and desolate.

"It's nearly finished," William lied. "I'm on the last chapter."

"Really? You're that close?"

"Sure. Look, it's Friday afternoon. Give me the weekend, and I'll get something over to you by the beginning of next week. Maybe Wednesday."

"You promise?"

"I promise."

There was a silence on the other end. Then, "You sound terrible, Will. Are you using again?"

The sun went behind a cloud.

"No." William sniffed and wiped his nose on the back of his hand. It was a nervous reflex. "Not at all. Not for ages. I'm just a bit groggy today. A cold, that's all."

He heard Max sigh. "Just make sure that first draft hits my inbox by Wednesday morning, or we're going to have words, you understand? Harsh words. You're in the last chance saloon, buddy, and it's high time to shit, or get off the—"

William opened his hand, and let the phone fall. It tumbled end-over-end and hit the water. A small splash, some ripples, and it was gone.

"Goodbye, Max." *Whisper your clichés to the drowned sailors and scuttling crabs at the bottom of the sea.*

William turned up the collar of his coat. The wool felt scratchy against his beard. Hands in pockets, he walked back, past the lock gates, and along the apartment-lined edge of the marina, heading home to where his laptop waited, the cursor blinking hopelessly on the first blank white page of his unwritten book.

Portishead was a coastal dormitory town in South West England, twenty minutes drive from the city of Bristol. It had a high street, shops, and a drive-through McDonald's. The town's marina had once been an industrial dockyard serving a coal-fired power station. Now, only the stone quay remained. The rest had been transformed in the early decades of the century. The bustling railway sidings had given way to cafés and a leisure centre, the cranes to waterfront apartments and a primary school. The dock itself had been retrofitted as a marina and, instead of the rusty cargo ships of old, now housed a flotilla of private yachts and pleasure boats. The rigging on their masts rattled in the wind; little turbine blades spun on their cabin roofs; and Union Jacks and French Tricolours flapped from their sterns.

William walked to the end of the quayside and out onto the road. Yellow leaves swirled from the trees and skittered around his feet. His latest apartment, which felt dank, lifeless and suffocating even on the sunniest of days, lay on the other side of the road, in a block overlooking a supermarket car park. In the summer, with the windows open, all he could hear was the rattle and crash of shopping trolleys and the slam of car doors.

Standing at the kerb, trying to summon the energy to cross the road and climb the stairs, he saw one of his neighbours emerge from the building. She was on her way to work, car keys in one hand and briefcase in the other, a triangle of toast clamped between her teeth. He didn't know her name, but gathered she was a nurse, working shifts at one of the local hospitals. They'd passed in the corridor a couple of times, but only ever exchanged superficial pleasantries.

*Maybe I should go into town,* he thought. *I could call in on Sparky, and pick up a couple of wraps to see me through the weekend.* Sparky was his dealer, and William had been buying cheap amphetamines, or 'cooking speed', from him for over a year now. For a moment he wondered if a few hits of the powder would get him going, fire up the old synapses and get the words crackling out onto the page.

He slipped a hand into his trouser pocket and pulled out his door key.

*No,* he told himself. *Sparky's the last person you need to be around. You've spent the last four days wired out of your damn mind, and you've produced nothing, not one word. The sooner you straighten up*

*and start writing, the sooner you'll have something
to give to Max. And if you don't get started soon,
you'll have to pay back the advance. And you can't,
because you've spent it already. You've frittered it
away on takeaways and whiskey, and drugs and
cigarettes.*

His neighbour crossed the street, and smiled
around the toast as she passed him. The sun emerged
again, and he blinked up at it, shading his sleep-
deprived eyes from its golden light.


AND THAT'S WHEN the first shot rang out.

He heard a noise like a car backfiring, and
something smacked into the wall of the leisure centre.
At first, he didn't know what had happened—a
spark of metal on brick, a puff of dust. Stupidly, he
thought somebody had thrown a stone. Then he saw
the car parked against the opposite kerb. The driver's
window was down, and an inhuman face snarled at
him from beneath a white fedora. He saw an ape-
like creature with a wide mouth and a bulbous
nose, and a gun held in its fist. Half man and half
beast, it looked like some sort of caveman, and he
frowned at it, sure his eyes deceived him. Then the
gun barrel puffed, and a bullet whined past his face.
Instinctively, he cowered back, covering his chest and
stomach with his hands. His body felt huge, exposed
and vulnerable. He turned his shoulder away from
the car. Every muscle cringed in anticipation, braced
for the impact of the next shot.

But the next shot never came. Instead, the car
exploded.

For an instant, William's world turned to light and noise. He felt the heat of the blast on his hands and face. His ears popped as he was thrown off his feet.

He hit the ground hard enough to drive all the breath from his body, and lay gasping, looking up at the trees. Leaves whirled down around him like snow. Car alarms shrilled. The air stank of the napalm tang of burning petrol. Across the street, the force of the explosion had shattered all the windows on the front of the apartment block. Pedestrians shouted and screamed. The girl with the briefcase crouched next to him. Her hair was a mess, and her jacket was ripped. She had a gash across one cheek like a ragged fingernail scratch. She asked him something, but he couldn't hear what she said. His ears were still recovering.

"Are you okay?" she repeated.

He swallowed. His throat and mouth were dry. "I don't know." His hands and face stung where shrapnel had nicked and scratched them. He eased an inch-long splinter of glass from the back of his hand, and let it fall onto the pavement.

"That man in the car." She spoke fast, gabbling with shock. "He had a gun. He was shooting at you."

William closed his eyes.

"Yes."

"But why? Why was he doing that?"

He tried to move, and winced at the pain in his back. He'd played football in high school, back in Ohio, and knew what it felt like to be flattened by a quarterback twice his size.

"I don't know. Is he—?"

She glanced at the tangled wreck.

"How did you do that?"

"Do what?"

"How did you make his car blow up like that?"

"Me?" William felt the world roll giddily around his head. His brain hadn't caught up yet, hadn't fully processed what had happened. He elbowed himself up into a sitting position. "I didn't do anything. How could I?"

The girl turned wide eyes to the black, greasy smoke belching up from the car's gutted shell.

"Well, *somebody* certainly did."

"It wasn't me."

Something popped in the wreckage, and they both flinched.

"Come on," his neighbour said. "I think we'd better move."

# CHAPTER TWO
## CITY LIGHTS

"WHO ARE YOU calling foul-mouthed, you twat?"

The tabloid journalist took a step back, brandishing his press ID like a shield. They were in the *Tereshkova*'s main passenger lounge, aft of the airship's bridge.

"N-not me," he stammered. "*I* know what you're like."

Ack-Ack Macaque's leather flight jacket creaked as he pushed up from his barstool.

"Then what are you saying?" The monkey rubbed the patch covering the socket that had once housed his left eye. He'd done a handful of interviews over the past twelve months, and hadn't enjoyed any of them. And now here was this clown, bothering him when he was trying to enjoy a quiet cigar.

"You're a national hero in the Commonwealth," the man said. The name 'Nick Dean' was printed beneath his photo. "But some parts of the British Press have criticised you as a poor role model for children."

Ack-Ack Macaque stood up straight. "Fuck them." He slapped the counter. "I stopped a nuclear war, what more do they want?"

Dean pocketed his card. A tiny camera drone hovered above his right shoulder like a tame dragonfly. "They say you drink, swear and smoke too much, and you play with guns."

"I don't play with guns."

"Yes, you do. You're fiddling with one right now."

Ack-Ack Macaque snatched his fingers away from his holster, and coughed.

"What can I say? When you've got a massive pair of Colts strapped to your hips, every problem coming your way looks like something that needs the shit shooting out of it."

"And that's why you were thrown out of the Plaza Hotel in New York, wasn't it?"

He bristled. "I wasn't thrown out. They simply asked me to leave."

"The neighbours complained about the smell. And the ricochets."

Ack-Ack Macaque grinned, exposing his yellow canines. "Hey, that wasn't my fault. The clock radio startled me."

"And so you blew it to bits?"

"When I left, they were still picking bits of plastic from the walls and ceiling."

Dean leant forward. "The *New York Times* said that if Nobel Prizes were given out for smoking cigars and wrecking stuff, you'd be top of the list."

"I suppose." Ack-Ack Macaque looked around the lounge. They were alone apart from the barman and a guy in a white suit. "Now, how about you fuck off and leave me in peace?"

Ignoring him, Dean pulled out an electronic notepad and moved his finger down to the next question on his list.

"We're currently approaching an airfield on the outskirts of Bristol," he read aloud. "This is the first time you've returned to the UK since last winter, when you helped overthrow the previous political regime. What have you being doing with yourself since then?"

Ack-Ack Macaque tapped his knuckles against the bar. "Lying on tropical beaches," he muttered. "Drinking cocktails, and taking pot shots at jet skis."

Dean frowned at him. He wanted a proper interview. "What have you *really* been doing?"

Ack-Ack Macaque took a deep breath, and made an effort not to plant a fist in the guy's stupid face. *May as well get this over with,* he thought. *Then maybe the bastards will leave me alone.*

"Well," he said, trying to force some enthusiasm into his tone, "I've been working as a pilot."

"Here on the *Tereshkova*?"

"Yes, here on the *Tereshkova*. We've been all over the North Atlantic. Middle America and the Caribbean; the East Coast of the United States; Newfoundland, and the North Polar Ocean."

Dean's finger tapped the notebook's screen. "The events of last year thrust you into the limelight. You went from being a cult figure in a computer game to being a real life celebrity. Everybody wanted to interview you. There was even talk of a TV series. Why'd you turn your back on all of that?"

"I'm not cut out for fame."

"You'd rather be a humble pilot?"

Ack-Ack Macaque caught hold of his tail and began grooming it, picking bits of fluff and lint from the hairs at the end. At a table across the room, the guy in the white suit sipped his coffee and pretended not to listen.

"For now. While I figure out what I'm going to do with my life."

"Any ideas?"

"None so far." He stopped cleaning his tail. "Moving from the game world to the real one takes some adjustment, you know." Learning that he'd been raised to sentience in order to play the central figure in a computer game had been something of a shock, especially when he found himself pulled from the make-believe online world and thrust head-first into a plot to assassinate the King of England. "And it doesn't help that I'm the only one of my kind."

"There were others like you, at the lab?"

"There was one." He scowled down at his fingernails, remembering a desperate scuffle on the deck of a flying aircraft carrier, and the obscene feel of his knife cutting into another monkey's throat. "Look," he said, "can we talk about something else? It's Friday night. I should be out drinking and puking."

Dean ran his finger down the list. "Okay, just a few more questions. You started life as a normal macaque. Then Céleste Technologies filled your head with gelware processors and upgraded you to self-awareness."

"I thought we were supposed to be changing the subject?"

"I'm getting there, okay? As my readers will know, they had you plugged into an online WWII role-playing game, didn't they?"

Ack-Ack felt his lips peel back. As the main character in the game, he'd been practically invincible. But he hadn't known that, and he hadn't known it was a game. As far as he'd been concerned, every day had been a fight for survival.

Since the events of last year, and the collapse of the *Ack-Ack Macaque* MMORPG, when he went from being one of the world's most iconic video game characters to its most famous living, breathing monkey, several new games had arisen to fill the niche left by its demise. *Captain Capuchin; Marmoset Madness; Heavy Metal Howler*—according to K8, none of them were as realistic or convincing as his game had been, because their main characters were animated using standard computer simulated AI, instead of the artificially-uplifted brains of actual flesh and blood animals. In fact, the whole uplifting process had been made illegal. There were no other walking, talking animals left in the world; he was the only one, and now always would be.

"I don't want to talk about this." He pulled out a cigar, bit the tip off, and lit up. Dean sighed.

"You're not making this easy," he said.

Ack-Ack Macaque shrugged. Smoke curled between his teeth.

"Hey, it's not my fault. This is my evening off, my chance to pull a Bueller. Spend all night drinking rum in the bath, that sort of thing. I didn't ask to be pestered."

Dean rolled his eyes. The camera drone hung in the air, a few centimetres from his ear. Its tiny fans made a gentle hissing noise.

"Don't you want to tell your story?"

Ack-Ack Macaque huffed again. He pinched the cigar between his forefinger and thumb, and puffed a smoke ring at the ceiling.

"No. Now, I've asked you to fuck off once." He fixed the man with his one good eye. "Do I have to ask you again?"

Dean picked up his notebook and pushed it into the pocket of his coat. The tips of his ears were bright scarlet.

"There's a story here, and one way or another, I'm not leaving until I get it."

Ack-Ack Macaque blew a second, smaller smoke ring.

"Suit yourself." His hand snaked out and plucked the camera drone from the air. In one fluid movement, he brought it slamming down against the edge of the bar. Its plastic casing shattered, and the little fan motors died.

"Hey!" Dean took a step forward. "Do you know how much those things cost?"

Ack-Ack Macaque grabbed him by the lapels and pulled him close enough that their faces almost touched.

"Do I look as if I give a shit?"

Dean flinched as spittle sprayed his face. He swallowed, and turned away from the smell of the cigar.

"You idiot," he said. "You stupid, bloody idiot."

Ack-Ack Macaque released him, and turned for the door.

Behind him, Dean said, "You'll be hearing from my solicitor. That's assault, matey. Assault and criminal damage." His voice rose, buoyed up by righteous fury. "You'll pay for this. I'll crucify you in print, you just see if I don't."

Ack-Ack Macaque closed his eye.

"Get lost," he said, voice low and dangerous.

Dean ignored him.

"I've got witnesses, haven't I?" He pointed to the guy in the white suit. "You just wait until you see tomorrow's headlines, pal. You just wait."

For a second, Ack-Ack Macaque considered turning around and punching the guy's Adam's apple out through the back of his neck. He imagined the crunch of knuckles hitting larynx, and ground his teeth. So tempting...

In the end, though, he had to content himself with walking away. He couldn't assault passengers, however annoying they might be. He couldn't even hurl his own shit at them. He'd had that drummed into him time and time again, and was in no mood for another lecture. Instead, he stepped out into the corridor and let the door swing shut behind him.

Fists clenched and cigar clamped in his teeth, he stalked to the dining room, where he found the evening buffet still in full swing, and the airship's owner drinking her first Martini of the night.

Victoria Valois had left her blonde wig in her cabin. Some days, she just didn't care what she looked like. Looking at her now, the smooth lines of her bald scalp were misshapen by a thick ridge of scar tissue bulging from her right temple, into which had been inlaid various input jacks, USB ports, and infrared sensors. The victim of a severe head trauma a few years back, half her brain had been replaced with experimental gelware processors, making her as much of an artificial creature as he was.

"Hey, boss." His voice was gruff. "How are we doing?"

She looked up from her glass. Her eyes were the same pale colour as the dawn sky. She wore a black t-shirt and blue jeans, and had a white military dress tunic draped over her shoulders. Her fighting stick lay on the table before her: a twelve-inch cylinder of metal that would, at a shake, spring out to almost six feet in length.

"We're about ten minutes from the airport, still running on autopilot." She picked the cocktail stick from the glass, and waved an impaled olive in his direction. "Do you want to bring us in, or are you still on leave?"

The tunic she wore came from the wardrobe of the *Tereshkova*'s former owner, the Commodore. An eccentric Russian millionaire with a proud military history, the Commodore had been killed in action while boarding the royal yacht during last November's shenanigans, and had bequeathed his elderly skyliner to Victoria, his goddaughter and only living relative.

"I might as well." Ack-Ack Macaque scowled around his cigar. "The evening's pretty much ruined now, anyway."

"How so?"

"That journalist who came on board in New York."

"Has he been pestering you?"

"Yeah."

"Have you hurt him?"

Ack-Ack Macaque shook his head. "He's fine. I just told him to sling his hook."

Victoria raised an eyebrow.

"Is that all?"

"Well, I may have squashed his bug."

She rolled her eyes.

"How commendably restrained of you." She dropped the cocktail stick back into her glass.

Ack-Ack Macaque grinned.

"Well," he said, "I'd better get to work." He threw her a floppy-armed salute and loped through the lounge, pausing only to snake an unguarded cheese and pickle sandwich from the buffet.

By the time he reached the bridge at the front of the gondola, brushing crumbs from the hairs on his chin and chest, the landing field had come into sight. Not that they would be landing, of course. Through the curved glass windscreen that comprised the entire front wall of the gondola, he could see helicopters and smaller blimps awaiting their arrival, ready to lift cargo and passengers to the helipads fixed onto the upper surfaces of the *Tereshkova*'s five hull sections.

He reached the pilot's station and settled himself behind the instrument console, in the familiar scuffed and worn leather chair. The controls of the *Tereshkova*, like those of all modern aircraft, were computerised. There was no joystick like there had been in his Spitfire, and no old-fashioned nautical steering wheel like there had been in the early Zeppelins— only a glass SincPad screen that displayed an array of virtual instruments and readouts. He could adjust the craft's heading and pitch by running his leathery fingertips over illuminated symbols, and control the vessel's speed and height using animated slide bars. It looked deceptively simple—so simple, in fact, that a child could grasp it—but he knew from experience that there was a lot more to piloting something this large. It wasn't as easy as it looked. For a start, the big, old airship would only turn sluggishly, and you had to finely balance the thrust to compensate for crosswinds and turbulence. If you wanted to bring it to a dead stop, you had to start slowing five miles in advance. Right now, as they approached the airfield's perimeter, they were crawling forward at walking pace. Each of the airship's engine nacelles could be controlled individually. Some were providing forward momentum, others reverse thrust, while the rest were pushing edge-on to the prevailing south-westerly, holding the big craft steady against the wind.

Looking forward through the big, curved windshield, Ack-Ack Macaque saw the city lights of Bristol laid out beyond the runways and hangars like sequins on a black cushion: the white and red streams of cars and buses; the twisted spider's webs of orange streetlamps; and the harsh daylight glow of a stadium's floods. The sight filled him with excitement. Nick Dean could go hang. Somewhere down there would be music and drinking, in a place with low lights and shadowy booths, where he could get comfortably shitfaced without attracting a large crowd. After a seventy-two hour crossing from New York, he intended to party: to get drunk with strangers, and see where the night took him.

Not that it would be enough, of course. It was never enough. Whatever he did, he couldn't scratch the itch that niggled him. He couldn't find anything to match the heady excitement of life in the game world, with the heightened reality of its constant action, and everything painted for him in the simple brushstrokes of a childhood summer's afternoon. The memory of it haunted him like an addiction, and sometimes it was all he could do to blot it out with drink.

He sighed.

Later, he'd take the new Spitfire out for a few hours, he decided. Nothing blew away the cobwebs of a hard night like the high, thin clarity of the dawn. For him, flying was the only thing in this world even close to the exhilaration of the game.

The Spit was an original, one of a number built during the Second World War, but then packed in crates as the War drew to a close, and buried by British forces in Burma. Since their excavation in the early 2020s, more than thirty had been reassembled and refurbished. His had been one of the first out of the ground, and had been lovingly restored to full flightworthiness. Victoria had bought it for him as a present. It was her way of saying thank you and, since inheriting the Commodore's billions, she could easily afford it.

Currently, he had the Spit housed in a hangar at the stern of the *Tereshkova*'s outermost starboard hull, along with the airship's complement of passenger helicopters. A four-hundred-metre-long runway ran diagonally across the top of the five hulls, to the opposite edge of the airship. It was just long enough for him to take off and land, providing the wind was blowing in the right direction and the *Tereshkova* wasn't moving too quickly.

Yes, a flight would be good. He'd enjoy getting up into the clouds: just him at the controls of the Spit, just the way it had been in the seemingly endless virtual summer of 1944, when all he'd had to worry about was the next dogfight.

Simian fingers tapping on the glass control screens, he brought the old airship into position above the airport's main apron, and eased back on the forward thrust, slowing it to a halt so that its shadow hung over the waiting choppers, blotting out half the sky like the footprint of an alien mothership. He puffed on his cigar, and rubbed his hands together. The city lay before him like an untended buffet table, ripe for plundering, and alive with tantalising possibilities.

Oh yes, tonight was going to be a good night. He could feel it in his bones.

# CHAPTER THREE
## BETTER ANGELS

"PLEASE, CAPTAIN." THE American threw his arms wide. "I'm desperate."

Victoria Valois considered him. Lack of sleep had left his eyes rheumy and red; the pores on his nose were enlarged; and his hair and beard were uncombed and wild, as if he'd dragged himself backwards through a hedge—an impression reinforced by the myriad nicks and scratches on his cheeks and forehead.

"I don't doubt it."

His name was William Cole. Apparently, he'd come aboard with the first of the passengers, and had immediately asked to see her, to request sanctuary. They were in her cabin now, behind the *Tereshkova*'s bridge, and she was sitting at her desk, in front of the large picture window that comprised most of the back wall. The office, like the skyliner itself, had once belonged to the Commodore, and there were still traces of him everywhere. She had hardly changed a thing. The books on the bookshelves were his, as was the ancient Persian rug covering the steel deck, and the cutlass sticking at an angle from the tasteless old elephant-foot umbrella stand.

She sat back.

"Pourquoi?"

"Because somebody's trying to kill me."

Victoria made a steeple of her fingers. "So you said, but why have you come here? Why have you come to me?"

Cole leant forward. Beneath the scratches, his face looked puffy and soft. She had him pegged for an alcoholic, or maybe a junkie.

"Firstly, because you're the only skyliner in town right now." He counted off the reasons on his fingers. "And secondly, because you've got a reputation for pretty tight security. Nobody can get on board without being scanned for weapons."

Victoria picked up one of the fountain pens that lay on the desk jotter. The brain surgery she'd undergone had left her unable to read or write, and so the pen was useless to her; but she still liked to fiddle with it while she talked, like an ex-smoker sucking on a plastic straw. "Who are you, Mister Cole?"

"I'm a writer."

"Oh?" She raised an eyebrow. "What sort of a writer?" She herself had been a journalist, back before the head wound that left her incapable of parsing written text.

Cole looked down at his hands. "I'm a novelist."

Victoria frowned.

"Who'd want to kill a novelist?" She drummed the end of the pen against the blotter. "Aside from another novelist, I mean. What sort of stuff do you write?"

"Science fiction."

"Ah, I see." She sat back in her chair. "Well, of course, I don't really read that stuff myself." She rubbed her nose with a forefinger. "But my husband does."

"Your husband?" It was Cole's turn to frown. "Forgive me, ma'am, but on the flight up here, I checked your public profile. It said your husband was dead."

Victoria narrowed her eyes. Even after a year of unwanted fame, she couldn't get used to the idea that strangers could be familiar with details of her personal life.

"Yes, he is." She put the pen on the desk. "But he still has his uses." She raised her gaze to the security camera above the door. "Paul? I assume you're listening?"

"Oh, yes." The voice came from an intercom speaker bolted to the metal ceiling. Paul had been murdered a year ago, for his unwitting part in the conspiracy to bring about Armageddon; but Victoria had managed to rescue a back-up copy of his personality. At first, she'd stored it in her own head, running it on the neural gelware prosthesis that filled half her skull; but that hadn't been a very satisfactory arrangement for either of them. She needed her privacy, and he needed something to occupy him. And so, a couple of months ago, with K8's help, she had uploaded his electronic essence to the *Tereshkova*'s main processors, where there was enough computing power to sustain him almost indefinitely. The process had been difficult and risky. They couldn't turn him off without resetting him to his initial state, which would have meant losing all the memories he'd accumulated since being reactivated. So they'd been forced to set up a seamless fibre optic link between Victoria's cranial processors and the computers in the *Tereshkova*, and then transfer him along it. Back-ups were notoriously delicate, prone to falling apart at the slightest disruption, but somehow they'd done it. He had the chance to survive a little longer. And their relationship, which had once been torrid, then awkward, seemed now to have settled into a deep, caring friendship. The love was still there. Love, for them, had never been a problem. They'd stayed close all through their disastrous marriage and subsequent separation; it was only his sexuality that drove them apart. He'd stopped finding her desirable, and it had broken both their hearts.

Now, a thirty-centimetre-tall image of him shimmered into existence before her, projected from a hologram generator built into the surface of the desk. He appeared to be in his late twenties, with spiky, peroxide blonde hair, and a blue and turquoise Hawaiian shirt worn over combat trousers. He'd been dead for a year, and they'd never been closer. Freed from the needs and desires of the flesh, he'd simply stopped caring about sex. That side of things had ceased to matter. What counted now, for both of them, was that the love remained. And love was what it was all about. They were both lonely, damaged creatures, but together, they had found some measure of companionship and contentment.

Her eyes flicked to a piece of paper stuck to the wall beside the desk. Paul had found a quote from an old short story, and printed it out for her. It said: '*Throughout history, love served a serious evolutionary purpose. It compelled us to look after those around us, and to allow them to look after us. This was the root of community, and the groups which survived and prospered were those with the most love.'* And that, for her, more or less summed it up.

She bent her face down to Paul's level and poked a thumb in Cole's direction.

"Have you ever heard of this guy?"

Paul's sprite turned to face the man in the chair. His fingers scratched at the pale stubble on his chin.

"William Cole? Hell, *yes*." He held his hands out. "Mister Cole, it's an honour to meet you. I've read all your Mendelblatt books."

Cole raised an eyebrow. The hologram couldn't really see him. His attentiveness was a carefully constructed illusion. Paul's actual 'eyes' were the security cameras set into the corners of the office ceiling.

"All *three* of them?"

"Absolutely. Jesus." The little figure rubbed his forehead with the back of his hand. He shuffled his trainers. "*Better Angels* is one of my top ten favourite books of all time. Seriously, I must have read it a dozen times over, at least."

Victoria flicked a finger through the projected image to get his attention. "Can you think of any reason why anybody would want to kill him?"

Paul put a hand to his garishly attired chest, fingers splayed. "Absolutely not. The man's a genius." He gave Cole a shy glance. "Like Dick, Ballard and Chandler, all rolled into one. Really, I mean. Wow."

Victoria sighed. "Please excuse my husband's nerdgasm, Mister Cole. What you have to understand is that, however free and bohemian we may seem to you, the truth of the matter is that, on a skyliner, everything is determined by weight and cost. We can only afford to feed so many mouths, and we only have room for a fixed number of passengers, and a fixed number of crew. If I were to grant you sanctuary aboard this vessel, you would either have to pay your way, or work your passage."

The American wiped his lower lip on the back of his hand. "I understand."

"Well, which is it to be?"

Cole patted his trouser pockets. "Being temporarily devoid of funds, I will have to opt for the latter." He smiled ruefully. "Tell me what I can do."

Victoria shook her head. It didn't work like that. "No, *you* tell *me* what you can do, and then *I'll* decide how best to use you."

Cole spread his hands. "I don't have a lot of skills. Beyond writing, obviously."

"Can you cook?"

"A little."

Victoria picked up the pen and tapped it against the edge of her desk. "The chef needs a new helper. The last one jumped ship earlier tonight. He got a better offer, apparently. Can you scrub pans and wash dishes?"

"If that's what it takes."

"That is exactly what it takes, Mister Cole." She rose, and extended her hand. "Welcome aboard. If you wait in the passenger lounge, I'll have one of my stewards show you to your quarters." They shook, and the author turned to leave. As he opened the door, she spoke again. "Oh, and Mister Cole?"

"Yes?"

"If it turns out you've done anything despicable to warrant this murder attempt, I'll throw you off this ship myself. Do I make myself clear?"

"Perfectly clear, Captain. And thanks."

TEN MINUTES LATER, William Cole found himself alone in a narrow cabin in the central gondola. In contrast to the passenger cabins, which were comparatively spacious, the crew cabins were narrow and utilitarian, with barely enough room to stand beside the bunk bed that took up the majority of the available space. There was no window, and nowhere to sit. The room smelled of garlic, farts and old cologne. Moving carefully in the confined space, William changed into a pair of pyjama trousers and an old t-shirt. The covers on the top bunk were mussed and grubby, so he climbed into the unused lower bed and closed his eyes.

He could hear his pulse thumping in his ears. The three hours since the explosion had been a frantic rout. Still groggy from the blast, he hadn't bothered waiting for the police to arrive. Instead, he was up and moving as soon as he felt able to stand. During last year's nuclear standoff with China, he'd developed an emergency plan in case the missiles flew, and now, he was following it. He wasn't going to hang around and wait for a second gunman to come looking for him.

Shaking off the protests of his neighbour, he crossed the road, taking care to give the burning car a wide berth, and picked his way into his apartment. The bomb blast had strewn fragments of glass across the front room, and they crunched beneath his shoes as he gathered up his passport and bank cards and stuffed them into his pockets. His hands were shaking. This wasn't drug paranoia: somebody really *was* trying to kill him.

He had a rucksack ready packed, containing everything he needed, from first aid supplies to powdered food and iodine tablets. It was his 'bug-out' bag, and it was stashed beneath his bed, where he could find it in the dark. All through the international crisis, he'd felt better knowing it was there. He knelt down and pulled it out by its canvas straps. He grabbed the electronic notebook containing the handwritten first chapters of the book he was working on, stuck it in a side pocket, and added a couple of spare batteries. Then he was out of the door and clattering down the concrete steps to the block's basement garage. He owned an old Renault with ninety-four thousand miles on the clock. It took him as far as the skyliner passenger terminal at Filton, where he abandoned it in the long-stay car park without a backward glance.

This was his plan: get airborne, and ride out the crisis. If somebody wanted him dead, he wasn't going to stick around long enough for them to take another pop. Better to get airborne and keep moving while he figured out his next move.

The gunman—if indeed the ape-like thing in the car had been a man—had been killed, but that didn't mean the danger had passed. The creature had been a pawn, and his death simply a way to protect the person, or persons, that had hired him. William knew enough to understand that the first rule of covering up an assassination was to kill the assassin. It had just been luck that the bomb had blown prematurely. Once whoever was behind the attack discovered their man had failed, they'd send somebody else, sure as eggs were eggs. The only thing that puzzled him was who 'they' might be. As far as he knew, he had no enemies. An obsessive fan would have acted alone and, as far as he knew, he hadn't said or written anything to anger extremist groups of any persuasion. He simply didn't have that many readers.

*After all,* he thought as he lay on the bunk in the *Tereshkova*'s cabin, *who pays attention to science fiction writers, anyway? We're the motley fools of literature. We caper and dance on the page, and nobody takes us seriously—certainly not seriously enough to send assassins.*

The mattress felt firm beneath him, and the sheets had the reassuring hotel roughness of cotton that had been washed and boiled a thousand times. Four days of amphetamine-charged wakefulness pressed down on his eyes; they felt like two peeled onions stuffed into the crevices of his face. He needed to sleep, to recharge his mental and physical batteries, yet he felt his heart jump at every unfamiliar creak and bang. The *Tereshkova* had her own soundtrack: a constant accompaniment made up of the hum of the engines and the purr of the air-conditioning units; the buffeting of the wind; the clank and gurgle of the water pipes; and the knock and slam of cabin doors up and down the corridor. He could even hear snatches of dance music from the passenger lounge.

He kicked off his shoes and turned on his side. Fleeing here had been instinct: simple self-preservation. Now, he had to work out his next move. According to her schedule, the *Tereshkova* was bound for Mumbai, by way of Paris, Prague, Istanbul, Cairo, and Dubai. If he kept his head down and his nose clean, he could ride her all the way to India, and after that, who knew? Perhaps he'd find passage to Hong Kong and Tokyo, and then across the Pacific to San Francisco, and the whole North American continent.

Or, he realised, he could alight at any one of those stops, and claim sanctuary on another skyliner, headed somewhere else. With a bit of planning and forethought, he could switch from one ship to another, criss-crossing the globe until his trail became too tangled to trace. He had his passport, and he had his notebook. He could work on his novel during his off-duty hours, without Max or Stella breathing down his neck. Or he could tear it all up and write something else. The Lincoln Mendelblatt books had made his name and attracted him a readership, but he was sick of the character. The Jewish private eye stories were set in a fictional world in which the UK and France had never merged, and England now stood on the edge of a federal Europe; a world of financial chaos and Middle Eastern oil wars, in which Westminster's loyalties leaned closer to Washington than Paris.

Stupid.

During the nuclear crisis, he'd had an epiphany; a moment of clarity in which he'd realised he didn't want to go to his grave remembered only for a series of trashy sci-fi detective novels. That realisation was, he admitted to himself, the real reason he was a month overdue on the latest instalment. He'd lost all enthusiasm for the setting. In the grip of real world events, his invented globe seemed paltry and irrelevant. Now, he wanted to be remembered for something nobler and more worthy. He had higher aspirations—aspirations that had become buried under the accumulated silt of convenience and expediency. He was tired of being passed over for awards and accolades, and tired of people's eyes glazing over when he told them what he wrote. He wanted to go mainstream and write serious literature. He wanted to write a book so searing and heartfelt that, one day, a girl in a library somewhere would read it and it would make her cry, and fall in love with him. If he had to depart this life, why not take a stab at literary immortality? Why not leave his mark on the world, once and for all?

He owed it to himself. Five years ago, when he'd hopped that first skyliner from Dayton to Liverpool, and then caught a freezing train south to Bristol, his plan had been to set up home with Marie and write the Great Transatlantic Novel. He'd been an overweight middle-aged man in love, but what great plans he'd harboured, what ambitions!

Lying on his back, staring up at the underside of the chef's bunk, he felt something harden inside him. He owed it to himself, and he owed it to Marie. She'd died believing he could do it, believing he could reach for the rarefied literary heights and escape the sweaty backstreets of pulp. When he'd started out, he'd been young and callow, with nothing original to say about the human condition. He'd been bored and lazy, and suffering through the slow motion car crash that had been his first marriage. No wonder he'd taken to writing escapism. Now, though, he was older, and could draw on the bitterness of two years of grief, disillusionment and drug addiction; and he had the rest of his life to gather more new experiences.

Exhaustion weighed on his bones like a heavy quilt, and yet, lying there, he felt the first tickle of optimism. Maybe this disruption was what he'd needed all along? Instead of moping around the flat, blitzing his grief with chemicals, he should have been out in the world, getting a change of scenery and dirtying his hands with some honest toil. Sweat would help him now more than speed ever could. Here on the *Tereshkova*, he'd labour as a kitchen hand during the days and write in the evenings, with no distractions, drugs or deadlines. He felt a moment's shame that it had taken a car bomb to shake him out of his rut, but now it had, he knew he'd been given a chance to make a new start, a clean start. All he had to do was seize it.

He scratched his nose. Hadn't Kerouac sailed out as a ship's cook during the Second World War? Maybe you couldn't write convincingly about life unless you were out there living it, shoulder-to-shoulder with everyone else—up to your elbows in the world, scraping your knuckles against its rough edges.

Lying there in the darkness, he curled his fingers into tight fists. For the first time in months, he felt alive. He didn't know who had tried to kill him, or why, but that didn't matter right now. What mattered more than anything else was that he suddenly had a reason to go on; he could see a path in front of him, and knew how to walk it. After years of doubt and misery, he could finally see how to become the writer he wanted to be.

His eyes were raw and dry. Closing them, he surrendered to his accumulated fatigue and, wrapped in an itchy blanket, on an airship bound for foreign parts, fell asleep dreaming of the places he'd see and the books he'd write.

HE WAS WOKEN by the squeak of the cabin door's hinges. The room was still dark, and he had no idea how much time had passed. The door had been opened a crack. A dim light pushed its way in from the corridor, and he rubbed his eyes. William tensed. With his mouth dry and heart hammering, he lay as still as he could. Through half-closed eyelids, he saw a shadow slip into the room. Hardly daring to breathe, he wished for a weapon. He heard the rustle of cloth, the soft tread of a shoe against the metal deck.

"William?" The voice was male, and American. "Are you there?" The figure crouched beside the bunk, and shone a torch at him. It wore robes, like a monk's habit. A cowl shadowed its face. Gulping down breaths, William shrank back into the corner, shielding the glare with a hand held in front of his eyes.

"Who are you, what do you want?"

The figure didn't answer. Instead, it reached up and lowered the hood, revealing its face, and William gaped as he found himself staring into features that were almost an exact reflection of his own.

"I know this is an awful shock," his double said, "but please try to relax." He spoke through a clenched jaw. Sweat shone on his brow and upper lip. "My name's Bill," he said. The words sounded forced. "I know you'll have a lot of questions, and I promise I'll try to answer them. But right now, you need to loosen your fists and listen." He let the robe fall open, revealing a black shirt and tie. The shirt had a hole in it. The material was sodden around it, and stuck to his skin. He coughed wetly.

"Is that blood?" The realisation seemed to jolt William out of his paralysis. He opened his mouth to cry for help, but Bill pulled a gun from the folds of his sleeves.

"I wouldn't do that, if I were you."

William looked into the black, unblinking eye of the barrel.

"Who are you?"

For long seconds, the gun remained unwavering. Then, with another cough, the man turned his hand sideways, and offered William the pistol's grip.

"I told you," he wheezed. "My name's Bill." He coughed again. "I'm here to save your life."

# CHAPTER FOUR
## THE GESTALT

With the *Tereshkova* stationary above the airfield, and passengers already disembarking, Ack-Ack Macaque switched on the autopilot to keep the vessel in place against the jostling coastal wind, and then knuckle-walked aft from the bridge.

"It's fuck-this-shit o'clock," he told the Russian navigator. Time to kick back with a couple of cold lagers, and maybe a rum daiquiri or two. Then later, catch a ride down to the airfield with one of the passenger 'copters, and hit a few bars. In New York, K8 had found him a fedora and raincoat and, as long as he wore the collar turned up, and the hat pulled low enough to shade his face, he hoped he wouldn't attract too much in the way of unwelcome attention.

Intent on his plans, he shuffled past Victoria's office. As he did so, the door opened and she beckoned to him.

"I've got someone in here who's extremely keen to meet you," she said. She still wore the military tunic but, since he'd last seen her, she'd replaced her wig: a platinum blonde bob which covered the jacks implanted into her temple, and the extensive scarring at the back of her head. Ack-Ack Macaque could smell the Martini on her breath. He looked past her to the figure standing by her desk. It was the same man who'd been in the bar when he'd had his skirmish with the reporter, Nick Dean.

"Who's that?"

"Mister Reynolds is here as a representative of the Gestalt."

Ack-Ack Macaque eyed the man up and down. "I should have guessed that." Like all members of the cult, Reynolds wore an immaculately white three-piece suit, with matching white shoes and a white tie, and his face held the same distracted, beatific calm they all radiated. "The question is: what does he want?"

Victoria's smile thinned. "Well, why don't you come in and *ask him*?"

She stood aside, and turned to her visitor.

"Mister Reynolds, please allow me to introduce our pilot. You'll have to excuse his manners, but he's only barely housetrained."

Ack-Ack Macaque glared at her. Reynolds bowed in greeting.

"Mister Macaque. May we say that this is indeed a pleasure?"

Ack-Ack Macaque scratched the chestnut-coloured hairs on his chest. "For you, maybe. But I've got places to be, and havoc to wreak."

The man's smile remained unwavering. "Of course, of course. We understand, and we are sorry for the intrusion."

Ack-Ack Macaque shivered. He'd run into a few of these Gestalt types in the States, and it creeped him out when they referred to themselves in the plural.

Part religion, part social experiment, the Gestalt used wireless technology to link its members' soul-catchers, networking them together in a web of shared thoughts and blurred identities.

"I met some of you weirdos in New York." Ack-Ack Macaque dug into the pocket of his aviator jacket, searching for a cigar. "I didn't know you'd spread to the UK already."

The man's dreamlike smile clicked up a notch. "We can assure you, we get everywhere." He held out a hand, and Ack-Ack Macaque made a face. He didn't want to shake. He didn't even want to be in the same room.

"So," he said, "what do you want with me?"

"We saw your unfortunate altercation earlier, and we thought maybe we could offer you our help?"

"Help? What sort of help?"

"We have a proposal."

"I'm not the marrying type."

The man's smile tightened. "Please, hear us out. We have been following your case with great interest. A humble monkey raised to sentience? What insights you must have, what unique perspectives."

Ack-Ack Macaque rolled his eye. He didn't like where this was going. He pulled the cigar from his pocket, bit the end off, and spat it into Victoria's wicker wastepaper basket.

"Look, don't get any funny ideas. I'm not going to join your little club, okay?" The idea made him queasy. He'd had enough scientists and engineers crawling around in his skull. He didn't need any more.

"But you would be so welcome." Reynolds rocked back and forth on his heels. "We have smoothed things over with Mister Dean, and reimbursed him for the cost of his camera."

"I didn't ask you to do that."

"It is our pleasure. Our Leader is so very keen to make your acquaintance."

"You guys have a leader?" Ack-Ack Macaque cocked an eyebrow. "I thought you guys were like some vast hive."

"Every hive has a queen." Reynolds licked the tip of his thumb, and used it to smooth his eyebrows. Two quick flicks. "Or, in our case, a king."

"And who is this king?" In his peripheral vision, Ack-Ack Macaque sensed Victoria tensing, bursting with unvoiced questions. He tried to ignore her.

"To find that out," Reynolds said smoothly, "you'll first have to agree to meet him."

"Sorry, but that's not going to happen."

"Are you quite sure?"

"Sure as shit."

"Please, Mister Macaque. Will you at least consider it? Your brain is mostly composed of gelware, so you wouldn't need additional implantation; at least, not much. The process of integration could be achieved in minutes, and quite painlessly. And I think it would be of great benefit to you."

"No, absolutely not." Ack-Ack Macaque rolled the cigar between finger and thumb, listening to the tobacco leaves crackle. Reynolds took a step closer.

"Welcoming you into the Gestalt would immeasurably enrich our whole." His breath stank of coffee and mints. Ack-Ack Macaque curled his lip, exposing an incisor.

"If you don't get out of my face right now," he growled, "I'll enrich *your* hole with the toe of my boot."

Reynolds ignored the threat. He reached out his arms as if asking for a hug.

"You wouldn't have to be alone."

*Alone.*

The word rang in the air like the toll of a funeral bell. Cold fingers gripped Ack-Ack Macaque's stomach, and squeezed. He felt his arms and legs shake. Then, without consciously willing it, he stepped forward and slapped Reynolds hard across the face. The man staggered back against the desk.

"Shut your mouth."

He pulled back his long arm for another strike, but Victoria stepped in front of him. She had her fighting stick in her hand, but hadn't yet flicked it out to its full length. He glared at her, his single eye wide and wild, but she didn't flinch. She didn't submit. Instead, she met his gaze and held it. In another monkey, this would have been tantamount to a direct physical challenge, and Ack-Ack Macaque had to fight down an instinctual surge of aggression. If he got hold of her, he could snap her like a twig. But Victoria was his friend, and saviour: he owed her everything. He might be the alpha male on this tub, but she was definitely the alpha female, and he knew she wouldn't tolerate any of his shit. She had no patience for insurrection or threats. The last person to raise a hand against her had been dropped from the *Tereshkova*'s cargo hatch, several thousand feet above Windsor Castle. He eyed the fighting stick in her hand, and let out a long, shuddering breath.

"Yes, boss." He dropped his chin. His palm stung where it had struck Reynolds' cheek.

"Thank you." Victoria gave him a final glare, and then turned to Reynolds, who leant drunkenly against the desk, his fingers dabbing at a split and bloodied lip.

"I am so sorry, Mister Reynolds." She took his elbow and helped him upright. "But I believe you've been given your answer. Now, do you require medical attention?"

Reynolds shot Ack-Ack Macaque a sideways glance.

"We are sorry you feel that way, Mister Macaque." His voice was quiet, the earlier self-assurance muted. "For what it's worth, we were only trying to help you."

Ack-Ack Macaque shrugged his leather-clad shoulders. He didn't need any help. He tossed the cigar into his mouth, and caught it in his teeth.

Victoria hustled Reynolds towards the cabin door. Looking back, she pointed a bony finger at Ack-Ack Macaque.

"You, stay here."

Ack-Ack Macaque harrumphed. He folded his arms and sat on the edge of the metal desk.

"I'm not going anywhere, boss."

He watched her escort the white-suited man to the corridor. Reynolds had a hand to his bruised face. He was lucky not to have a broken jaw.

It would have served him right, Ack-Ack Macaque thought.

He fished around for his lighter. When he looked back up, Reynolds was watching him, ignoring whatever apologies Victoria was making.

"You will come to us and let us help you eventually, you know." Not even the cut lip could disguise the certainty in the man's voice. "After all, where else can you go? Where else can someone like you ever truly belong?"


WHEN VICTORIA CAME back, her cheeks were flushed and her lips almost white.

"Putain de merde," she said. "What was that all about?"

Ack-Ack Macaque's jacket creaked as he shrugged a shoulder.

"You're lucky I didn't shoot him."

Victoria looked him up and down, nostrils flared. "If you had, you'd be in the brig right now, and we wouldn't be having this conversation."

Ack-Ack Macaque flicked his lighter into life. It was a Zippo with a brushed aluminium case, and he was rather fond of it, even though it stank of petrol fumes.

"I can't help it," he grumbled. "Those Gestalt bastards make my pelt crawl." He thumbed the wheel to ignite the wick, and then used the flame to light the cigar. As he puffed it into life, he heard the air-conditioning fans whisper into action.

Victoria wrinkled her nose and flapped a hand in front of her face. "Mine too. But I can't have you slapping passengers around, especially in my office. Are we clear?"

He tapped a pair of fingers to his forehead in salute. "Clear as crystal, boss."

She narrowed her eyes. "You haven't been on the espresso again, have you? Because we all know what happened last time."

Ack-Ack Macaque waggled his head.

"No, boss."

Victoria drew herself up. Then she let out a long, cleansing breath, and threw her blonde wig onto the desk.

"Right, now that's out of the way, what are you planning to do with the rest of your evening?"

Ack-Ack Macaque was used to her mood shifts. He shrugged. Reynolds's final words still rankled him, like a fleabite he couldn't scratch.

"Drink imported lagers until I puke?"

Victoria smiled. She straightened the collar of her white military tunic, and slipped the retractable fighting stick into one of its pockets.

"That sounds like a damn fine plan, monkey-man. If you don't mind a little company, the first round's on me."

# CHAPTER FIVE
## UNCOMFORTABLY PARANOID

THE MAN WHO called himself Bill slumped back against the cabin wall, and stretched his legs out before him. One of his hands pressed at the wound in his stomach, and he sucked air through his teeth in tight, rapid breaths.

"I haven't got long. I have to. Warn you. About the virus."

Transfixed, William slid forward on the bunk. The gun Bill had given him felt heavy, cold and solid in his grip.

"Who are you? Why do you look like me?"

Bill coughed. Where William's hair was long and wild, his had been carefully cropped.

"I *am* you." He had trouble speaking and breathing at the same time. "Sort of. I'm a different version... of you."

William felt his face flush. "What, you're like my twin brother or something?"

"No." Bill's head shook loosely on a neck that seemed loath to support it. "I really am... you. But I'm a version of you from a different... world. A parallel... world."

"Bullshit."

Bill winced in pain. "You write... science fiction,"

he said between clenched teeth. "You know how... this works."

William fought the urge to curl into a ball and pull the covers over his head.

"No way," he said, voice unsteady. Parallel worlds were just a bit of fun, a thought experiment at best. Writing about them was one thing; he didn't necessarily believe in them. Despite setting his books in one, he'd never on a gut level accepted the idea of them as being *true*. "How did you get here?"

"Doesn't matter."

"But—"

Bill raised an arm. "We don't have time... for explanations. You're in danger. I'm here to help."

William leaned forward. "So, you know who's been trying to kill me?"

"Yes." Bill's breathing was shallow. The sweat glistened on his brow. "We didn't think... they'd find you. Not so quickly. We have to move you. Before they try—" His words dissolved into a convulsive fit of coughing. His shoulders shook and his back arched. By the time the fit subsided, his lips were dark, and shone red in the torchlight. Feeling panicky, William tried to stand.

"I'll get help."

Bill's hand locked around his wrist like a cuff. "No, it's too... late." The words were a bubbling whisper. "They're going to release the virus. You have... to stop them. Find Marie. She'll help you..."

William pulled back. "Marie's dead." His mouth was so dry he could barely speak. "She died two years ago."

Bill turned his head and spat a wad of red phlegm onto the deck.

"Not. That. Marie." His body shook in a final spasm, and then fell back against the wall. His chin dropped to his chest, and a line of bloodied drool unwound slowly from his lips, onto his beard. William heard the last of the air wheeze from his blood-filled lungs, and knew for sure that the man was dead. Dumbfounded, he sat and stared into Bill's face, with the uncomfortably paranoid feeling of just having watched his own demise.

K8 HAD THE *Tereshkova*'s kitchen more or less to herself. The radio on the shelf played a concert from the BBC's Paris studios, and the cook, a large Russian with a drooping moustache, snored in a chair by the open porthole, his feet up on an upturned bucket.

Much as she loved living on the *Tereshkova*, K8 treasured moments like these. In the rattling boxes of the skyliner's gondolas, peace and quiet were scarce commodities.

K8 was a young former hacker from Scotland, and one of Ack-Ack Macaque's most trusted friends. A pair of headphones dangled around her neck as she mixed ingredients in a bowl: flour, eggs and sugar, a handful of white chocolate chips, and a chopped banana. The cookies she was making were for the monkey. They were his favourite, and she called them 'macaque snacks'.

Not that he'd ever thank her, of course. Not out loud. He seemed embarrassed when people did nice things for him, and so the most she could expect would be a grunt. But she knew he liked them, and that was enough. Besides, she enjoyed having somebody to cook for. At school, the only subjects in which she'd shown any interest had been computer science and home economics; and, to her, cooking and hacking had always had their similarities. Both required concentration and the methodical combination of ingredients. If you followed the procedures, and threw in a dash of creativity, you could perform magic. The right components, put together in the right order, were capable of conjuring forth perfection.

And, she thought as she spooned the thick, sugary mixture into blobs on a baking tray, if you knew the rules you could find ways to break them. You could hack your taste buds with new combinations of flavours, such as white chocolate and banana.

She made two rows of blobs, leaving plenty of space for them to spread out as they cooked, and then bent down to slide the tray into the oven. As she slammed the door, the chef muttered in his sleep.

She'd been Ack-Ack Macaque's wing woman for a year now, having helped him escape the clutches of her former employer, Céleste Technologies. And she'd seen and done more in that time than she'd ever believed possible. Since the company plucked her from her mother's two-bedroom tenement in Glasgow, her life had been a mad whirl of travel and adventure. But, however unfamiliar or dangerous things had become, she'd always felt safe because he'd always been there. She was more than capable of taking care of herself, of course, but when he was there, she didn't have to.

He was her commanding officer, and her best friend; but, more than that, he was a shield against the world. In that respect, he reminded her of her ratty old teddy bear—the one she'd slept with every night of her childhood; the one she'd clung to during the arguments and recriminations of her parent's divorce; the one who'd kept her company during the lonely evenings spent with her finger jammed in one ear and the pillow jammed in the other.

When she was near him, she felt safe the same way as she had when she squeezed that bear. Except, she couldn't imagine Ack-Ack Macaque letting anybody hug him. The thought brought a smile to her face. Whatever else he might be, he certainly wasn't cuddly.

She checked her watch. The cookies would take a few minutes to bake through. She'd wait for them, and then she'd hit the lounge while they cooled. She was only seventeen, but had an arrangement with the bar staff. As long as she didn't ask them to serve her directly, and as long as she limited herself to a few glasses of wine in an evening, they turned a blind eye to her age. The *Tereshkova*'s rules said you had to be eighteen or over to drink in the bar—but as long as Ack-Ack Macaque ordered the drinks, the stewards were quite happy to pretend they didn't know that one of the glasses he wanted was for her.

She tapped her foot.

Yes, it would be good to kick back and have some laughs. It was Friday night, after all.

\*    \*    \*

WILLIAM COLE WONDERED what his next move should be.

Here he was, in a cabin with a dead body—a body with a face that clearly resembled his own. How could he explain what had happened? Who in their right mind would believe such a story? He was only here on Captain Valois's sufferance. What would she say if he came to her with this? His mind raced. Was there any way he could dispose of the body? Or should he leave it here, and try to disappear himself?

His earlier tiredness had gone, washed away by adrenaline.

He shuffled forward on the bed and, placing the gun on the covers beside him, reached out a hand to touch Bill's still-warm cheek. Even closeup, the resemblance was striking. The hair might be shorter and the beard tidier and more neatly trimmed, but this was definitely the face William saw every morning in the mirror above his bathroom sink.

He took a deep breath and tried to stop his hands from trembling. Apart from the ugly guy in the car this morning, he'd never seen anybody actually die before—and to see 'himself' do it filled him with nauseous revulsion. He hadn't even been there when Marie went. When she'd finally slipped away, he'd been outside, in the hospital corridor, taking a call from his agent. By the time the nurse found him and brought him back into the room, it had been too late.

*Find Marie,* the man had said. But what did that mean? How could he find her? He'd scattered her ashes on their favourite beach, in accordance with what he thought her dying wishes might have been. She was one now with the sand, the wind and waves. How could she possibly help him?

And yet…

If Bill had been William's double, did that mean—dare he hope—that there could be another Marie out there? Was his wife's doppelganger walking around somewhere? If so, he had no idea how to find her.

He took another long, deep breath, trying to calm himself. He couldn't stop opening and closing his hands. They fluttered like startled birds. Before he did anything else, he had to decide where he was going to go when he left this room.

The gun lay on the blanket next to him. He picked it up and turned it over and over. He could smell the sooty oil used to lubricate its mechanism. He had a weapon now. The thought made him feel better. He had no idea how 'Bill' had smuggled the pistol on board, but that didn't matter right now. The important thing was that he wasn't defenceless any more.

But where was he going to go?

He tried to analyse the situation as calmly and rationally as he could, as if working out the plot for one of his novels. On balance, the *Tereshkova* still seemed like his best bet. It was a self-contained state, with limited access; but if he wanted to stay here, he'd have to find a way to explain the body.

So be it, he thought, pulse racing. He had a weapon. What he needed now were allies.

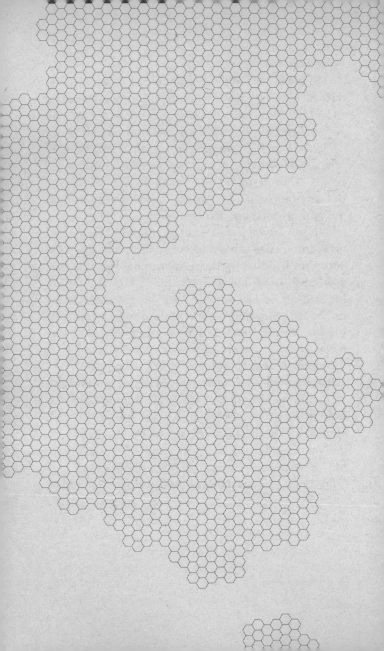

## BREAKING NEWS

From *The South West Messenger*, online edition:

### Police Try to Trace Missing Writer

Police in Somerset are trying to trace the whereabouts of reclusive science fiction author, William Cole. Cole, whose works include the 'Lincoln Mendelblatt' novels, disappeared from his home this morning, following an explosion in the street outside his apartment block. Eyewitnesses say that shots were fired before the explosion, possibly at Mister Cole, and police are very concerned for his safety.

Cole, aged 44, is known to have past convictions for the possession and use of controlled narcotics, and a history of depression, and police are appealing to members of the public to get in touch if they can shed any light on his whereabouts.

Cole, who is often compared to Philip K. Dick and H.P. Lovecraft, first came to public attention when a damning review of his debut novel, *Better Angels*, went viral on the Internet. Since then, two sequels have followed—*Die Robot* (2058) and *The Collective* (2060).

Speaking at a hastily convened press conference in London, Cole's agent, Max Morrison, said, "I spoke to Will this morning, just prior to the attack. He was in good spirits, and working hard on his next book, the fourth in the Mendelblatt series."

Online, fans have speculated that the author's disappearance could be a media stunt, designed to promote his forthcoming novel, *A Thousand City Whispers*. However, when asked if he had a message for William Cole, Morrison simply said, "We're all worried about you, buddy. If you're listening to this, I want you to get your act together and call me, okay? We've got important things to do, and time's getting tight."

Police are urging anyone with information concerning the author's whereabouts to come forward as soon as possible.

Read more | Like | Comment | Share

**Related Stories**

Merovech and Julie: date announced for royal wedding.

Diplomats from Commonwealth and China 'close to deal' on Hong Kong.

Car bomb rocks North Somerset town.

Members of the Gestalt cult petition for UN recognition as independent 'state of mind'.

Skyliner Tereshkova returns to British shores for the first time since 'Le Combat de La Manche'.

Culture: art world stunned by new Da Vinci sketches found in Paris cellar.

Sport: Eight Nations tournament kicks off at Twickenham.

Space: controversial Céleste probe still on course for Mars.

# CHAPTER SIX
## DON'T FUCKING MOVE

Victoria decided she was too tired to accompany him into town, so they agreed to have a quick drink in the *Tereshkova*'s passenger lounge. They took a corner table, and Victoria signalled one of the white-gloved stewards.

"An Amstel for me, and rum for the monkey."

The steward bowed. Like most of the airship's staff, he was Russian. The Commodore, a former pilot and cosmonaut in the Russian air force, had preferred to hire his own countrymen.

The steward turned to Ack-Ack Macaque.

"Single or double rum, sir?"

Ack-Ack Macaque grinned around the cigar in his teeth.

"Bottle."

"Very good, sir."

This early in the evening, few people were in the lounge. Victoria knew that most of the transatlantic passengers had already disembarked. They would complete their journeys by fast trains to London, Manchester, or Edinburgh. The remaining passengers, who intended to stay with the airship for her onward journey to London and Paris, had also mostly gone ashore for the evening, glad to be back on terra firma after three days in the air, ready to sample the nightlife and historic tourist attractions of Bristol and Bath.

When the steward had fetched their drinks, set them down, and withdrawn, she leant across the table.

"Are you all right, now?"

The monkey glanced at her with his one good eye. In the light of the art deco electric wall lamps, his fur had a rough, bronzed sheen.

"I've been better."

Victoria wiped her thumb across the condensation on the neck of her beer bottle. She couldn't read the label, but she could recognise the maker's logo by its colours and shape.

"Would you care to elaborate?"

On the other side of the table, Ack-Ack Macaque unscrewed the cap of the rum bottle and, ignoring the glass the steward had brought, took a hefty glug from the neck. He smacked his lips, and replaced the cigar.

"Not particularly."

"Was it something he said?"

"Who, Reynolds?"

"Of course, Reynolds."

The monkey made a face and hunched over the table. His leather jacket creaked. "You know what they say: It takes a hundred and forty-three muscles to frown, but only fifty-two to grab somebody by the lapels and bite their face off."

Victoria wasn't amused.

"There's been too much violence on this ship. If you want me to carry on trusting you, you can't lash out like that."

Ack-Ack Macaque drummed his fingers on the side of the rum bottle.

"It was everything he said. Especially all that stuff about being alone." He ran a fingertip around the rim. "It got to me."

"But, you're not alone. You have K8. You have a place here." She reached out a hand. "You have me."

"I know." Ack-Ack Macaque scowled. "But it's not easy being the only talking monkey in the world."

"You feel like a freak?"

He gave a shaggy shake of the head. "You wouldn't understand."

Victoria felt her cheeks colour. She tapped the ridge of scar tissue at her temple. The surgery to repair the damage to her brain had been extensive and life saving; but it had left her bald and scarred—an oddity.

"Oh, really?"

She saw him glance at her scalp, then back down to the bottle in his paw.

"Sorry, boss."

She gave a shrug. In truth, she knew how he felt. She used to feel the exact same way when passengers tried not to stare at her. For a while, it had bothered her; but last year's unpleasantness had given her confidence, and a certain notoriety, and now she no longer cared what anyone thought of the way she looked.

She accepted his apology with a gracious nod.

"C'est rien." Her beer was cold and sharp, just the way she liked it. She savoured the bubbles on her tongue before swallowing.

The sad truth was, the camaraderie she shared with Ack-Ack Macaque was about the closest thing she had to a relationship with an actual, physical being. She had Paul, of course, but, however much she loved him, he was still just a face on a screen, or a tiny hologram on her desk. The monkey was, tragically, the nearest thing she had to a living, breathing friend.

"You know," she said, "I don't trust them, either."

His eye swivelled up to meet hers.

"The Gestalt?"

"There's something about them." She thought of Reynolds, and wondered how many minds had been peering at her from behind the man's mild, cornflower-blue eyes. "They freak me out."

Across the table, Ack-Ack Macaque took another hit of rum. She gave him a long, thoughtful look.

"I wonder why he wanted you," she said. "In particular, I mean. After all, I've got nearly as much gelware in my head as you do, and yet he didn't even ask me."

"Feeling left out?"

"Hardly." Her thumbnail worried the edge of the beer bottle's label. "But doesn't it strike you as odd?"

"Everything they do's fucking odd."

She dipped her heard, conceding his point. "Still, there's something about it that doesn't ring true. Something that tells me he wanted to do more than simply recruit you."

Ack-Ack Macaque regarded her from beneath a lowered brow. "Your journalist instincts acting up again, boss?"

Victoria smiled. "Something like that."

Ack-Ack Macaque ground out the butt of his cigar, then fumbled in his jacket pocket and pulled out another. "I thought as much." He put the fresh cigar into his mouth, but didn't light it. "Don't go digging around on my behalf. I couldn't give a damn what they want." He grinned. "I'm just glad I slapped the silly sod when I had the chance." He stretched in his seat. "Now, if you'll excuse me, boss, I'm going out for the evening."

Victoria sat back with a sigh. Her curiosity would have to wait. She peeled off the label and screwed it into a ball.

"Are you going anywhere nice?"

"I hope not." He gave a toothy grin. "Are you sure you don't want to come?"

"Quite sure, thank you."

Victoria watched as Ack-Ack Macaque got to his feet, with the cigar clamped in his jaw and the bottle dangling from his fingers. *This is my life,* she thought: *an uplifted monkey, an electronic ex-husband, a teenage hacker and me; four wretched creatures drawn together because we have nowhere else to go; because we're all artificial, made things— with patched-up souls, and cortices covered with other people's grubby fingerprints. Maybe that's why the Gestalt frightens us so much: because, instead of feeling incomplete and ashamed, they embrace their artificiality. They make it a central part of themselves. And they want to help us.*

With a flick of her finger, she sent the screwed-up label skittering across the table.

"Well, have a good time, won't you?"

Ack-Ack Macaque caught the paper ball and dropped it into his unused glass.

"I'll give it a try."

A shout came from the corridor behind him. Victoria looked over, just in time to see a figure burst into the room—a wild-haired, bearded man in a white t-shirt and saggy pyjama bottoms, with pale, gooseflesh arms, and a gun clenched in his fist.

*Oh hell, Cole.*

The gelware processors in Victoria's head kicked into combat mode, pumping adrenaline into her system and ramping up the speed of her thoughts. The chair went flying behind her, and her fingers curled around the neck of the beer bottle, ready to hurl it. At the same time, in her peripheral vision, she saw Ack-Ack Macaque throw himself sideways across the lounge, dragging his huge silver Colts from their holsters. By the time Cole staggered to a halt a few paces inside the door, he found himself facing a woman and a snarling monkey, both pointing weapons at him, and both poised to defend not only themselves, but also everybody else on the skyliner. His eyes rolled from one to the other, and then down to the pistol in his fist.

"Don't shoot!" He let go of the gun as if scalded. The weapon clunked onto the deck, and he raised his hands.

Lying on his side, with both guns trained on Cole's forehead, Ack-Ack Macaque spat out his cigar.

"We won't fucking shoot," he said in disgust, "if you don't fucking *move*."

\*    \*    \*

ACTING ON VICTORIA'S instructions, Ack-Ack Macaque and two of the white-jacketed stewards manhandled William Cole to her office, where they handcuffed him to the chair in front of her desk. She followed behind, examining the fallen gun.

"So, Mister Cole," she said when he had been firmly secured. "Would you care to explain what you were thinking?"

Cole looked bad. Beneath the scratches, his face was pale, and his eyes bugged out. His breathing came in heaves.

"Yeah," the monkey said, growling around his unlit cigar. "Because bursting into rooms waving guns is a very good way to get your fucking head blown off."

Cole looked between them. Sweat glistened on his balding forehead.

"I want to report a murder."

Victoria sniffed the barrel of the gun she'd picked up. It had been fired recently.

"Have you killed somebody, Mister Cole?"

"No!"

"Then, tell me, what's happened?"

Cole swallowed. "A man came into my cabin." He pulled experimentally at the cuff on his right wrist. The chain rattled. "He looked just like me. He said he'd come to help, that somebody was trying to kill me."

"But you already knew that." Victoria weighed the pistol in her hand. "You told me as much when you came on board."

"Yes."

"Did you shoot him?"

Cole shook his head. "He was already wounded. I didn't realise at first."

"And now he's dead?"

"I think so, yes."

Victoria turned to one of the stewards. "Get a medic to the chef's cabin. Go armed. Report back."

The man gave a salute, and left the room.

Cole squirmed in his chair. "I didn't kill him. That's his gun you're holding. He gave it to me before he—" He swallowed again. "Before he died."

Victoria looked him up and down. She knew he hadn't smuggled the gun aboard himself. Given his claim that somebody had tried to kill him, she'd made sure his bag and clothing had been thoroughly searched.

"All that remains to be seen," she said. "In the meantime, I'd like you to take a deep breath, and start from the beginning." As a former correspondent, she'd had plenty of practice at talking to the distraught. She slipped off the military jacket and draped it over the back of her chair, to make her look more informal. Then she sat and placed her hands on the desk, palms down. "Now," she said as calmly as she could, "who was this man? Did you recognise him?"

Cole's jaw tightened. "Of course I recognised him!"

Beside his chair, Ack-Ack Macaque spat out his cigar. "Then who was he? Don't keep us in suspense."

Cole turned a baleful eye on him.

"I told you. He was *me*."

# CHAPTER SEVEN
## DOPPELGANGER

THE DEAD BODY lay wrapped in its habit, on a bunk in the *Tereshkova*'s infirmary. Ack-Ack Macaque looked from it to the man standing at the foot of the bed.

"That," he said, "is fucking uncanny."

Standing next to him, Victoria Valois was forced to agree. Aside from a few cosmetic differences—tidier hair, a better maintained beard, and a bullet hole in the stomach—the man lying on the bed seemed to be the exact double of William Cole. At the end of the bed, Cole himself seemed transfixed.

"He said his name was Bill," he said.

"Who is he?"

"I don't know." Cole's hands were crossed in front of his chest. Despite the cold, he still wore only a t-shirt and pyjama trousers. "But he said he'd come to warn me. Something about a virus."

"Any idea what he meant?"

"Sorry, none." With nails bitten down to the quick, the writer scratched at each of his wrists. "What happens now? Do we go to the police?"

"No." Victoria looked up at the ceiling. She felt warm and tingly inside. First the Gestalt guy, and now this? So many questions suddenly needed answering. "The *Tereshkova* is mine." She pulled the Commodore's white dress tunic more firmly onto her shoulders. "For now, I'll lead the investigation."

"But—"

"No buts." She fixed Cole with her firmest stare. "The local *flics* don't get a sniff of this." She panned her gaze around the assembled faces. "Do I make myself clear?"

One by one, they nodded their assent. They knew as well as she did that international treaties protected the autonomy of each skyliner: that each functioned as an independent city-state, unaffected by the laws of whichever territory it happened to be flying over, and that the local police had no jurisdiction.

She looked over at Ack-Ack Macaque.

"What do you say, monkey man? Are you up for a challenge?"

Ack-Ack Macaque fixed her with his one-eyed squint.

"What do you have in mind, boss?"

Victoria smiled. She could tell by the way his tail twitched, and by the way the fingertips of his right hand drummed against the handle of the revolver at his hip, that he'd been just as bored as she had during the Atlantic crossing.

"First off, we need some facts." She gave a nod towards the dead man on the bunk. "Like who this guy was, and how he got aboard. And how he got dead."

Ack-Ack Macaque leaned over the corpse and sniffed.

"He smells fresh." His pink nostrils twitched. "I mean, apart from the fact that he's shat himself, but everybody does that when they die, don't they?" He looked up at her. "What does the doc say?"

Victoria had already spoken to the airship's medical officer—a grey-haired old alcoholic by the name of Sergei.

"Gunshot wound to the large intestine. Died from internal haemorrhaging. Otherwise, nothing unusual."

"Was he wearing a soul-catcher?"

"Unfortunately not." If the man had been wearing a catcher, they'd have been able to electronically revive and quiz the copy of his personality held within. That was how she'd saved her husband, Paul, after he ran afoul of a killer in London.

"So, no help there, then?"

"Not much." She reached out to touch the hem of the dead man's robe. As she moved, the medals on her chest tinkled together like distant wind chimes. "Mister Cole, do you have any idea why this man's dressed as a monk?"

The writer shook his head. He was calmer now than he had been when he'd burst into the lounge, but his eyes were still wide and bloodshot. It seemed to be their default setting, and gave him the look of a hermit dragged from a cave.

On the other side of the bunk, Ack-Ack Macaque gave a grunt. "Maybe he's a fucking monk?"

Cole blinked at him. "Who would shoot a monk?"

Victoria drew her hand back from the bed. "You didn't go to Catholic school," she said, "did you, Mister Cole?" He frowned, and opened his mouth to protest, but she silenced him with a raised hand. "You said his name was Bill. Did he tell you anything else? Give you any idea where he was from?"

Cole licked his lips. His eyes settled on her for a moment.

"You wouldn't believe me if I told you." He massaged the bridge of his nose between forefinger and thumb. "Hell, I'm not even sure I believe it myself."

Victoria narrowed her eyes.

"You're talking to a cyborg and a monkey. If you can believe that, you can believe anything."

The American put a hand to the small of his back and straightened his spine, visibly trying to pull himself together. Victoria could see the gooseflesh on his bare arms.

"Okay," he said. "What do you know of parallel worlds?"

"Quantum theory." Having been married to a sci-fi fan, and been obliged to sit through seemingly endless movies and TV shows, she had a pretty good handle on the concept. "The idea that there's a multiverse of endless alternate realities, each with a different history. Like in *Star Trek*, where everybody in the parallel world has a beard."

Cole gave her a reappraising look. "Yes, that's it. Essentially, every choice we make spawns two or more alternate worlds. In one, we take the first choice, in the other, we take the second choice, and so on."

Victoria glanced down at the dead man's face.

"And so this guy's supposed to be you from a different reality?" She didn't believe it for a second. "Alternate worlds are just fiction, Mister Cole. They're plots from bad movies about Nazis; they don't really exist."

Cole held out his hands. "I know. Trust me, I write books about them and even I can't believe in them.

But that's what he told me; that he was me from another reality."

"Maybe he was having you on?"

Across the bunk, Ack-Ack Macaque gave a snort. "Who jokes with a bullet in their gut?" He waved a hand from the writer to the corpse, and back again. "Look at the two of them. They're completely identical. What other explanation is there?"

"Twin brothers?"

"Surely he'd know?"

"Plastic surgery?"

The monkey rubbed the leather patch covering his empty eye socket. "Who'd go to all that trouble and expense, just to kill this dickhead?"

Cole frowned.

"No offence taken, I'm sure."

Ack-Ack Macaque flashed his yellow canines.

"Shut the fuck up, asswipe."

Victoria still had the dead man's gun in her hands. It was a small, compact pistol, made of thick plastic and devoid of markings or serial numbers. She passed it across to Ack-Ack Macaque.

"Do you recognise the make?"

He dangled it between finger and thumb.

"Nope."

"But that doesn't mean anything, these days, does it?"

"Guns are as easy to make as anything else." He shrugged; if there was one thing he knew about, it was weaponry. "This could have come out of a 3D printer anywhere from Cape Town to Bucharest, and all points in between."

"Then it could have come from anywhere, as could our friend here."

Ack-Ack Macaque harrumphed. "So, we've no idea where to start?" He stuck out his bottom lip, and Victoria guessed he'd been hoping for some action, or at least the chance to kick an arse or two.

"Not yet." She ran a hand over her bare scalp. "But it's getting late, and I don't know about you, but I'd kill for a coffee." She took back the gun, and slipped it into her pocket. "And besides, I think I'm going to have to have a word with my husband."

THE *TERESHKOVA*'S AUTOMATIC systems were perfectly capable of holding its bulk in position above the airfield; and so, with the old skyliner at rest, the crew had no need to man the bridge around the clock. At this time of night, Victoria had the room to herself. Through the curving windshield, she could see the bright city lights of Bristol and, far across the black waters of the Severn Estuary, the orange lights of Newport and Cardiff. With a tin mug of fresh black coffee cradled in her hands, and the Commodore's jacket still draped over her shoulders, she perched on the edge of the Captain's chair.

"Are you there, Paul?"

In front of her, one of the screens on her workstation blinked into life.

"Hey, Vicky. What can I do for you?" The image on the display was of him as she remembered him: short, peroxide blond hair, rimless glasses, and a loud yellow and green Hawaiian shirt.

"I assume you already know about the dead guy in William Cole's cabin?"

Paul's fingers fiddled with the gold stud in his right ear.

"Yeah, I heard about that."

"Have you been eavesdropping again?"

"Maybe just a little."

Victoria raised the mug to her nose and inhaled steam. "I need you to review the security footage. Follow it backwards. Find out who the dead guy is, and where he came from."

"I can do that."

"Will it take long?"

Paul grinned at her. By rights, he shouldn't still be here. Most personality recordings fell apart after a few months. They just couldn't sustain themselves. But somehow, letting Paul loose in the *Tereshkova*'s memory had kept him intact—even if it meant he was now confined to the ship

"Just give me a moment..." He trailed off, and his image froze. Victoria sipped her steaming coffee. It was very good. After years of drinking cheap and nasty swill in newspaper offices, she now insisted that the *Tereshkova*'s quartermaster stocked only the very best.

From her chair, she watched the nocturnal bustle of the airport, and hummed to herself a little tune she'd picked up from that morning's radio.

When Paul came back, a few minutes later, he gave her a suspicious look.

"Why are you so happy?"

Victoria gave a start.

"Me?"

"You're practically singing."

"It's nothing." She tried to wave him away, but he raised an eyebrow.

"It doesn't look like nothing to me."

Victoria drummed her fingernails against the side of the tin mug. She let out a sigh. "It's just good to have something to do," she finally admitted.

Paul smiled knowingly.

"Running a skyliner's not enough for you, eh? You still need that extra excitement, don't you? The thrill of the chase?" He shook his head, pretending to despair of her. "Some things never change."

"And some things do." She put the tin cup down on the chair's padded arm. "Now, what have you got for me?"

Paul's smile widened, and he puffed his chest forward. "Well, I've reviewed the footage."

"Any luck?"

His eyes twinkled behind his glasses.

"Let me show you." A second screen lit, displaying grainy footage from the security camera in the corridor outside Cole's cabin. "Right, here's our man." A hooded figure appeared from the right side of the screen, moving awkwardly and hunched over to the right, as if trying to curl around a pain in his side.

Victoria said, "You see where he's holding himself? That's where he was shot." So, Cole's story held up. The man *had* been shot before entering the cabin, just as he'd said. "Okay, let's back it up."

The picture froze, and then began to rewind. Victoria watched the robed figure shuffle backwards along the corridor. Moving from one camera to another, the pictures retraced his steps to a tiny berth in one of the outermost gondolas.

"According to records, the cabin was occupied by a man calling himself Bill Cole," Paul said. "He came aboard shortly after William." The picture jumped to show a shot taken by a camera up on the main helipad. It showed a middle-aged man stepping down from one of the passenger choppers. He wore an expensive-looking business suit, and clutched a leather briefcase. Mirrored sunglasses covered his eyes.

"That's him?"

"Yeah. He must have the robe in his suitcase, but it's definitely him."

Victoria leant close to the screen. "He seems to be moving okay." In fact, he looked like a typical business traveller. "Which means, he hadn't been shot when he came on board."

Paul frowned. "So, whoever shot him might still be here somewhere."

"Oui. And Cole could still be in danger. Where is he now?"

The screen changed to a real-time view of the passenger lounge. Cole, now wrapped in a white bathrobe, sat at a corner table with Ack-Ack Macaque and K8. The monkey's revolvers lay on the table, within easy reach.

"He should be safe enough there," Paul said. "Nobody's going to tangle with the Ack-ster."

Victoria frowned.

"Let's hope not." She ran a hand up her forehead and over the rough scar tissue at the back of her scalp, dreading to think what mayhem might be unleashed if someone engaged the monkey in such a confined space. "Right," she said, "access the room records. Find all the information this 'Bill Cole' gave us when he came aboard."

Paul waved his hands like a conjuror, and the data appeared on the screen beside him: a copy of the man's electronic boarding pass, and a scan of his passport.

"Here it is. Bill Cole, aged forty-eight. British citizen. With an address in the city."

"This city?" She glanced forward, at the lights beyond the windshield.

"Yeah." Street maps appeared on the screen. "It's not too far from here, in fact. A couple of miles, at the most."

"Can you load it into my head?" Victoria's neural prosthesis held a satellite map overlay.

"Sure." Paul's eyes narrowed as he watched her slip her arms into the sleeves of the jacket draped over her shoulders. "Why, what are you going to do? Talk to the police?"

Now it was her turn to grin.

"No, of course not." She began fastening the shiny brass buttons on the front of the tunic. "I'm going down there to check it out myself."

# CHAPTER EIGHT
## RAY GUN

HALF AN HOUR later, they were driving through the city streets in a rented black Mercedes. K8 had the wheel, Ack-Ack Macaque rode shotgun, and Victoria Valois and William Cole shared the back seat. As they negotiated their way through the early evening traffic, Victoria kept track of their progress using a map uploaded to her mind's eye from the *Tereshkova*'s database. A small green dot marked their current position, a red one their destination.

In the front passenger seat, Ack-Ack Macaque wore dark glasses, a wide-brimmed fedora, and a long coat with the collar turned up. He'd even wound a scarf across the lower half of his face. This was his idea of going incognito—never mind the fact that nothing could disguise his lumbering walk, or the way his tail poked out of the vent in the back of the coat.

Victoria watched the passing buildings. They were moving through the affluent suburb of Clifton, with its steep, tree-lined streets and three-storey Georgian town houses. She saw sturdy-looking churches; corner pubs with traditional signs and black railings; newsagents with handwritten headline boards; supermarkets with glittering holographic window displays; and beautiful old houses retrofitted as solicitors' offices and estate agencies.

Despite being too young to hold a British driving licence, K8 handled the big Mercedes like a pro. She claimed to have been able to drive from the age of eleven, having been taught by joyriding classmates on the estate where she grew up. Right now, she was chewing gum and listening to punishingly loud techno on her earphones. As she turned the big wheel this way and that, her spiky ginger head bobbed in time to the music.

Victoria tapped her on the shoulder.

"Just down here, on the left."

With a squeal of tyres, they slithered to a halt in the middle of the road. Parked cars lined both sides of the street. Victoria nudged Cole, and they both climbed out. The air outside felt fresh in comparison to the heated comfort of the Mercedes, and Victoria was glad she had a fleece cap to keep her head warm. At the top of the street, between the buildings, she could see one of the towers of Brunel's famous Suspension Bridge. Originally the fevered dream of an eighteenth century wine merchant, the bridge had been designed by the engineer in the stovepipe hat and completed after his death. It spanned the gorge almost three hundred feet above the muddy River Avon, and was a magnet for sightseers and suicides alike.

Ack-Ack Macaque emerged from the front passenger door, and the Mercedes drove off to park.

William Cole had dressed in a pair of black jeans, an old sweatshirt, and a worn-looking tweed jacket. His thinning, unruly grey hair still stuck up at odd angles, despite his frequent attempts to smooth it into place.

"Which building is it?" he asked.

"This one." Victoria walked to the front door of one of the houses. An intercom had been screwed to the wall beside the door, with a separate buzzer for each of the six flats within. She dug in her pocket and pulled out the keys she'd found in the dead man's luggage. One had obviously been cut for an external door, the other for an internal lock. She tried the first, and it turned. The door was heavy and made of black-painted wood, and she had to shove to get it open.

Ack-Ack Macaque and William Cole followed her into an unlit hallway with a wide wooden staircase and black and white floor tiles.

"We want flat number three," she said, looking at the numbers on the doors to either side of her. "My guess is that it's on the next floor up."

They trooped up the stairs, and found the right door on the upper landing. Inside, the little flat smelled faintly stale. Threadbare curtains hung across the windows. By the light of the orange streetlamps, she could see that the main room was a sparsely furnished studio flat, with a futon at one end and a small kitchen area at the other. Another door led off into a cramped and damp-smelling bathroom, comprising no more than a shower stall, toilet and sink.

"This is it." She reached out a hand and flicked the light switch. Beside her, Cole gasped. The walls were covered in photographs and handwritten notes; and most of the photographs seemed to be black and white surveillance photos of him. He stepped into the room, gawping around at the pictures, and Victoria followed. The glossy prints showed Cole shopping in his local supermarket, a basket in the crook of his arm; standing on the edge of a marina on a bright morning, holding a mobile phone to his ear; getting into a battered-looking blue Renault in an underground car park; browsing bookshop shelves; struggling back from the off-licence with carrier bags filled with bottles of whiskey and gin...

"These go back months," Cole said. "How long was he watching me?"

In the doorway, Ack-Ack Macaque pulled the scarf from his face. He pocketed the dark glasses, and then fumbled around in his coat until he found the bag of banana and white chocolate cookies that K8 had baked, which he proceeded to eat.

"It looks as if you've got a stalker," he said, spraying crumbs. "I had one of those for a while last year. One of those gamer nerds who couldn't let go."

This was news to Victoria. She raised an eyebrow.

"You did? What happened to him?"

The monkey grinned, exposing dirty yellow teeth.

"Poor guy broke both his legs."

Victoria started to ask how, but then stopped and shook her head, deciding she'd be better off not knowing. Instead, she walked up to Cole, who was leaning close to the wall, reading the handwritten notes pinned beside each picture.

"Any clues?" To her, the scribbled words were just squiggles on paper, utterly indecipherable.

Cole tapped a picture of himself kneeling at a stone in a snowy memorial garden, a paper-wrapped bunch of flowers clutched in his hand. "It seems I've been under scrutiny for some time. At least since last Christmas."

"Any idea why?"

"Not so far." He turned to her. "But do you want to know something weird?" He pulled a note from the wall and held it out to her. "His handwriting is *exactly* the same as mine. Absolutely, spookily identical." He shivered.

Victoria peered at the paper trembling before her.

"I'll have to take your word for that." She watched as he opened his shaking fingers and let the note fall, spiralling down to the floorboards. "Why don't you sit down?"

Cole rubbed his beard. He seemed agitated.

"None of this brings us any closer to finding out who shot him." He tapped his ribcage. "Or who's been trying to kill me."

"I think we can assume for now that the same people are responsible for both," Victoria said.

The writer's nose wrinkled. "Even if that's the case, the question is: what am I going to do about it?" He glanced around at the walls, and crossed his arms over his chest. "Because poking around in this hovel isn't getting us anywhere."

Victoria felt her fists tighten at her sides. She licked her dry lips, and swallowed her irritation.

"Sit down," she said quietly. She took a breath. "We won't be here much longer. Have a rest."

Cole glared at her, but he sat on the futon. She left him there, muttering to himself and stroking his hairy chin, and went to see what the monkey was fiddling with. He'd been rummaging in the kitchen drawers.

"What's that you've got?"

He held it out to her.

"Another gun," he said.

"Is it the same as the last one?"

"No, boss." He tipped it into her outstretched hand, and she felt its weight. It was lighter then she'd been expecting. Also, it was like no gun she'd ever seen before. It looked like a pocket flashlight with a pistol grip fixed to the underside.

"What does it do?"

Ack-Ack Macaque reached out and took it back. He held it at arm's length and aimed the 'lens' at the far wall.

He pulled the trigger. Nothing seemed to happen.

"Is it broken?"

The monkey shook his head, and pointed a leathery finger at the wall. Amongst the papers, a small spot of plaster smouldered, molten red. The notes around it were charred at the edges; the photos had curled and melted, as if shrinking away from a flame.

"Good, huh? It must be some kind of ray gun."

Victoria scratched her chin. "Or an x-ray, perhaps?" She wished Paul were here, as she was sure he'd know. "Anyway, be careful where you point it."

Ack-Ack Macaque gave a gleeful simian grin. "Yes, boss."

She turned. "Hey, Cole. Have you ever seen anything like this?"

The writer looked up from wringing his hands. "What?" He stood upright, and shuffled over. "What is it?"

"A ray gun," Ack-Ack Macaque said.

"Let me see." Cole snatched the gun from the monkey's hand, and glowered at it. He turned it over and over in his hands. His tongue poked into the side of his cheek as he inhaled a long breath. "Ray gun, indeed." He stopped turning it and held it by the grip, forefinger resting on the trigger guard. He extended his arm and closed his left eye, drawing a bead on the futon.

"Be careful," Victoria said.

He turned to her. "I'm not an idiot."

"I never said you were..." Victoria trailed off. It was quite obvious that Cole had stopped listening to her. His eyes were focused on something she couldn't see: a thousand yard stare into the middle distance. His lips were working soundlessly, opening and closing, forming words she couldn't hear. The breath rasped in and out of his nostrils. "Uh, Cole?" He didn't react, and gave no signs of having heard her. She put a hand to his shoulder, and he went rigid. She could see beads of sweat forming at his temples. "What's happening? What's the matter?" She turned to Ack-Ack Macaque. "Is he having a fit?"

"How the hell would I know?"

Cole let out a moan. Every limb shook, and she thought he would fall. Then whatever was holding him seemed to relax its grip, and he sagged instead.

"I have to go." His voice was hoarse.

"Go? Go where?"

"Get away from me." He shook her off angrily. "I'm not waiting around here to be killed. I've got to go. Got to get out."

Holding the pistol at waist height, he blundered backwards until he stood in the open doorway.

Ack-Ack Macaque made to follow.

"Hey, Cole, wait."

The writer brandished the strange pistol in the monkey's face.

"Stay back!" His eyes were manic-looking slits. His lips were drawn back from his teeth. As Victoria watched, his knuckle whitened on the trigger. The shot drilled a smouldering hole through the top of Ack-Ack Macaque's fedora. "Stay back, or I'll kill you both!"

THEY LISTENED TO the American's footsteps clump down the stairs.

Ack-Ack Macaque turned to Victoria. "Should I go after him?" He had his hat in his hand, one finger exploring the charred puncture. The beam had burned its way in at the front, and out at the back, singeing a few hairs on the top of the monkey's head.

Victoria waved him on. "Yes, but be careful."

"What about you?" He flexed his leathery fingers, and drew one of the silver Colts from beneath his coat. "No offence, but I can probably move faster without you."

Downstairs, they heard the front door bang.

Victoria didn't have the energy for a chase. She couldn't keep up with the monkey, and she knew it. "I'll get a taxi back to the *Tereshkova,* and do some digging around. Find out if Cole had a twin, that sort of thing. Meanwhile, you and K8 find Cole and get him into the car. Call me when you're on your way back."

The monkey touched the barrel of the revolver to his brow. "Right-o."

"And Ack-Ack?"

"Yes, boss?"

"Try not to blow anything up."

# CHAPTER NINE
## THE MEN IN WHITE

WILLIAM'S HEART WAS a hunk of uranium: hot, heavy and crackling with toxicity.

Crashing out of the house, he turned right, and ran along the street until he reached an area with shops and bright lights. The boulangeries, patisseries, newsagents and offices were closing, and the pubs were filling up for the night. Rickshaws cut between the cars and vans; three-wheeled tuk-tuks chuntered past, farting petrol fumes. As he blundered past an open door, he got a whiff of stale beer, a blast of warm air and jukebox music.

Seeing the handwritten notes had shaken him. Up until that point, he'd been clinging to the idea that—however unlikely and fantastical it all seemed after four days without sleep—there would be a rational, mundane explanation for the sudden appearance of his doppelganger. Seeing the handwriting had changed all that. His understanding of the world had been shaken, and now all he wanted to do was flee.

Flee from the strangeness, and from the people who were out to kill him.

He didn't know what he could trust, or who he could count on. All he knew for sure was that somebody wanted him dead.

*Marie,* he thought. *Bill told me she'd help. And if there's a chance she's alive, anywhere or anyhow, I have to find her.* Wild hope surged against entrenched grief, and his legs wobbled beneath him. His knees felt soft like butter, and he couldn't remember the last time he'd eaten. He was empty. For the past four days, before boarding the *Tereshkova,* his body had been living off its own fat reserves while the speed quashed his appetite.

At a street corner, momentarily overcome by dizziness, he fell against the cast iron shaft of a Victorian-style lamppost.

How could his wife be both alive and dead? And which was the real Marie? And why had reality stopped making sense?

Parallel worlds?

Talking monkeys?

Car bombs?

Clinging on, he screwed his eyes tight. How could he comprehend any of this right now? As a habitual amphetamine user, he was used to a certain amount of craziness; but nothing on this scale, nothing of this magnitude. Like a frightened child, he wanted to run and lose himself in darkness and endless movement, until the world dwindled to a speck far behind him, and all its dangers and terrors were lost in his wake.

Releasing his grip on the lamppost, he blundered forward through a blur of pale faces. His eyeballs seemed to throb in time with his breathing.

In the past, when he'd been afraid to sleep, when his brain cells crackled with coffee and speed and he found himself gibbering at his keyboard at three am, his hands shaking too violently to type, his peripheral

vision itching with half-glimpsed phantasms; when
the chemicals got too much; when paranoia or
depression knocked the wind out of him or the walls
of his room tried to engulf him like the petals of a
carnivorous plant—when all that happened, he'd
known where to turn. There'd always been one
person who could straighten him out; one person
who could claw him back onto solid ground. When
he needed someone to talk him down and help him
get his shit together, he called his dealer, Sparky.

*Yeah,* he thought, *that's what I'll do. I'll go and
see Sparky. He lives near here. He'll help me. I
need to hole up somewhere and ride this out. He'll
understand, and maybe he'll have something to
straighten me out. A few dabs of the good stuff on
my gums, maybe, just to take the edge off.*

He staggered onwards, trying to ignore the
looks of the passers-by, and straightened his collar,
smoothed down his wild hair. His head spun and his
innards writhed like hooked eels, but at least he had
a direction. He had a goal. Like a drowning man
reaching for a lifebelt, he knew what he needed, and
where to get it. He was going to see a familiar face,
and he was going to clear his head. Only speed could
give him the clarity needed to cope with everything
that had been happening; and Sparky's place was as
good a bolthole as any.

*Yes,* he thought, *I'll go find Sparky. Good old
Sparky. He'll fix me up.*

BY THE TIME he reached the block of student flats
where Sparky lived, stumbling and cursing all the

way, he'd begun to feel calmer, and more rational. As quickly as it had come, the panic passed, leaving him washed-out like a beach at low tide. In the aftermath of its onslaught, the events of the day seemed less overpowering, and more like the leftover hallucinations of a particularly vivid dream.

Panting for breath, he stood in the shadow of the gnarled trees at the edge of the square, looking up at the rectangle of Sparky's fourth-floor window, wondering if the car bomb and his doppelganger had all been part of some kind of fit—perhaps the result of a seizure, or maybe even the first stirrings of a brain tumour?

Was he having some sort of paranoid breakdown? Was he going mad?

His hands trembled with the fear that he might, at any moment and without warning, slip back down that rabbit hole of delusion and madness. He could feel it there, like a dark sea beneath the icy crust of his sanity, just waiting to draw him in.

The cold air felt sharp and real on his cheeks and fingers. He tried to concentrate on it as he scratched his beard. Above, the light was on in Sparky's room. He knew he should go back to the house, try to find Captain Valois and the monkey, and apologise—but that light was warm and familiar. Looking at it, he could almost smell the flat's familiar mingled fug of chickpea curry and hash smoke. What would it hurt if he popped up for a few minutes? Sparky would be pleased to see him. The guy was pleased to see everybody. And maybe he'd have a few samples for his favourite customer?

*Maybe enough,* William thought, *to give me a little clarity?*

Clarity was what he needed now, more than anything; clarity, and the strength to stop himself coming apart at the seams. But he couldn't do it alone. He was too tired, too strung-out. He needed a little chemical pick-me-up. He could always make his way back to the *Tereshkova* afterwards. He could get a taxi. The speed would give him the energy and the nerve to do it. It would straighten him out, and hold him together.

He stepped out of the trees, onto the road. The buildings around the square were tall Georgian townhouses, fronted in pale stone. They had steps up to their front doors, and steps down to their basements. Some had wrought iron balconies, and several had been converted into offices, or subdivided into flats. He looked left and right. Two men stood at the corner of the square, watching him. They wore long white raincoats, white fedoras, and matching gloves. Even their shoes were white.

William frowned. They were dressed the way he thought angels might dress; yet something about them seemed to radiate menace.

"William Cole?" They spoke in unison. Startled, he stepped back, away from the light.

"Who are you?" He didn't feel up to talking. All he wanted was to get inside, and get fixed up.

The one on the left spoke.

"I am Mister Reynolds, and this is Mister Bailey. We knew you'd come, eventually, and we've been waiting."

Cole took another step back. They watched him with expressionless calm.

"What do you want?"

"We want you to come with us."

"Where?" He was playing for time, shuffling back towards the shops and crowds on the streets beyond the square. Moving in step, they kept pace.

"You know where," Reynolds said.

He blinked at them.

"What?"

"Don't try to stall us, Cole. You cannot change what must happen." Without breaking stride, they opened the left sides of their white coats, revealing ivory-handled pistols. Seeing them, William wanted to turn and flee, but his knees were still weak, and he knew he couldn't outrun a bullet. Instead, he fumbled in his pockets, until his fingers closed on the gun he'd taken from Bill's house.

Seeing what he was doing, the men in white drew their pistols in one smooth, coordinated sweep, and aimed them at his head.

"Don't try to pull that out," Reynolds warned.

With his hand still in his pocket, William felt for the trigger. He could hardly breathe.

"We wanted you to come with us, Cole," Bailey said.

"But if you're going to be awkward," Reynolds finished, "we'll have to shoot you where you stand."

Side-by-side, their gun barrels stared at him like the soulless, empty sockets of a metal skull.

In his pocket, his finger closed on the trigger, but he made no move to pull out his hand. Instead, heart squirming in his chest, he squeezed, firing through the material of his coat. Mister Bailey gave a grunt, as if he'd been punched, and dropped to his knees, pawing feebly at a charred spot on his chest. Reynolds looked down at him in confusion.

Moving as if in a dream, William turned his hips and fired again. Reynolds yelped, and his gun clattered to the floor as his hands went to the pencil-thin hole speared through his left thigh. Without even thinking, William had fired twice through the lining of his coat into the two men in white. The beam had burned through their skin and bone as easily as it had through paper.

And it had set light to the fabric of his coat. With his hands beating at the flames, and his nostrils filled with the stink of bonfires, he turned and ran for all he was worth.

# TECHSNARK
**BLOGGING WITH ATTITUDE**

### Legion of the Bland?
**Posted:** 08/11/2060 – 16:00 GMT
| Share |

Wave of the future, or totalitarian techno terror? Whatever your opinion on the white-suited Californian cult, one thing's for certain: the 'Gestalt' is here to stay.

Since its inception a mere two years ago, the cult's grown at an unprecedented, and some would say alarming, rate. Their website boasts more than a million linked-up members across the world and, just yesterday, they petitioned the United Nations in New York, demanding to be recognised as a sovereign nation – a nation without geographical or ethnic boundaries.

Adherents to the faith use adapted soul-catcher technology to broadcast every thought and image in their heads to every other member of the cult. They can 'hear' what each other is thinking, twenty-four hours a day, three hundred and sixty-five days per year; and they claim this makes them the ultimate democracy, with 100% participation in every decision. Human language is, they argue, too limited and imprecise a medium to truly and reliably communicate the complexities of our innermost nature; only by linking brains, they say, can we fully engage in meaningful discourse.

According to its literature, the Gestalt cult aims to create a 'global consciousness' and free humanity from the hatreds and conflicts that have dogged its history. And yet, despite all this techno-utopianism, the individual members (if they can still be described as 'individual' in any meaningful sense) exhibit a disappointing blandness – the complacent vacuity of born-again converts whose troublesome personalities have been sterilised in the name of conformity. Yes, they seem happy but, speaking personally, I don't trust them. There's something sinister about the way they move and talk in unison. I grew up believing in freedom and individualism, but the men and women of the Gestalt seem dedicated to wiping out every quirk and foible, turning us all into mindless drones. They might wear white, but don't let that fool you. Beneath that smiling, angelic exterior, they're no better than ants in a nest or bees in a hive.

Read more | Like | Comment | Share

# CHAPTER TEN
## UGLY SONOFABITCH

THE DOWNS WERE an expanse of green parkland that ran along the lip of the Avon Gorge, sandwiched between its cliffs on one side and the city on the other. They ran a couple of miles downstream from the Suspension Bridge, eventually blurring into the leafy avenues of Sneyd Park and Henleaze. Having left the house, Ack-Ack Macaque figured Cole would have come this way, trying to lose himself in the darkness beyond the streetlights; but, so far, all he'd found had been a pair of urban fox cubs rooting through a bin, a drunken reveller asleep on the grass, and a misted-up car full of dope-smoking teenagers listening to Parisian techno.

Freed from the encumbrance of his overcoat, which he'd stashed beneath a park bench, and wearing only a t-shirt and holsters, he moved like a wraith through the cold November night, scampering on all fours from one clump of trees to the next, his breath steaming like cigar smoke from his mouth. Most of the Downs had been given over to rough grassland, and he tried to stick to the overgrown areas, hoping that if anyone saw him, they might mistake him in the dark for a dog.

From certain vantages, he could see right down into the bowl of the city. Bristol nestled around the old harbour side, where tall ships had once tied up, carrying tobacco and slaves, bringing in the wealth that had paid for much of the city's construction. Those docks had been a major global port; a hub of commerce and piracy; and the jumping off point for expeditions to far-flung lands of unexplored exotica. Now, all he could see down there were the glittering hologram signs that strutted and danced above the nightclubs and restaurants, and the advertising blimps drifting like goldfish between the church spires and high-rise hotels of the city centre—from which the surrounding districts spread, clinging to the sides of the ancient arterial roads like frost accumulating around the strands of a spider's web.

Like a dog, he was trying to pick up the writer's scent, but the smells of the city were too strong. They came drifting across with the omnipresent buzz of traffic and the occasional wailing siren. The ground around him smelled of moss and dog shit. The wind brought the oniony tang of fast food from the streets at the edge of the park, and animal scents from the nearby zoo; and, he had to admit, all those cigars hadn't done his sense of smell any favours. Nevertheless, he kept searching until his SincPhone rang.

"What?"

"It's me, boss." K8 sounded annoyingly perky. "I'm parked across from the flat."

"I'm not there anymore."

"I know, Captain Valois told me. Have you found Cole?"

"What the fuck do you think?"

"No sign, huh?"

Ack-Ack Macaque looked at the orange streetlamps, and the lit windows of the shops and houses, wondering if he'd made the right call. He'd assumed Cole would have made for the cover of trees and darkness; but maybe that was his own instinct talking. What if the old guy had gone into the city instead, trying to lose himself in the crowd? "A city this size, he could vanish forever."

"Do you think he might have jumped off the bridge?" K8's tone held the ghoulish delight of a teenager. "I hear people do that sometimes."

"Nah." Ack-Ack Macaque let his free hand drop to the gun at his side. "He was frightened, not suicidal." His leathery fingers drummed against the holster, and he scanned the horizon. "I just keep wondering: if I were an unstable, gun-toting psychopath, where would I go?"

K8 laughed. "You *are* an unstable, gun-toting psychopath."

Ack-Ack Macaque harrumphed. He was about to end the call—his thumb was actually on the button—when she took a sharp intake of breath. He heard the Mercedes'z leather seat creak beneath her as she wriggled lower.

"What is it?" he asked, all humour gone. "What's happening?"

"A car just pulled up." Her voice had dropped to a breathless whisper. "A guy got out. Now he's letting himself into the flat. The car's leaving."

Ack-Ack Macaque looked around at the empty park. "Is he a cop?"

"I don't think so. That wasn't a police car, and the guy at the door doesn't look like a policeman. He's big and ugly-looking, and I think he means business."

Ack-Ack Macaque huffed. Tonight was supposed to have been a party night, and here he was, chasing a madman on a common when he could have been lying drunk under a table somewhere. "Okay, I'll be with you in a couple of minutes. Keep your head down until then. Don't let them see you."

"You don't need to tell me twice, Skip." Even over the phone, her excitement was palpable.

He sighed. Teenagers…

"Just do it, fuckwit."

HE RETRIEVED HIS coat and hat, and retraced his steps. When he reached the house, he saw the Mercedes parked at the opposite kerb, in the shadow of the Avon Gorge Hotel. He opened the passenger door and slid in beside her.

"Is he still up there?" He couldn't see any lights behind the first floor windows.

"No-one's come out yet."

He dumped his hat and coat onto the back seat, and hunched down beside her, with his feet pressed against the dashboard. "If he's sitting in there in the dark, I'd guess he's planning to jump somebody."

"The dead guy?"

Ack-Ack Macaque pulled out one of his Colts and checked the cylinder. "Chances are, he already knows he's dead. I'm guessing he had something to do with it, and now he's come back to stake out this place." All six shells were where they should have been, so he snapped the cylinder back into place, and re-holstered the gun.

"But why?" K8 wriggled closer to him. "Who's he waiting for?"

"Cole."

Her eyes widened. "Cole?"

"Somebody tried to kill him, then his double turned up dead." He pulled out his second revolver, and flicked it open. "The two events have to be connected."

"But why would big-and-ugly in there expect Cole to come here?" A furrow appeared between K8's eyebrows. She may have been exceptionally bright when it came to computers and electronic systems but, like most teenagers, adult motivations were still largely a mystery to her.

"He did though, didn't he?" Ack-Ack Macaque glanced at the copper shells nestling in the second gun. All six were present and correct, which meant he had twelve shots altogether, should he need them.

"Yes." K8's frown deepened. "But that's because we brought him with us."

Ack-Ack Macaque returned the second gun to its holster and cracked his hairy knuckles.

"In which case, as far as the bloke in there's concerned, we're Cole's allies."

K8 wriggled lower in her seat. She had a flick knife in her sock, and a small Beretta in the glove box.

"Skipper, all that stuff Cole was saying about parallel universes?"

"Sounded like bullshit to me."

"You don't think it's possible?"

"I haven't a clue." Ack-Ack Macaque scratched his belly beneath the t-shirt. "Just remember he writes science fiction. Those guys are all nuts. They've all got a screw loose somewhere."

K8 jerked a thumb at the unlit window. "So, who do you think our friend is?"

Ack-Ack Macaque let his lips peel back over his yellow incisors. "There's only one way to find out."

"Does it involve violence, by any chance?"

"Hell, yeah." He reached for the door. "You stay here, I'll grab him, and we can beat it out of him."

IN THE OLD days, back in the game, he wouldn't have thought twice about kicking down the front door and going in with both guns blazing. It was his style, his *modus operandi*. But he wasn't in the game anymore; oh no, those days were long gone, along with his invulnerability. He wasn't bulletproof anymore. Like it or not, over the past months, he'd had to get used to operating in the real world. Out here, actions had consequences, and injuries were real. He'd had to learn that the hard way. He'd had to wise up and find a way to temper his natural recklessness.

So, now, despite being tempted to mount a screeching frontal assault on the flat, he instead made his way around to the back of the building, where the waste water pipes from all the sinks and toilets clung to the outside wall like a giant, multi-limbed stick insect. If the building were alive, these pipes would be its digestive system. He had to climb over some bins to reach them. The main pipe was about the width of his thigh, and moulded from some kind of hard black plastic. Hardly breaking stride, he wrapped his hands and feet around it, and began to climb.

Reaching the first floor took a few seconds. A tributary pipe branched off, disappearing into the wall beneath the frosted glass of a bathroom window. Hanging by one hand from the main pipe, he stretched for the windowsill. The height didn't bother him; he was only about twenty feet up, and, in his time, he'd scaled much taller trees. Having made the sill, he saw that the window came in two parts: ones which opened outward like a door, and the other, smaller one above it, which hinged upwards like a flap. Right now, only the smaller one was open.

Clinging to the sill by his toes, he reached in and carefully unlatched the bigger window. Then he was inside, perched on the edge of a ceramic sink in a darkened bathroom no bigger than a large closet. His nostrils twitched at the damp reek of mouthwash, hair product and black mould. And there, behind it all, something else: a trace of something unfamiliar, something that hadn't been in the flat earlier; something that smelled of wet hair and stale, almost oniony sweat. Whoever this guy was, he smelled more like an ape than a human.

Leaving the window open behind him, Ack-Ack Macaque dropped silently to the floor and reached for the door handle with his left hand. As he did so, he drew one of his pistols with his right. If he wanted to get the jump on the guy in the flat, he had to be stealthy.

*Like a motherfucking ninja*, he thought to himself. But the door fittings were old. As he gently tugged the handle, the hinges squeaked. The living room light snapped on, and he found himself staring down the barrel of a fat silencer.

So much for stealth.

He leapt back and slammed the door, and dropped to the bathroom's tiled floor. Muffled shots blew splinters from the door panels and spanged off the sink, spraying him with chips. He rolled onto his back and fired both Colts through the gap between his feet. Three times he squeezed the triggers. In the enclosed space, the noise was thunderous. When he'd finished, most of the lower half of the door was gone.

Groans came from the other room. Ack-Ack Macaque slid his ass across the tiles, and kicked the remains of the door from its hinges.

"Anybody alive out there?"

No reply came; at least, none that he could hear. His ears felt as if spikes had been driven into them.

He had to move fast. Firstly, he knew K8 would have heard his shots, and he didn't want her blundering up here, not until he was sure it was safe. Secondly, half the city had probably heard them too, and he had no doubt the police would be on their way.

Standing, he edged around the doorframe, guns held out in front of him, ready to empty the rest of his bullets into anything that moved.

His shots had scythed through the flat at shin height, splintering wood, cloth and bone. Now, a thick-set man lay curled around a bloody leg wound, trying to stem the flow of blood from where a clean, white shard of bone stuck out from the back of his calf.

Ack-Ack Macaque pointed both revolvers at the man's head.

"Drop the gun, sweetheart," he said. The man glared up at him from under a heavy brow, and he did a double take. When K8 had told him that the guy was ugly, she hadn't been kidding. The man—if indeed he was a man—had a large, bulbous nose, with cavernous, hairy nostrils; his stubble-covered lower jaw seemed too large for his face, and his shovel-like teeth too numerous for his mouth. With one over-sized hand still clamped over the wound in his leg, he tried to raise his gun; but Ack-Ack Macaque sprang forward and stamped on the weapon, forcing the tip of the silencer into the floor. "I said, drop it, dickhead." He slammed the butt of one of his Colts into the man's temple. The man's head snapped sideways, hit the wall with a smack, and he slumped to the floor unconscious.

For a few moments, the only sound Ack-Ack Macaque could hear in the flat was the sound of his own panting breath. He holstered the gun in his left hand, but kept the right one drawn, in case of trouble. Then he bent over to take a look at his fallen opponent. The guy wasn't particularly tall, but he had powerful, muscular arms, broad shoulders, and a barrel-shaped chest. He wore a shabby overcoat and a cheap brown suit. The ridge on his forehead was far more pronounced than it had first appeared; and his unusually large jaw and protruding chin made his face look as if it had been somehow pulled forward.

"Ugly sonofabitch, aren't you?" Keeping the Colt aimed at the guy's face, he slipped a hand inside the raincoat, looking for a wallet, or anything that might identify who—or what—he might be. As he rummaged, he heard the front door slam, and the sound of shoes on the stairs. His SincPhone rang, but he didn't answer it. Instead, he stood up and faced the open door, gun at the ready.

A couple of seconds later, Cole stood swaying at the threshold. His eyes were wide, and he was out of breath. His coat had a blackened hole in it.

"Monkey?" The word was a croak from dry lips.

Ack-Ack Macaque raised his revolver.

"Don't move, fucknuts."

But Cole didn't seem to hear him. Without another word, the writer lurched forward, and collapsed into his arms.

# CHAPTER ELEVEN
## ANDROGYNOUS SEVERITY

VICTORIA VALOIS RETURNED to the *Tereshkova* by helicopter. Almost three years had passed since her helicopter crash in the South Atlantic, and yet she still thought about it every time she climbed into one, remembering the helplessness and terror that had possessed her as the ailing craft hit the slate grey sea and started to sink. The raised scar on her temple served as a constant reminder that she'd been lucky not to die in the accident—that she'd only survived thanks to the gelware that had been used to replace the damaged areas of her brain.

Now, when the helicopter from Bristol touched down safely on the pad fixed to the *Tereshkova*'s upper surface, she felt her clenched fingers and toes relax. Today had been a long day, and she was ready for a hot shower and a good night's sleep, but she knew she'd get neither for a while yet—not with her professional curiosity aroused and prowling, hungry for answers.

Moving slowly, she made her way down through the hatch that led into the body of the skyliner. A flight of metal stairs took her down past one of the main gasbags, to a draughty walkway that ran the length of the *Tereshkova*'s central hull—almost a full kilometre in length. If she felt the need, she could walk all the way to bow or stern, past storage areas housing passenger luggage, freight, and essential supplies; additional gas bags; and a thousand other nooks and crannies containing who knew what. For thirty years, the *Tereshkova* had been the Commodore's private fiefdom, filled with souvenirs and trophies from a life hard lived and dearly sold; it had been his home and his attic, and now it was hers, and she didn't have the heart to start rooting through its alcoves, chucking out his stuff.

A series of companionways took her down through another four levels, until she reached the one that led down to the main gondola. She could hear piano music swirling up from the passenger lounge, where a cocktail pianist tinkled on an electronic keyboard, and smell the remnants of the evening's dinner from the kitchen. Her head was bare, and the top two buttons of her tunic undone. As she clomped down the grille metal steps, she saw someone waiting for her at the bottom. At first, she could only see their shoes; then their baggy cargo pants. The build and stance looked familiar but, for a second, she couldn't place it. Then she spotted the tattoos on the figure's arms, and her heart bucked in her chest like a startled horse.

"Paul?"

She took the last couple of steps in a daze, and there he was, waiting for her with a stupid grin plastered across his face.

"Do you like it?"

She couldn't let go of the metal banister. Paul was dead; he'd been murdered, and his brain had been removed; she'd seen the body, been at the funeral; and now all that was left of him was the electronic copy of his mind that lived in the *Tereshkova*'s computer. And yet here he was, standing before her, as apparently solid and alive as she was.

"I don't understand. What's going on?"

He held up a hand.

"Don't freak out, Vic."

"I'm not freaking out, I'm just—" She stopped, and narrowed her eyes. Then, very slowly, she pressed her hand into his chest. Her fingers passed through the material of his garish Hawaiian shirt without resistance, and pushed in up to the wrist. "You're a hologram?" Her heart sank. For a moment she'd allowed herself to hope that, however unlikely it might seem, he'd found a way to reincarnate himself. Now she knew what she was looking at, it became obvious he was a projection: a little pixelation here, a little blurriness there.

"Yeah, pretty good, don't you think?"

She pulled her hand back, feeling her breathing slow, and her pulse return to normal.

"How do you do it?"

He gave a modest shrug. "I had the idea while you were away, and got one of the mechanics to cobble it together for me." He pointed at his feet. "There's a little remote controlled car down here on the floor, with a tiny projector mounted on it. I control it using the skyliner's WiFi, and I use cameras on the front to see where it's going."

"Wow. That's pretty good. I have to admit, you had me there for a second." She bent down and reached into the image of his trainers. Her hands closed around something hard, and she pulled it out. His image flickered and died, and she found herself holding a toy car. It was around twenty centimetres in length, with fat rubber tyres and several projection lenses protruding from its roof. A tiny camera sat on its bonnet.

"Sorry if I startled you." Paul's voice came from a speaker bolted to the side of the car. Victoria turned the vehicle over, looking at the wiring.

"So, what's the range on this thing?"

"It can go anywhere on this deck."

"Only this deck?" Victoria bent at the knees, and placed the little car back on the floor. When she straightened up, Paul's image reappeared, looking almost as deceptively solid as before.

"I haven't found a way to make it climb stairs yet." He looked down at his hands. "It's just a prototype. Perhaps I'll build the next version into a little remote-controlled helicopter or something. Maybe one of those floating cameras, like the one the monkey smashed. Or maybe one of those quad copter drones, they look pretty cool."

"So, are you in there?"

"I'm still in the ship. This is just a remote. But it has the capacity. I could download into it if I needed to." He shrugged. "Anyway, how did it go for you? Did you find any clues?"

"We lost Cole."

"You lost him? You mean he's—?"

"No, he's not dead. He just ran off."

"Where'd he go?"

"I don't know." Victoria's eyes felt suddenly tired. She pinched the bridge of her nose between thumb and forefinger. "I sent the monkey to find him."

"Was that wise?"

"Damned if I know."

Paul took off his glasses. "I don't understand why you have to be involved." He wiped the lenses on the hem of his brightly patterned shirt. "Why don't you turn the case over to the local *federales*, and be done with it?"

Victoria stretched.

"Things have been a bit sedate around here recently, and I need a change of pace."

"Let me guess, you're just a simple journo at heart, right?"

Victoria pushed her fists into her pockets. "What can I say? I miss that stuff."

"Things have changed."

"You don't need to remind me." The helicopter accident had put an end to her career as a writer, but the old urges were still there, and she couldn't walk away from a mystery.

She made to step around Paul's ghost but, as she did so, he held up a hand to stop her.

"Hold on."

She paused. "What is it?" He was made entirely of light. If she wanted to, she could walk right through him; but, somehow, to do so seemed impolite.

"It looks as if you were followed."

"What do you mean?"

"There was a stowaway on your chopper. She was in the luggage compartment at the back. God knows how she got in there."

Victoria's tiredness vanished. "Where is she now?"

"I've got her on camera. She's making her way down one of the service ladders."

"Where's she going?"

"Looks like the accommodation section."

Victoria hurried through the lounge, along the connecting corridor, and into her office. Paul's image followed, the little battery-powered car whining as it kept pace. "Anyone we know?"

"Apparently not."

She shrugged off her tunic and sat behind the desk. "Have you run her face against the passenger manifest?"

"First thing I did."

"And you got nothing?"

"Well, duh."

"Show me." A few years ago, the Commodore had installed a SincPad in the top of the desk. Being unable to read, Victoria usually kept it switched off, using its glass screen as little more than a surface on which to rest her elbows. Now, for the first time in months, the display brightened into life, showing a grainy black and white feed from a camera in the corridor outside the crew's quarters. A slim, black-clad and obviously female figure was trying to jimmy the door to Cole's cabin. "Is this live?"

"Yes, it's happening right now." Paul reached up to fiddle with the gold stud in his ear. "How do you wish to respond?"

Victoria peered at the picture. She didn't know who this woman was but, as there'd already been one murder on the airship, she wasn't about to take any chances.

"Get some crew down there. Make sure they're armed, and have her brought to me."

"Aye-aye, Captain."

\*      \*      \*

VICTORIA WATCHED THE screen as three of her stewards approached the intruder. By this time, the woman had gained access to cabin, and was crouched over Cole's luggage, her hands rummaging through its contents. She froze when she heard the stewards in the corridor outside. Then, when they pushed the door open, she backed up against the wall, hands spread flat against it, ready to spring.

"Don't move," Paul said. Although his image stood at the side of Victoria's desk, she knew his consciousness—if you could call it that—still lurked in the skyliner's computer systems, where it could monitor everything that happened on board, and that his voice was being relayed to the woman in the cabin via the intercom system. "We have you surrounded. There's nowhere to go."

On the screen, Victoria saw the woman glance upwards. Her eyes found the CCTV camera, and she smiled. It was a smile of recognition, and resignation. Without taking her eyes from the lens, she relaxed her stance, and raised her hands.

"We've got her," Paul said.

Victoria watched the stewards cuff her, and then switched off the screen. She sat back and pulled the Commodore's cutlass from the umbrella stand.

"Tell them to bring her straight here."

"Have done."

Paul walked to the picture window that took up most of the wall behind the desk. Patting the flat of the blade against her palm, Victoria turned in her chair and looked out, trying to imagine what he was seeing through the little camera stuck to the front of the toy car supporting his image.

Beyond the window, she could see the whale-like undersides of the *Tereshkova*'s hulls, and the lit windows and red and green running lights of the other gondolas. Below, at the edge of the airfield, a motorway cut southwards like a ribbon of orange light. She could see cars and trucks skimming its surface. Further away, the lights of the two Severn crossings, their humped backs carrying other motorways westward across the river, into Wales.

Although she'd been here a few times over the years, this wasn't a part of the country she knew well. Nevertheless, it felt good to be back in England. However far the skyliner took her, the United Kingdom of France, Great Britain, Northern Ireland and Norway would always be her home—and she guessed Paul felt much the same.

He watched as she placed the cutlass on the desk and retrieved her white tunic. The shiny buttons were large and easy to fasten in a hurry. When she'd finished, she stood straight and looked at her reflection in the glass of the window: a tall woman in a military jacket, her bald, scarred head and strong-boned face lending her a handsome, almost androgynous severity.

She heard footsteps in the hall, and Paul said, "The stewards are outside."

With a tug, she straightened the hem of the tunic. Then she picked up the cutlass and stuck it through her sash. "How do I look?"

"Totally badass."

She smiled despite herself. "Then, I guess you'd better let them in."

# CHAPTER TWELVE
## NOVEMBER RAIN

HALF-CARRYING THE half-conscious Cole, Ack-Ack Macaque staggered out of the building's door. Across the street, K8 was in trouble. A couple of uglies had pulled open the door of the Mercedes and were trying to haul her from the car. They were short and stocky, just like the one he'd left in the apartment above, and he wondered again who—or what—they were.

"No time for guessing," he muttered. Inside the car, K8 scratched and bit at the hands that clawed at her. Thrashing like a trapped animal, she tried to reach the gun she'd stashed in the glove box, but the uglies were strong, with big hands, and seemed impervious to her blows. As he watched, she let fly with a kick that would have broken the arm of a normal man.

"Get away from me, you creeps!"

With his left hand still supporting Cole, Ack-Ack Macaque drew one of his Colts and put a bullet through the nearest of her attackers. The report was loud in the empty street, and he winced at the stab of pain from his already-damaged ears. The guy he'd hit fell against the car, and then slid down to the tarmac. He had a bullet in the spine. If he lived, he'd never walk again.

Ack-Ack Macaque gave a grunt.

"That'll teach you to pick on kids."

The remaining attacker let go of K8 and spun around. He had the same thick brow ridge and protruding lower jaw as the others. Like them, he reminded Ack-Ack Macaque of a hairless gorilla.

"Hold it right there, Delilah." Ack-Ack Macaque waved the Colt at him. "Step away from the irate teenager." He glanced at K8. She had a split lip, and her sleeve was torn. "You okay, kid?"

"I've had worse." She climbed out of the car and came over and took Cole from him. As she helped the writer into the back seat of the car, Ack-Ack Macaque kicked the dead thug aside, and led the other around to the rear of the vehicle, where he popped the boot.

"Get in." The ape-man scowled, and shook his head, stance defiant. Ack-Ack Macaque let his fangs show. "Don't fuck with me, Tinkerbell. I've already shot two of your friends tonight. No reason I shouldn't make it three."

He heard sirens: distant now, but closing fast. In minutes, the place would be swarming with police. If this lunkhead wouldn't move, there was only one thing he could do.

"Don't say I didn't warn you." He squeezed the trigger and the Colt leapt in his hand. The shot bit a bloody chunk from the man's thigh. As he bent in pain, Ack-Ack Macaque brought the gun barrel up in a vicious swing that caught him under his over-sized chin, knocking him back into the waiting trunk.

The sirens were close now. Ack-Ack Macaque grabbed the man's dangling legs and stuffed them inside. "Try not to bleed on the upholstery," he said, and slammed the boot shut. "How are we doing, K8?"

Cole had been laid out across the back seat, still insensible. K8 closed the door and hopped into the front seat.

"Get in, Skipper." She turned the key and the engine boomed to life. Ack-Ack Macaque bounded onto the roof, and slid over to the passenger side. The door was open, and he swung in. He was still closing it when she let the brake off, and the big Mercedes leapt forward, throwing him back in his seat.


WITH THE PEDAL pressed firmly to the metal, and a mile-wide grin on her face, K8 flung them through a maze of narrow terrace streets. She had one eye on the road, the other on the Sat Nav screen. Her hands and feet moved in sharp, precise jabs, spinning the wheel and stamping the brake, then the accelerator. In the seat next to her, Ack-Ack Macaque clung to his armrest. As they slithered around a particularly tight turn, the wing mirror on his side splintered, snatched away by the rear light of a parked car.

"Jeez!"

K8's grin grew wider than ever. She was obviously having the time of her life. The car moved like an extension of her will.

"Drive it like you stole it, Skip."

She gunned the gas again, and they tore down a steep, tree-lined hill, at the bottom of which, Ack-Ack Macaque saw a busy main road. His fingers dug into the armrest but, just before they reached the junction, K8 stood on the brakes, and the heavy Mercedes squealing to a stop.

In the sudden silence, K8 cracked her knuckles and smiled at him. The air smelled of burned rubber.

"I think we're out of trouble," she said, glancing in the rear view mirror. "And, fun as that was, we'd better stop drawing attention to ourselves."

She changed gear and pulled out into the traffic. Keeping to the speed limit, she drove the big Mercedes along the road, which ran alongside the city docks. Across the water, Ack-Ack Macaque saw the masts and floodlit prow of Brunel's *SS. Great Britain*—the first iron-hulled steamship to brave the Atlantic, and a direct ancestor to the *Tereshkova* and all the other skyliners now plying the trade routes of the world. Nervously, he looked behind them, but saw no flashing blue lights. They were just one car among dozens now, going with the flow.

During the violent manoeuvres, Cole had been thrown from the back seat and now lay sprawled across the floor, with his head in one of the foot wells and his legs in the other. Ack-Ack Macaque decided to leave him there. He swivelled back to face the front, and stuck a finger in his ear. Firing his guns in the enclosed space of the bathroom had been a bad idea. He could have burst an eardrum. As it was, who knew what long-term damage he'd done to his hearing? At the moment, everything sounded muffled, as if he'd stuck gum in his ears, and waggling his finger in the hole brought no relief, no matter how hard he did it.

"Everything okay, Skipper?"

"Huh?"

"I said, are you okay?"

He sniffed the tip of his finger, and then slipped it into his mouth.

"Nothing serious," he said around the taste of the earwax. "Just a little deaf from the gunshots." He tried to sound cavalier, but the truth was he couldn't get away from the thought that, like the grey hairs around his muzzle, the damage to his ears was a sign that he was as mortal as anyone else—something he'd never had to worry about when he'd been immersed in the game, back before Merovech and friends busted him out of the Céleste Tech labs; back when he'd been the indestructible WWII flying ace, and all he'd had to worry about were enemy planes and banana shortages; back where guns never jammed, parachutes always opened, and the skies were forever a bright, brilliant blue.

They passed office blocks and bus stops. At the end of the road, K8 took a left up Park Street to avoid the city centre. The shops on the hill were arranged in a neatly stepped terrace, at the top of which the dramatic Neo-Gothic tower of the Wills Memorial Building loomed over the university.

Ack-Ack Macaque watched the reflection of the Mercedes as it flickered from one shop window to the next. He still wore only his t-shirt and ammo belt, and found himself wishing for the warmth of his flight jacket, which he'd left in his cabin, back on the *Tereshkova*. His coat and fedora were folded on the back seat, but he didn't like them as much as he liked the jacket. It had been a present from K8. She'd also given him a matching leather flying cap and a pair of goggles. They were the same as the ones he'd worn in the game; and that was the whole point. The outfit was his brand. When he wore it, people recognised him. He wasn't just a monkey then, he was a character.

He'd been the star of one of the world's most popular online virtual reality games; and then last year, after he and Victoria helped thwart a plot to trigger nuclear Armageddon, he'd become one of the most recognisable faces on the planet. Photos of him had been splashed over every newscast and web bulletin. His existence had been big news: a monkey raised to sentience via brain implants. They painted him as a walking, talking marvel; a cartoon character made real; a real-life superhero. He was the monkey who'd saved the world.

And then, at the height of it all, he'd walked away. He couldn't handle the fame, and he didn't want it. He had been trying to get his head around the fact that he was living in the middle of the twenty-first century and not, as he'd thought, in 1944. He needed rest and relaxation; so he stuck with the *Tereshkova*, and her new owner, Victoria Valois. Victoria needed a pilot, and he needed sanctuary. The deal worked for both of them.

He had a strange relationship with Victoria, and he didn't have the emotional vocabulary to describe it. She was his commanding officer, and she was his friend. The species gap ruled out any hint of romance, and yet there was something between them that was deeper than mutual respect: a recognition of kinship, perhaps. When they looked into each other's eyes, they saw a little of themselves staring back. They were both artificial creatures. Both their minds ran like software on the synthetic gelware neurons packed into their skulls; and both had been products of the Céleste Technologies lab in Paris. They were abandoned prototypes, and therefore both unique. But uniqueness led to loneliness. The *Tereshkova* was the closest thing he had to a home, K8 and Victoria the closest thing he had to any sort of family; but there was nobody who really understood him; no other talking monkeys to sympathise and share his pain.

And nobody he could fuck.

He rubbed his leather eye patch. The empty socket itched sometimes, especially in cold weather.

In California, some pony-tailed Buddhists had tried to explain to him about Karma and the journey of the soul.

*What savage atrocity did I commit,* he wondered, *to have to live this life as a talking monkey?*

Whatever it was, he hoped it had been spectacular.

Thinking about loneliness reminded him of the Gestalt, and the offer Reynolds had made earlier that evening.

How would it feel, he pondered, to be permanently hardwired into the thoughts and feelings of hundreds of other people; to be part of a larger, emergent personality; a single thought in a vast torrent of consciousness?

He could see how that kind of surrender might be a comfort, for some. Humans, like most primates, were social creatures. They clustered together in packs, seeking the safety, reassurance and approval of the tribe. Outcasts were miserable, distrusted and frowned-upon, and had a tendency to die early. If joining the Gestalt meant an end to loneliness, he could see how they might find doing so attractive; but it wouldn't work for him. He'd still be the only monkey in a sea of apes; still just as alone, however many humans he had crawling through his head, chattering away about their human feelings, and human problems.

Reynolds could go fuck himself. It was bad enough having to talk to humans, without being forced to hear all the crap that bubbled around inside their swollen brains. He'd rather be lonely than submerge himself in babble.

And yet, he had to admit, the white suits they wore did look kind of cool.

A raindrop hit the windscreen. Then another. As their patter became an insistent drumming, K8 hit the wipers.

Ack-Ack Macaque looked out at the suddenly slick and shiny road. Back in the game, he hadn't had to worry about rain; the weather had always been perfect: a perpetual high summer just right for dogfights. Of course, he'd seen rain before that; he wasn't a stranger to it. He'd spent the early part of his life in Amsterdam, made to battle other monkeys and apes in illegal backstreet knife fights. That was how he'd lost his left eye. His memories of that time were vague, to say the least. He hadn't been fully self-aware in those days; he'd been an average monkey, unable to speak. And without language, there had been no naming of things, and hence, no memory of having seen them. All he had were a few images, fuzzed by his lack of understanding, and blotted by the clumsy footprints of his subsequent neural surgery. If he concentrated, he could remember rain dappling the waters of a wine-dark canal at night, breaking up the reflections of the neon shop signs; and thunder that cracked and growled over the city like the very wrath of God. But how much of that was actual memory, and how much had his newly expanded brain backfilled over the years?

His real memories began with the game. His sentience and, to some extent, his personality, came preloaded on the synthetic gelware processors they stuffed into his skull. He'd been created to prove a point. He was a spin-off from AI weapons research, employed in a computer game to show the validity of using uplifted primate brains as CPUs for military drones. He hadn't been the first monkey those bastards at Céleste Tech had uplifted, nor was he the last—but, thanks to the fallout of last year's brouhaha, all the scientists were in jail, and all the other monkeys were dead.

He was, and now always would be, the only one of his kind.

# CHAPTER THIRTEEN
## MARIE

THE WOMAN STOOD before Victoria's desk, her hands bound before her, her feet apart, and her shoulders thrown back. She was, Victoria guessed, somewhere in her mid-to-late forties, and wore a black fleece top, black jodhpurs, and knee-length fur boots. Frizzy orange hair tumbled around her cheeks.

"I'll ask you again. Who are you, and why were you on my helicopter?"

The woman returned her stare. The lines at the corners of her eyes made her look as if she were permanently squinting against a bright light.

"I want to see William Cole." Chin raised, she spoke in a clear Home Counties accent. Victoria might have lost her ability to parse written text, but she could still read people, and if this woman weren't military in some way, she'd eat her wig. And with that in mind, perhaps she ought to try another tack.

Taking a deep breath, she pulled herself up to her full height and fixed the woman with her hardest stare. Then, trying to channel the Commodore's best parade ground bark, snapped, "What's your name, soldier?"

The prisoner blinked in surprise, and her posture straightened. If she hadn't been wearing cuffs, she would have snapped to attention.

"I'm not saying another word until I see William." She sounded less sure of herself now, but her continuing stubbornness revealed itself in the way her hands and jaw tightened. Seeing this, Victoria sighed inwardly. From long experience, she could sense when someone was likely to open up to her, and when they weren't. Still, the drill sergeant routine had been worth a try. Now, she'd have to think of something else.

When the *Tereshkova*'s stewards had apprehended the woman, she had been unarmed. If she was a killer, she was an unusually empty-handed one. All Victoria really had on her was that she'd stowed away in order to get aboard, and had broken into Cole's cabin; but her insistence on seeing Cole suggested her motive hadn't been burglary.

If she wasn't a killer or a thief, what was she?

Victoria walked around the desk, and stood close to the prisoner.

"Are you a friend of his?"

The woman looked sideways at her.

"You could say that."

"Then why won't you tell me who you are?"

The eyes swivelled to face forwards again, staring across the desk at the large picture window and the darkened skies beyond. "Because the less you know, the better."

"And why is that, pourquoi?"

"I can't say. Just let me see him."

Victoria perched on the edge of her desk. She could feel the cold of the metal through her jeans.

"I'm afraid he's not here."

"Not here?" The woman blinked rapidly. A tendon stood out on her neck. "Then where is he?"

"He went ashore."

"Is he all right?"

Victoria smiled to herself, knowing she'd found a way in, a crack in her opponent's armour.

"You answer one of my questions," she said, "and I'll think about answering one of yours." She crossed her arms. "So, tell me: why are you so keen to see Mister Cole?"

The woman's shoulders slumped, and she shifted her weight onto one hip.

"I'm concerned about him."

Victoria sucked her bottom lip.

"Pourquoi?"

"Because he's in danger."

"Yes, I gathered that. But you're not the first person tonight to come looking for him. I've got another one down in the infirmary. His name's Bill. Maybe you know him?"

"Is he okay?"

"He's dead."

The woman stiffened. "How?"

Victoria shook her head. That wasn't how the game was played.

"First, tell me who you are, and why you're so interested in Cole."

The woman's chin dropped to her chest as she looked down at her bound wrists. She rubbed the back of one hand with the fingers of the other.

"My name's Marie." She spoke quietly, without looking up. She seemed to be fighting a battle with herself. "And I'm his wife."

Victoria frowned. "Cole's wife is dead." She'd been reading through the writer's online biography, trying to figure out who Bill might be, and knew Marie had died over two years ago, from an infection contracted during a routine appendectomy.

The orange haired woman raised her eyes, expression bleak.

"Apparently not."


WHEN THE CHOPPER carrying Ack-Ack Macaque, K8 and William Cole touched down on the *Tereshkova*'s main helipad, Victoria was there to meet it. Wind and rain whipped in from the Bristol Channel, making her wince. Two stewards flanked her. It was past midnight now, and she was ready for her bunk.

K8 stepped down from the helicopter first, followed by Cole. Both had cuts and bruises. Cole seemed dazed, but he was upright, walking with one hand to his head. Ack-Ack Macaque came last, moving stiffly, dragging a body.

"Who's that?" She had to shout over the noise of the rotors.

Ack-Ack Macaque had been pulling the guy by the lapels; now, he let him drop onto the wet rubber of the pad.

"We got into a fight."

"You don't say?"

Without being asked, the stewards stooped, took hold of the body by its legs and arms, and carried it below decks. Standing there, in the helicopter's wet downdraught, Victoria gave silent thanks to the Commodore for having trained them so well.

The helicopter couldn't stay on the pad for long.

The wind was too strong. The noise of its engines increased as it throttled up, preparing to depart. As it thundered away into the midnight sky, Victoria led the writer, the girl and the monkey down the main companionway, through the body of the airship, and into the warmth of the main gondola; but instead of heading for her office, she took them aft, past the passenger cabins and infirmary, to the brig.

"Why the brig?" Cole asked. He had some colour in his cheeks, and his breath smelled like a distillery. Apparently Ack-Ack Macaque had been using shots of rum to revive him during the helicopter flight.

Victoria paused at the door. "It's the safest place on the ship. And besides, there's someone in here I want you to meet."

The brig was a small room, just large enough to accommodate a narrow bunk and a stainless steel toilet. Its door was made of thick, soundproof glass. Inside, Marie stood with her back to them and her head down. Her hands were still cuffed together in front of her. Cascades of orange ringlets curtained her face. When Victoria pressed the keypad that unlocked the door, she turned, and the light caught the side of her cheek.

William Cole blinked.

"Oh!"

Victoria put a hand on his shoulder.

"Steady."

He turned to her, eyes bulging.

"I'm sorry, I can't—" Victoria felt his knees wobble. The vestibule held no chairs. As carefully as she could, she helped him over to the riveted metal wall. He leant his shoulder against it, and put his face in his hands.

When she looked around, Ack-Ack Macaque and K8 were staring at her. The monkey had one of his pistols in hand, just in case. He jerked a thumb at Marie.

"Who the *hell* is this?"

Cole trembled. Perhaps springing this on him had been a mistake; and yet, Victoria had been half-expecting him to denounce the woman as a fraud. She'd done some research and, as far as she could ascertain, Marie Cole was definitely dead. At least, the Marie Cole from this world...

The woman with the orange hair walked up to the open cell door, and leaned out.

"Hello, William."

He wouldn't look at her. Instead, he slid down into a crouch, and then bent forward with a tormented moan, wrapping his arms around his head, trying to block her out.

Victoria looked up at Marie.

"I'm sorry."

The other woman shrugged. "Don't be. It must be a terrible shock for him."

"And not the first he's had today."

Standing beside the cell door, Ack-Ack Macaque cleared his throat.

"Okay, I'll ask again." His tail twitched ominously. "Who the hell is this?"

Marie turned to him.

"I'm William's wife."

"Bullshit."

Marie held up her hands. The cuffs clanked together. "I can prove it."

"How?"

"Run any test you like. Fingerprints, DNA, whatever."

Ack-Ack Macaque looked her up and down, and then turned his sepia eye on Victoria.

"Can we do that, boss?"

Victoria shook her head. "Sorry. I already thought of it, but we just don't have the equipment."

Cole's hands fell from watery, bloodshot eyes.

"It's her," he said. His voice silenced the room. "Only you're not *her*, though, are you?" He curled his lip. "You look just like her, but you're not really *her*. I saw her body. You're no more the real Marie than your dead friend was the real me."

Marie lowered her arms.

"I am her, William. At least, I was until her baby died. That's where we split." She swallowed nervously. "She lost a child, I didn't. But up until that point, we were essentially the same person, identical in every way." She brushed a wisp of orange behind her left ear. "I am what she would have been, had things been different."

Cole glowered up at her from beneath his wiry eyebrows.

"But things weren't different, were they?"

Marie flinched at the bitterness in his voice.

"I loved you every bit as much as she did."

"No you didn't." Cole knuckled his eyes. "You loved the other one, the dead one. Bill. What was he, your husband?"

"He was. But in many ways, so are you."

Cole rubbed his forehead, hard, as if trying to dislodge a stuck thought, or an embedded arrow. "Where are you from?"

"You know," Marie said. "Deep down, you know. You've been writing about it for years. That's why we came to find you."

Cole looked blank. Marie took a step towards him, and Ack-Ack Macaque brought his gun up, covering her, making sure she made no sudden moves.

"Mendelblatt's world," she said, "Where the UK and France never merged, and there aren't any Zeppelins in the skies over London."

"Mendelblatt?" Cole's face was a mask of anguish and confusion. "You mean—?"

She raised her cuffed hands, imploring him to believe her.

"That isn't sci-fi you're writing, my darling; it's memory."

**BREAKING NEWS**

From *The Commonwealth Sentinel*, online edition:

**Palace Moves To Block Movie**

LONDON 15/10/2060 – This morning, Buckingham Palace issued a statement expressing its opposition to the making of a movie based around the events of last year's attempted royal coup d'état.

Titled *Ack-Ack Macaque*, after the world-famous monkey, the multi-million dollar movie will tell the story of events leading up to the death of King William V, and the subsequent ascension to the throne of HRH King Merovech, then Prince of Wales. While some details of the so-called 'Combat de La Manche' have been made public, much remains classified, and royal sources fear that the gaps will be filled in by 'guesswork and fabrication, making any attempt at an impartial enquiry impossible.'

The film will be directed by BAFTA-winning British director, Tonya Field, who co-wrote the script with her husband and long-time collaborator, Tim Duncan. In 2057, the pair won an Oscar for their controversial screenplay, *Andre's Choice*, about the life of a surgically enhanced male prostitute on the streets of Berlin.

No actors have yet been named, but insiders tip teen favourite Brad Foley to play the Prince, and expect motion-capture specialist Ashton Stanislavski to be brought in to play the monkey. A veteran of sci-fi epics, Stanislavski is probably best known to UK audiences for his portrayal of the alien in 2053's horror blockbuster, *Death Station*. If the rumours are true, he will be playing one of the world's most unusual and enigmatic celebrities: an intelligent monkey with a passion for cigars and alcohol, and a pathological dislike of the paparazzi.

Having spent several years portraying the main character in an online video game, the real-life 'Ack-Ack Macaque' somehow escaped from the headquarters of Céleste Technologies in Paris, and made his way to the coast, where he joined forces with Prince Merovech and became embroiled in the fight against Céleste Tech's owner, the Duchess of Brittany, thereby averting a potentially catastrophic nuclear confrontation with China. Since then, the monkey has been living as a recluse aboard the skyliner *Tereshkova*, and has refused all requests for interviews or publicity.

In its strongly worded statement, the Palace called the forthcoming movie, 'a cynical and ill-informed attempt to turn a serious international event into a tawdry spectacle.'

Ack-Ack Macaque himself was unavailable for comment.

Read more | Like | Comment | Share

**Related Stories**

'Gestalt' members among four injured in multiple shootings.

North Sea fish stocks 'beyond recovery'.

European Commonwealth leaders meet for crucial budget summit.

Netherlands announces 'massive' flood defence scheme.

Royal wedding set for June 5th.

US carries out fatal drone strike in Nepal.

Elephants declared extinct in the wild.

Missing writer's car found at airport.

# CHAPTER FOURTEEN
## SPECIAL CIRCUMSTANCES

As a cool and watery sun rose beyond the portholes, Ack-Ack Macaque stood at the foot of another infirmary bed.

"We seem to be collecting bodies," he said. The room smelled of antiseptic and disinfectant. In front of him lay the guy he'd shot and dumped in the car. Somehow, despite the blood loss, the man had survived. Monitors and drips had been plugged into him to keep him alive.

Paul's hologram stood to one side of the bed, stroking his chin.

"How are you doing?" Ack-Ack Macaque asked.

Paul's face fell. He scratched at the wispy suggestion of a beard around his chin.

"You've never been killed, have you? Not even in the game, I mean."

"Not so far."

"Then you don't know what it's like, being a ghost, always on the outside of everything."

Ack-Ack Macaque thought of the hat and coat he had to wear in public. "Maybe I got some idea."

Paul wasn't listening. He held his palms out in front of him, and turned them over as if inspecting them for dirt. "I have hands, but I can't touch anything." He looked up. "I have a tongue, but I can't taste."

Ack-Ack Macaque rolled the cigar from one side of his mouth to the other. "You can complain though, can't you?"

Paul blinked at him. "I beg your pardon?"

Ack-Ack Macaque made his hand into a puppet's flapping mouth. "Yap, yap, yap." He laughed, and the tips of Paul's ears reddened. "So, you don't like being a ghost? Don't be a fucking ghost. Be something else."

"Like what?"

Ack-Ack Macaque waved his arms in an impatient gesture that took in the gondola and the five hulls above it. "Hell, you're practically running this ship. Why not plug yourself right in? Stop pussyfooting around. Stop being a ghost, start being an airship."

Paul's forehead grew lined in thought. He removed his glasses, blew on the lenses, and polished them on the hem of his long white coat. As a hologram, Paul had no need to clean them, and the action achieved nothing; but Ack-Ack Macaque knew he clung to these old habitual gestures. They were part of who he was, part of what made him Paul.

"You know, you could be on to something."

Ack-Ack Macaque clacked his teeth together. "Hey, you know the old saying: If life gives you lemons, pull a gun on it and say, 'Fuck your lemons, where are the goddamn bananas?'"

Paul smiled, and tapped an index finger against his chin. "If I could hook myself into the navigation software," he said slowly. "If I could somehow wire into the telemetry, and maybe co-opt the main bridge computers..." He looked up. "Yes, it could be done. I could totally run this whole ship." His eyes were shining. "Ack-ster, you're a genius."

Ack-Ack Macaque waved a hand. "Yeah, yeah." He looked down at the unconscious ape-man on the infirmary bunk. "Back to business. You were about to tell me about good-looking here."

"Yes, sorry." Paul hooked his glasses over his ears. In life, he had been a medical researcher, specialising in brain implants. "Well, the thing is, I've never seen anything quite like him before. I don't even think he's human. At least, not in the strictest sense."

"If he ain't human, what is he?"

"I'm not sure." Paul reached out a hand to indicate the figure's upper arm. "His bones are shorter and thicker than most people's. And take a look at the shape of the skull. The shape of his nose, and that ridge above his eyes."

Ack-Ack Macaque chomped the cigar between his molars, but didn't light it. "He's certainly one ugly motherfucker."

"He's more than that." Paul straightened up. Somehow he'd edited his appearance. The Hawaiian shirt and cargo pants were gone, replaced by blue jeans and a faded red sweatshirt, which he wore beneath a pristine white doctor's coat, complete with pens in the breast pocket and a stethoscope slung around his neck. "At least, he might be."

"Might be what?" Ack-Ack Macaque spoke around the cigar.

Paul pushed his glasses more firmly onto the bridge of his nose.

"Do you know what a Neanderthal is?"

"A type of cocktail?"

"Neanderthals were a type of intelligent hominid." Ack-Ack Macaque frowned. "A what?"

"Like a cave man."

"Gotcha."

Paul pointed to the man's arms. "They had thicker bones than modern people, bigger jaws; and they lived in Europe around the time of the last ice age."

"Great, so now we know what he is."

"Yes, but that's left us with a much bigger question."

"Why does he smell so bad?"

"No." Paul put his hands in the pockets of his white coat. "It's that the last Neanderthals disappeared thirty thousand years ago. He shouldn't even be here."

"They're extinct?"

"They died out, or interbred with modern humans." He shrugged his shoulders. "The point is, there hasn't been a Neanderthal on the Earth for thirty thousand years, and suddenly you run into three of them, all on the same night, in Bristol."

Ack-Ack Macaque patted the Colts at his sides. "And I made two of the bastards extinct, all over again."

Paul didn't hear him. "It just doesn't make any sense." The skin between his eyebrows furrowed. He started to pace back and forth beside the bed, talking to himself. "Unless somebody's breeding them from fossil remains. But that's ludicrous. This one here's at least twenty-five years old. How could you keep it a secret that long; and, assuming you could, why would you risk exposure now?"

"Beats me, I only work here." Ack-Ack Macaque pulled the damp, oily-tasting cigar from his mouth. "Did you try going through his pockets?"

"One of the stewards did. He found a wallet. It's on that table in the corner." Paul held up his holographic hands. "I can't touch it."

Ack-Ack Macaque replaced his cigar and shuffled over to the table. The wallet lay on a shiny steel tray, along with a few coins, a flick knife, and a black plastic comb. The knife had a yellowish ivory handle. The comb had seen better days. He picked up the wallet and opened it.

"Not much here." He pulled out a dog-eared business card. "Only this."

A tiny electric motor whined as Paul's image 'walked' over to him.

"What does it say?"

"It's from a company called Legion Haulage. There's a number, but no address." Ack-Ack Macaque turned the card over. "The back's blank."

"Legion Haulage?" Paul tapped his chin. "They're not in my database. Maybe K8 can find them?"

Ack-Ack Macaque slipped the card into his gun belt. "She's asleep right now. I'll ask her when she wakes up." He looked down at the bed and wrinkled his nose. "In the meantime, what are we going to do with smelly here?"

"Victoria wants him kept alive, to see if he can tell us who he is, and where he came from."

The monkey cracked his knuckles. "Wake him up, and I'll slap it out of him."

Paul shook his head. "He's sedated at the moment. And she strictly forbade torture."

Ack-Ack Macaque huffed. "She can talk." He leant over the bed towards Paul. "Wasn't it her that dropped an assassin off this ship?"

Paul looked uncomfortable, and Ack-Ack Macaque knew he'd been present at the time, existing as a virtual ghost inside Victoria's neural gelware.

"He was more robot than man."

"Yes, but she didn't know that at the time, though, did she?" While interrogating the prisoner in one of the *Tereshkova*'s cargo bays, Victoria had allowed the man to fall to his death, from several thousand feet above Windsor Castle.

"Those were... special circumstances." Paul looked away. "That man was Cassius Berg. He killed me. He cut my brain out, and tried to do the same to Vicky. And he was threatening the safety of everyone on this airship."

Ack-Ack Macaque grinned around his cigar. "Hey, I'm not criticising, I would've dumped the fucker myself."

Paul's hands moved jerkily. He rubbed the back of his neck. "You don't understand. It really cut her up inside to do it. She doesn't want anything like that happening again. It nearly destroyed her."

"Even with a scumbag like that?"

Paul sighed. "Perhaps you don't know her as well as I do."

Ack-Ack Macaque bridled. He'd been flying for Victoria Valois for over a year. "I know she's a hell of a lot tougher than she thinks she is." He spared the caveman a final glance, and turned for the door. "Where are you going?"

He didn't turn around. "Up and out."

"Taking the Spitfire up for a jaunt?"

In the doorway, Ack-Ack Macaque pulled out his lighter. "You'd better believe it, my friend." He struck a flame and puffed the cigar to life. "It's been a long night, and I've got a lot of aggression left to work off."

# CHAPTER FIFTEEN
## SCOURGE OF THE SKYWAYS

AN HOUR LATER, at the other end of the main gondola, Victoria Valois sat behind the desk in her office, and regarded Marie over the steeple of her fingers. William Cole wasn't there; the writer had been sedated. The man hadn't slept in God only knew how long, and he'd had more than enough surprises for one day. Between the drugs, the car bomb, and everything else, his sanity had been dangling by a thread. Knocking him out had seemed by far the kindest option.

Sitting across the desk, Marie returned her gaze. Her hands, now unbound, were resting comfortably on the arms of her chair.

"So," Victoria said. "You really are his wife?"

The other woman brushed back an orange curl. "A version of her."

"From a parallel world; yes, I get it." Victoria dropped her hands to the desk. "The question is: what are you doing here, now?"

Marie straightened in her chair. "I've come to protect him."

"From whom?"

"Certain parties."

Victoria chewed her lower lip. "You said he was

writing memories. Is that why they're trying to kill him, because of something he's remembered?"

"William's special. He's creative, and like a lot of creative people, he's sort of attuned to the probabilities and possibilities of the timelines. Without knowing it, he's picking up on the experiences of his other selves. Not memories as such, more like glimpses of the other world. I can't really explain it, except to say that it's like the rapport you get between identical twins. Sometimes, when something happens to one of his alternate selves, he senses it. He has dreams, and they feed into his writing. He thinks he's making all those stories up, but he isn't. He's just trying to get down on paper what's going on at the back of his head."

"And what is that?"

Marie rubbed the bridge of her nose with her index finger. She stifled a yawn.

"Look, Captain, I probably shouldn't be telling you this, but you seem a reasonable sort."

"Telling me what?"

"That there's a war going on."

Victoria raised a sceptical eyebrow. "A war?"

"William knows nothing about it, but he's involved nevertheless, whether he likes it or not."

"How so?"

"Because of his gift." Her fingers picked at a loose thread on the armrest. "The truth is, the war hasn't been going so well for us. We've been losing territory, falling back."

"So, why come here?"

"Because the battle's spreading."

"I don't like the sound of that."

"Nor should you."

From beyond the walls of the gondola, she heard the scream of a Rolls Royce engine; Ack-Ack Macaque was out there, putting his Spitfire through its paces, throwing it into loops and rolls above the airfield. She picked up a pen from the desk and clicked the end of it. Then she held it to her ear and clicked it again, two or three times. She could feel that they were getting close to the truth of things now; but her experience told her to stay quiet. People often divulged more than they wanted to if she simply gave them the space to do it. Her silence unnerved them, and they spoke to fill it. Leaning back in her chair, she tapped the end of the pen against her lower lip. Would the tactic work here? She liked to think of herself as a pretty good judge of character, and Marie struck her as a sharp cookie. Nevertheless, she held her tongue, and waited to see what would happen.

Part of her was convinced that, all evidence to the contrary, the whole 'parallel world' story would fall apart. After all, how could it possibly be true? The idea ran counter to every instinct in her body. And yet, how else to explain William Cole's doppelganger, and the reappearance of his dead wife? Across the desk, Marie's position hadn't changed. Her hands still rested loosely on the arms of her chair, and she showed no sign of agitation or discomfort, and certainly no burning urge to talk.

Okay, Victoria thought, this fish isn't biting. She gave the pen a final click, and tossed it back onto the desk. But, before she could marshal her next round of questions, somebody tapped on the office door.

"Come in."

K8 stepped into the room.

"I've got a result for you." She walked up to the desk and laid the printout in front of Victoria.

"What does it say?"

The teenager ran her tongue around her teeth, and glanced at Marie.

"I found Legion Haulage. They're a transport business, based in Rotterdam." She leant over and tapped her finger on some of the words. Victoria looked, but the black marks on the paper might as well have been written in Martian for all the sense they made. "They're a front for another company, who are a front for another in turn. If you follow the chain of front companies back far enough—" Her finger traced down the page. "You find out that they're owned by the Gestalt." She straightened up with a what-do-you-think-about-that look on her face.

Victoria smoothed a hand backwards across her bald scalp.

"Are you sure?"

"It's all there, in black and white."

"So it's possible the things that attacked you—"

"Were working for the men in white, yes. At least, it's a possibility."

Victoria frowned. "But what would the Gestalt want with William Cole?"

K8 shrugged. "Who knows? What would anyone want with him?" She glanced at Marie. "No offence."

The woman with the orange hair dipped her head and smiled. *None taken.*

"It still doesn't explain where the Neanderthals came from." Victoria hadn't slept all night, and she'd spent much of the past hour listening to Paul's speculations on the caveman nature of their prisoner. Now, she could feel her neural implant upping her production of adrenaline, fighting to keep her sharp. "I mean, where did they get them?"

Marie cleared her throat. Sitting up in her chair, she raised a hand.

"Perhaps I can help, Captain?"

Victoria pulled her fighting staff from the pocket of her tunic.

"I was just thinking the very same thing." With her head throbbing with fatigue, she clonked the staff onto the desktop. *Time to stop acting like a journalist,* she thought, *and time to start behaving like a skyliner captain.*

Under international law, skyliners were classed as autonomous city-states, able to travel where they wished, and govern themselves however their captains saw fit. They had been carrying passengers and freight around the world for almost a hundred years, and had become so vital to global commerce that now no country would risk interfering with the neutrality of a single vessel, for fear of boycott by the rest. On board, the captain's word was law. They were the undisputed masters of their little flying cities, and had the final say on everything from criminal trials to business deals and marriages. Yet, they weren't tyrants. At least, the majority weren't. Passengers tended to avoid skyliners famed for repressive laws or unusual punishments, and so, in order to survive economically, captains were obliged to run their ships with a modicum of fairness and equitability—but only a modicum. Skyliner captains enjoyed a reputation for eccentricity and ruthlessness unsurpassed by any profession since the eighteenth century sail ship captains of the Spanish Main.

Among them, Victoria was something of an oddity: she hadn't risen up through the ranks, and had no experience. But, as the Commodore's appointed heir and successor, she had the respect of her crew, and a burgeoning reputation based on her striking physical appearance and the fact that it was the *Tereshkova* she commanded: a vessel now famous to the public as the skyliner which, last year, had rammed the royal yacht in the middle of the English Channel. The well-documented fact that she'd also thrown an assassin out of a cargo hatch helped. According to the British tabloids, she was Victoria Valois, the half-human scourge of the skyways. Sometimes, it took her a while to remember that.

With a French curse, she pushed back her chair and rose to her feet.

"I have a dead guy in my infirmary, and a caveman in the bed next to him." She waved a finger in Marie's face. "Now, how about you start talking. I want to know why you're here, and how you got here!"

Marie's knuckles whitened on the arms of her chair.

"I told you—"

"That you're here to protect Cole? Yes, I know. But there's more to it than that, isn't there? You didn't just come here to find him, did you?"

The other woman's eyes widened. Victoria saw her nostrils flare.

"No."

"Then, what?"

Marie looked down at her knees. She ran her tongue around her lips, and her shoulders tensed. She seemed to be steeling herself to speak. When she looked up, her eyes were bright with desperation.

"It's my daughter."

"Your daughter?"

Marie glanced at K8. "She's about your age. Her name's Lila."

Victoria leant forward across the desk, her palms either side of the retracted fighting staff.

"What about her?"

Marie thrust her chin forward defiantly. Her eyes glittered.

"They have her."

"Who?"

"The Gestalt. They have her, and I'm here to get her back."

"By yourself?"

"Bill was helping me." The woman ran a hand across her eyes. "They killed him."

"And Cole?" Victoria bent her elbows, leaning closer. "Where does he figure into this?"

Marie squeezed her hands shut. She looked at K8.

"Lila's his daughter too."

# CHAPTER SIXTEEN
## FIRE POSITION

K8 LEFT THE Captain talking to the orange-haired lady, and wandered back in the direction of her cabin. As she passed through the gondola's main lounge, the sun shone through the brass-rimmed portholes. Motes danced in the light. Uniformed stewards bustled back and forth, serving breakfast to a handful of passengers, clustered in ones and twos around the small, circular tables. As a plate went past, she caught the smell of bacon and scrambled eggs, and her stomach growled. She'd been awake all night, and hadn't eaten anything for hours. For a moment, she dithered, trying to decide whether to sit down and eat, or head back to her cabin and crash in her bunk.

In the end, sleep won out. She was young, and needed her rest. Pausing only to snag a slice of toast from the serving table, she went aft, along the main accommodation corridor.

As she walked, she nibbled a corner of the toast, and pondered the events of the night. One thing particularly bugged her. She'd heard Marie claim the Gestalt had killed William Cole's doppelganger. But if Reynolds had been with the Captain when Bill was shot, he couldn't have done the deed—which meant

Bill's killer could still be on board, somewhere, waiting for the chance to strike again.

How many members of the Gestalt were on the current passenger list?

She needed to talk to Ack-Ack Macaque. He'd know what to do. He always knew what to do. Just being around him made her feel safe. Partly it was his proclivity for violence—she knew he'd rip apart anyone who tried to harm her. He was like the big brother she'd never had, and the pet she'd always wanted: a big, sweary monkey who drank and smoked and was dangerous to other people, but always safe, safe, safe for her.

Not, of course, that she'd ever admit to such feelings. Where she came from, you learned to keep your emotions to yourself and never show a hint of weakness, or dependence on anyone else. And besides, she knew that if she tried to tell him how she felt, he'd laugh at her. Not in a cruel way, maybe; but not in a sympathetic way, either. As far as he was concerned, they were comrades in arms. She was his wingman, and that was all there was to it.

They'd first met in the game world. Impressed by her hacking and gaming skills, Céleste Tech had brought her in to help monitor the monkey's behaviour. They plucked her from the slums of Glasgow and flew her to their labs on the outskirts of Paris, where they had the monkey strapped to a couch in a lab, his artificially enhanced brain hooked into the simulated world, believing the dogfights and battles around him were real. They'd already used up four previous primates, and couldn't work out why the monkeys kept cracking up. It was K8's job to keep the latest, Ack-Ack Macaque himself, sane and operational. Instead, when he escaped into the countryside outside Paris, she went after him—not to get him back, but rather to help him bring down the company, and everything for which it stood.

When she'd gone to Paris, it had been the first time she'd left her native Glasgow. Most of her teens up until that point had been spent in her bedroom, illuminated by the blue glow of a computer monitor. Now, just over a year later, she'd been all around the world working as a navigator on the *Tereshkova*, playing co-pilot to an ill-tempered, cigar-chomping monkey. She'd walked the streets of New York and San Francisco, feeling like a character in a movie; seen the sun set over the Pacific; looked down from her porthole at the splendour of the Grand Canyon. And yet, despite it all, she was still the shorthaired little ginger kid from the Easterside estate, acting tough because she had to; because that was the only way she knew how. The irony was, she no longer had to worry about the mean kids, the schoolyard bullies, or her parents' fighting. Her hacking skills had taken her out of Scotland, and anyone who tried to intimidate her now would first have to deal with an angry and heavily armed primate; but she'd been putting up a front so long she couldn't let go of it. It had become a part of who she was. She'd been acting the plucky little tough girl so long that now she couldn't tell exactly where the role ended and the real her began.

Her shoes echoed on the metal deck. The doors to the passenger staterooms were made of polished wood. The door to Ack-Ack Macaque's, which was situated farther back, in the crew section, was metal.

It was an oval hatch, with a lip like the hatch of a cabin in a seagoing ship. As she reached it, she heard the howl of the Spit's Rolls Royce Merlin engine, and knew he was still out there, flinging himself around the sky, reliving his glory days as a fighter pilot.

Disappointed, she thought about going back to her own cabin, but didn't feel like being alone. Instead, holding the toast in her mouth, she pushed down on the handle, intending to curl up on his spare bunk. He wouldn't mind, and she could barricade herself in his cabin while she waited for him, wrapped in the reassuring, homely scents of old cigar smoke, leather and animal sweat.

She shouldered the door open and, taking the toast from her mouth, stifled a yawn with the back of her hand. The room was dark. Still yawning, she fumbled her hand along the inside of the wall, searching for the switch. As she did so, she heard the rustle of clothing, and became aware of another presence in the room.

Before she could cry out, gloved hands closed firmly around her arm. Other hands closed over her mouth and nose, and squeezed her throat, holding her head still. She kicked out in the darkness, but their grip only tightened. There were at least two people holding her. The pressure on her larynx stopped her from being able to shout. She couldn't even breathe. Frantically, she kicked and thrashed, but the hands held her in place. Something cold pressed against her neck, and she flinched, expecting a gunshot. Instead, there was a loud, mechanical click, and a needle punched through the skin above her collarbone, into the muscle beneath.

\* \* \*

THE SPITFIRE'S COCKPIT was cold, and smelled like a zoo, but that was just the way Ack-Ack Macaque liked it. Six thousand feet above the airfield, high above the uppermost antennae of the hovering *Tereshkova*, he wheeled the plane through the crisp morning air. From up here, through the perspex bubble of the cockpit, he could see down the length of the Estuary, towards the distant southerly hills of Exmoor; and west, across the rolling landscape of Wales, to the bracken-brown peaks of the Brecon Beacons. No trace remained of last night's rain. The sky was an endless blue, the air as fresh and clear as a melt-water stream, and his heart sang an accompaniment to the engine's holler.

Wrapped in his leather flying jacket and favourite silk scarf, he pushed his goggles up onto the top of his head, and peered down at the city streets whirling beneath his wings. He wondered how many people were still asleep in the houses on the outskirts of the airfield. Pushing the stick forward, he put the Spit into a screaming dive and held it—ignoring the screams of protest from air traffic control—until the altimeter dial had almost wound down to zero. At the last possible moment, less than a hundred feet above the deck, he hauled back and pulled up the nose, booming over the suburban roofs and gardens at three hundred miles per hour, rattling windows and setting off car alarms.

Cackling, he kept low, only pulling up once the houses gave way to fields and industrial units. Then, throttle pushed forward, he aimed the old plane's nose at the sky. The Spit leapt like a prancing horse, eager to kick up its heels, and he gave it the beans, glorying in the shuddering roar of the engine. This was what he was, what he'd always been: first and foremost, a pilot.

"To slip the ugly bonds of Earth," he misquoted around his cigar. "To punch the stupid, smiling face of God." His voice sounded muffled. His ears still ached from last night's gunfire, and the changes in pressure caused by these manoeuvres weren't helping. He opened his mouth wide to let them pop, then pushed aside his left earphone and waggled his little finger in the hole. His whole head felt like a bubble that refused to burst. "Fuck it," he muttered. Time to go home. A bit of rest and recuperation would do him more good than titting about in a plane, however chary he was to admit it.

He levelled out his climb at five thousand feet. By now, he was over the bronze-coloured waters of the Severn, so he put the plane into a wide turn, intending to bring it back to the *Tereshkova*.

He passed over the Second Severn Crossing, flashing through the gap between its massive concrete towers, and brought the nose around to face the rising sun.

As the cigar-shaped silhouette of the airship hove into view ahead, he clocked a helicopter lifting from its upper deck. But it wasn't one of the tubby passenger choppers that belonged to the ship. This was a sleek, small, and expensive-looking dragonfly; able to carry no more than two or three people; maybe four, at a push.

"Special delivery," he muttered, wondering if the 'copter had just picked someone up, or just dropped them off. He watched it climb into the sky, heading eastwards over the city, away from him. In his experience, an expensive 'copter like that usually belonged to a high-ranking business person or celebrity—or, he thought with a scowl, that bloody film crew who wanted to make a movie about him. Couldn't they get it though their thick, coke-addled heads that he wasn't the slightest bit interested in seeing a Hollywood version of his life? If he'd wanted fame, he could have had all he could handle last year in the wake of that scrap in the Channel. But he hadn't. He'd chosen to fly away on the *Tereshkova* instead. Couldn't those people take a bloody hint?

For the past half an hour, he'd been ignoring the radio chatter from the ground. Mostly, they'd been shouting at him for breaking rules and flying dangerously, and he'd sort of tuned them out. Now though, as he watched the helicopter pull away, he became aware of a new note of urgency in their voices.

*Ack-ster, Ack-ster, respond please. This is Paul. Respond please.*

"Hey Paul, what's up?"

*Oh, man, where have you been? I've been calling you.*

"I'm here, I'm here. What's the problem? Are the Hollywood people here again?"

*It's K8. They've got K8.*

Ack-Ack Macaque felt the hairs prickle on his neck. "Who's got her?"

*The Gestalt. They grabbed her from your cabin. They were disguised as passengers. They disabled some of our cameras, but I caught them taking her up to the roof. She looked drugged.*

His hands squeezed the stick.

"Where are they now?"

*They had a helicopter waiting. It was registered as a courier from Legion Haulage.*

Ack-Ack Macaque glared forward, through the bulletproof windshield.

"Small, pricey-looking job?"

*Yes.*

"I see it."

*What are you going to do?*

The push-button control for firing the Spitfire's eight machine guns was mounted on the stick. A cover prevented accidental firing during manoeuvres.

"What the hell do you think I'm going to do?" He took the cover between finger and thumb, and rotated it a quarter turn, from the 'safe' position to the 'fire' position. "I'm going to get her back."

# CHAPTER SEVENTEEN
## MY EYES

WILLIAM COLE LAY on his bunk, staring up at the painted metal ceiling. He felt washed-out and his thoughts, trodden down by the sedatives he'd been given, were soft and gloopy.

"My daughter?" His mouth was dry, his voice a croak.

"Yes, my love." Marie knelt beside the bed, and placed her hands on his arm. "Lila, our daughter."

"But, I don't have a daughter."

"Yes, you do. Or rather, you should have done."

"I don't follow." In the gloom of the curtained cabin, she looked and sounded so much like *his* Marie that he felt a hard, hot lump in his chest. Even her breath smelled the way he remembered.

"Do you recall when you and your Marie first got together, about sixteen years ago?" They'd run into each other at a book launch in Greenwich Village, for the autobiography of some flavour-of-the-month artist with hardly enough years behind her to fill the pages. Marie had been covering it for *The Guardian*; he'd been trying to buttonhole a literary agent with one of his manuscripts. Somehow, they'd ended up standing next to each other at the bar.

"How could I forget?" Two weeks after that first meeting, she'd come out to visit him in Dayton, and stayed for six months.

"And Marie had that miscarriage?"

William felt his eyes widen. "How do you know about that?" He and Marie had never spoken of it to anyone. It had been something they kept to themselves, even though the fact of it had driven them apart. After it happened, they just couldn't be around each other. She went back to England, to her job at *The Guardian*, and he didn't hear from her for another five years; didn't see her for another ten. By the time he came to the UK to live with her, they were both in their very late thirties, both divorced, and both still childless. It was going to be a second chance for both of them; but, five years later, she was dead, and he was left alone again, this time on the wrong side of the Atlantic.

*So many wasted years.*

He felt Marie's fingers squeeze his arm through the bedclothes.

"Well," she said, "in my timeline, the baby lived."

He turned towards her. "I *beg* your pardon?"

"The miscarriage never happened." Marie let go of him and put a hand to her abdomen. "The baby survived. She grew up fit and strong."

William frowned in confusion.

"So we stayed together? You never went back to England?"

"We were a family."

William let his head roll back onto the pillow, trying to imagine all the what-ifs and if-onlys.

"But, she's not my daughter, is she? Not really. She's yours. You and the other me, from your world."

Without looking up, Marie shook her head. He saw her orange ringlets move in the corner of his peripheral vision.

"No, she is yours. The worlds didn't split until she died." She looked up at him, and he could see the care lines in the skin around her eyes. "She has your DNA. She came from you, before our worlds diverged. Just because she's from a different version of events, doesn't mean she isn't your flesh and blood." She reached up and brushed a loose hair from his forehead. The touch of her fingers sent little shivers though the muscles in his neck and jaw. "It doesn't mean you aren't her father."

William bit his lip. "I'm not sure I understand."

Marie cocked her head to one side.

"What's to understand? You fathered a child, but then the timelines diverged, and you got stuck on one and she got stuck on another. You got separated, but now you can be together again, after all this time."

He swallowed.

"How? How is this even possible?"

"There are machines. Big powerful machines that can nudge a person from one timeline to another."

"And you used one of those?"

"The Gestalt on our world have them. Bill, Lila and I used one. We broke into one of their facilities and sent ourselves here."

"So, you didn't bring it with you?"

"Strictly a one-way trip. We couldn't even choose our destination, they already had it programmed in, but that's okay. We don't want to go back. We were trying to escape."

"Escape what?"

Marie dropped her gaze and shook her head.

With great effort, William elbowed himself up until he was half-sitting, with his back against the pillows and his head against the cabin wall.

"If you want me to help find your daughter," he said, "I want to be sure I know what I'm getting myself into."

Marie pursed her lips. She rocked back on her heels, and got to her feet. "Okay, then, here it is." Her voice had become brusque and businesslike. "There are an infinite number of identical worlds, all occupying the same space but separated by wafer thin membranes of probability. A decision taken in one world will be reversed in the next, and so on to eternity. Every time one of us makes a choice, every time the wind blows left instead of right, every time a subatomic particle wobbles one way instead of another, the timelines fork, and new worlds are born. Trillions every second."

William was familiar with the concept, but when he tried to imagine it, he couldn't grasp the scale.

"That's hard to visualise."

"Think of them as branches." She clasped her hands behind her back. "Forks in the timelines."

"An infinite number of worlds?"

"Only a tiny percentage are inhabited by humans, but even that percentage accounts for a number so big that to write it down would take longer than the remaining age of the universe."

He licked his lips. They were rough and dehydrated.

"So, why are people trying to kill me?"

"Who?"

His face darkened. "There was a guy in a car yesterday afternoon, and those two Gestalt guys outside Sparky's place last night."

"You've met the Gestalt already?"

"They wanted me to go with them. They were armed."

For the first time in the conversation, she seemed off-balance. "I was hoping we'd get to you first. What happened?"

"I shot them."

She gave him a long, thoughtful look.

"Okay," she said at length, "I'll level with you. Bill and I, we've been fighting for a long time, trying to free our world."

"Free it from what?"

"From the Gestalt."

William raised an eyebrow. The Gestalt was a cult, a curiosity. They were rich and secretive, but nobody took them seriously. The media lumped them in with groups like the Scientologists or the Jehovah's Witnesses. They were eccentric, a little secretive, but essentially harmless. Until last night, he would never have thought them capable of carrying guns, let alone threatening anybody.

Marie said, "They evolved on a different parallel to ours. We don't know which one, but they've been trying to spread ever since." Her fingertips brushed the edge of his blanket. "They want to turn the whole multiverse into one giant hive mind. In order to do it, they recruit locals and convert them, then use them to spread their message and build support."

"Can't they be stopped?"

Marie shook her head. "That's just the first stage.

On our world, they started kidnapping people and converting them by force. They bought up media companies and used them to broadcast propaganda. And in the end, when they got numerous enough, they staged a coup."

"They have soldiers?"

"Human and Neanderthal. They recruit the Neanderthals as muscle, from timelines where the species never died out."

"You think that's what they're planning here?"

"From what I've seen, I'd say they're almost certainly planning an invasion. Maybe even something worse."

"Worse than invasion?"

Marie looked tired. An orange curl fell across her forehead and she flicked it aside with her finger. "The Gestalt have been here on your world for a while now. They will have been studying your soul-catchers, finding out how they work; and you can bet they've thought of half a dozen ways to subvert the technology. When their main force gets here, they'll unleash something—could be a signal or a virus, depending on the way the technology works; maybe even something nanotechnological—to turn those implants against their owners, and assimilate them into the Gestalt."

William tried to sit up. Half the people he knew wore soul-catchers. Although the gelware recording devices sat comfortably beneath the skin at the base of the skull, their tendrils extended deep into the grey matter of the brain, recording and monitoring everything. If the Gestalt had some way to reverse the process, to turn output to input, the results could be catastrophic.

Beside him, Marie laced her fingers and stretched her arms, popping the knuckles. "The good news is, we've got people fighting them on my world, and we can fight them here."

"But why are the Gestalt trying to kill me?" Spoken aloud, and weighed against the idea of an impending battle, the thought sounded petty and selfish; but still, he needed to know. "I haven't done anything. I didn't even know about any of this."

Her head tipped to the side again. "In my world, Bill was one of our leaders. For years, he kept us going, and kept us united. And now he's dead." She gave a matter-of-fact shrug, but he could see the pain in the way the lines bunched around her eyes. "So it goes. But the Gestalt worry that another version of him might rise up in his place. And they know about you. They've seen your work, and they know you're getting glimpses of our world. Your last book, *The Collective*, was a dead giveaway."

"They're trying to kill me because of my books?"

"No, they're trying to kill you because they're concerned you might warn the people of this world of their plans. That you might use your knowledge to lead the fight against them the way Bill did. The fact they're here, now, means they're ready to make their move on this world, and they don't want you standing against them."

"And where does Lila come into all this?"

Marie pulled a photograph from her pocket, and handed it to him. It was a snap taken outdoors, on a bright day. Maybe it had been taken at the seaside; it had that quality of light. A teenage girl looked back over her shoulder, laughing into the camera.

She wore a thick coat, and a strong wind teased her hair into long, dark straggles.

"She came here with Bill, looking for you. She wanted to warn you that the Gestalt were after you."

"And now they have her?"

He saw the muscles tighten as Marie clenched her jaw. Her fists were at her sides.

"We have to get her back," she said.

She looked so much like his own poor, dead Marie that he spoke without thinking.

"What can I do?"

"William, I know that right now you're a burned out writer with a drug problem. But in another reality, you were a guerrilla leader, and I need your help."

He glanced down at the picture in his hand, at a face that was somehow strange and familiar, all at the same time.

"She has my eyes."

"Will you help me get her back?"

He could feel the warmth of her breath; smell her unwashed skin.

"Do you think I can?"

She grasped him by the shoulders, her hands warm where they brushed the skin of his neck.

"My darling, I *know* you can."

## BOOK REVIEW

From *Mega Awesome Sci-Fi Magazine*, October 2060 (online edition):

**The Collective**
William S. Cole
(Avuncular Books, £17.99)

Reviewed by Jared Easterbrook

*The Collective* is the third of Cole's 'Mendelblatt' books. In the opening chapter, private eye Mendelblatt's partner, Al Lemanski, turns up dead, killed in a gruesome, occult manner, and with his right hand chewed off and missing.

The police arrest Mendelblatt on suspicion, but his partner's client—the millionaire, Bradley Knox—intervenes, bailing him out of prison to investigate Al's death and retrieve the valuable briefcase that Al was transporting for him.

And so begins another adventure for the hard-bitten Mendelblatt—only this time, he's operating alone, without the back up of his partner. Personally, I was a bit sad to see Al killed, as I felt he added a much-needed sprinkling of comic relief to the earlier books. Without him, the world of the novel feels much darker, and Mendelblatt's loneliness is palpable, and almost overpowering.

Despite the gloom, the plot gallops ahead, and

Cole pulls out all the stops. Within a few short chapters, Mendelblatt finds himself dealing with magic amulets, sinister cultists, mystic portals, and the threatened return of Lovecraftian horrors from beyond our dimension. Somehow, Cole also manages to cram a fairly tender storyline into the mix, and it is in the passages where our hero encounters his estranged daughter that the writing really comes alive.

The evil cult at the centre of the story provides a set of suitably sinister villains, prone to brainwashing recruits and bumping off enemies, and I particularly like the scarily plausible way that Cole shows them insinuating themselves into society.

All in all, I'm going to give this one an eight out of ten. The story's exciting and fast-paced, and certainly a page turner—but I could have done without so much existential moping on behalf of the main character, as it made him look like the disappointingly soft centre of an otherwise tough and enjoyably hardboiled tale.

Read more | Like | Comment | Share

# CHAPTER EIGHTEEN
## BRINGING A MONKEY TO A DOGFIGHT

PUSHING THE OLD Spitfire to the limits of its performance, Ack-Ack Macaque soared high into the bright morning sky, his right eye never leaving the dragonfly silhouette of the departing helicopter. It looked fast, but he was sure he could catch it; and it never hurt to have the high ground in a dogfight.

Paul's voice came over the radio.

*Hey, Ack-ster. What are you doing, man?*

"I'm going after K8."

*But how are you going to stop them? You can't shoot them down with her on board.*

"I'm not going to shoot them down, I'm just going to shoot bits off their chopper until they agree to land."

*Are you serious?*

Ack-Ack Macaque grinned around his cigar, his earlier tiredness gone.

"Damn right."

The altimeter nudged ten thousand feet, and he tipped the nose forward and down, aiming it at the back of the fleeing chopper. He wanted to come at it from behind, exploiting the blind spot caused by the bulk of its rotor mounting. With any luck, they wouldn't see him coming until he was already on top of them, and he'd be able to get a couple of good shots through the engine before they started weaving around.

The engine's pitch changed as the Spitfire began its dive, and his lips drew back from his teeth. He hadn't had a proper dogfight since being pulled from the game. Ahead, his target barrelled eastwards into the morning sunlight, seemingly oblivious to his pursuit. He watched it grow in his crosshairs.

He gripped the stick with both hands, and clamped his cigar tightly between his teeth. He wanted to get good and close before he opened fire. The chopper could stop in the air, he couldn't. He needed to make his first shot count. They were over farmland now— that great swathe of patchwork fields that stretched along either side of the M4. If he could get a quick burst through the engine without peppering the cockpit, he might be able to force it down without killing anyone—especially K8.

So intent was he on his target, he didn't see the attack drone spiralling down from above until it opened fire. Cannon shells punched through his wings and fuselage. The cockpit canopy shattered.

"Yowch!" He dragged the stick back into his left hip, throwing the plane over, trying to roll out of the line of fire. As he did so, he caught a glimpse of a shark-like profile, with two enclosed engines and short, stubby wings laden with missiles. The drone was an unmanned, jet-propelled weapons platform, and the Spitfire was no match for it. He could twist and turn all over the sky, but all that the drone had to do was follow and shoot. A single missile would be enough to finish him, and that thing looked to be packed with them.

"Fuck, fuck, fuckity-fuck."

He'd lost sight of the chopper but that, right now, was the least of his concerns. Squinting against the rush of cold air, he clawed his goggles down over his one good eye, and shoved the stick as far forward as it would go, throwing the Spitfire's nose at the ground. If he stayed up here, his life expectancy would be less than a few seconds. His hundred-and-fifteen-year-old plane was no match for a modern, computerised targeting system. His only hope was to get low, and try and lose himself in ground-level scenery.

For a moment, he missed his days in the game. Although he hadn't known at the time that he was, as far as the other players were concerned, technically immortal, he'd at least had the reassurance that he'd never be pitted against anyone with a better plane than him. The Spitfire and the Messerschmitt ME109 were reasonably matched in terms of weaponry and performance. The playing field had always been level, and the conflicts decided by the respective skills of the pilots involved. But in these days of autonomous decision engines and laser guidance, skill meant a hell of a lot less than it used to. All a drone pilot had to do was steer his craft within a mile or so of his target and press a button.

Creaks and groans wracked the airframe as the Spit drilled down through the air, hammering towards the green baize billiard table of a grassy field. Ack-Ack Macaque, head half-frozen by the wind, held his nerve for as long as he could; until he fancied he could see each individual blade of grass. Then he hauled back on the stick, pulling out of the dive with his wings in serious danger of clipping the trees and hedgerows at the field's border. If he could stay low enough, with the belly of his plane almost kissing the dirt, the drone's missiles wouldn't have enough room to manoeuver; they'd plough into the soil or hit a pylon before they could zero in on him.

At least, he hoped so. But being so low had its own share of hazards. Not only was he in constant danger of smashing into a telegraph pole, lamppost or church spire; he was also too low to bail out if something went wrong. If the Spitfire were hit, he wouldn't have time to leap out—and if he did, his parachute wouldn't have time to open—before he hit the ground at three hundred miles per hour.

He weaved from side to side. He had no idea where the drone was, only that it was behind him somewhere. He didn't dare tear his one good eye from the onrushing scenery. With trees whipping past his wingtips like the skeletal fingers of ghouls trying to snatch him down, a moment's inattention would be fatal.

His lips drew back in a fierce grin.

"Ah, to hell with it!"

Sparing one hand, he reached into the side pocket of his flying jacket and pulled out his petrol lighter. A quick flick of the thumb, and a blue flame roared in the wind. He used it to light his cigar. If he had to go down, he was going to do it in style.


THE FIRST MISSILE hit an old oak tree a few metres behind and to the right of the Spitfire's tail, with an explosion that threw Ack-Ack Macaque forward and sideways against his harness. He saw a fireball in the shattered remnants of his rear-view mirror, but didn't have time for more than a quick glance. "Damn and blast!" He threw the stick to the left, and then hauled it back over to the right, hoping to throw off his enemy's aim. If there were more missiles, he couldn't see them. He flashed across a motorway at streetlamp height, and crossed a set of train tracks. Ahead, a line of hills stood like a frozen wave. Pylons marched across the ridge. And still he couldn't see the drone. The thing was built for stealth. It was designed to flit across warzones, raining death and mayhem on convoys and bunkers. His fingers curled around the firing controls, aching to shoot back. In the game, he'd taught his pilots to turn and face any attack. The drone might be a state-of-the-art killing machine, but a well-placed volley of tracer rounds would fuck it up the same as any other plane.

He hopped a hedge, into a long, wide field. With nothing to hit but brown soil, he risked a peep back, over his shoulder. The drone was a speck in his wake, above and behind him, black against the bright blue sky. As he watched, a flame shot from beneath its starboard wing: another missile on the way.

Ahead, the ridge of hills bore down upon him. He could go up and over—but when he reached the crest, he'd be plainly visible against the skyline, exposing his backside to the drone's cannon. Better, he thought, to stay low and fight dirty.

To his left, the motorway carved into the hills, and he angled his nose in the direction of the cutting. If he could get low enough, he could squeeze under the twin bridges of the junction, and emerge on the other side with a barrier between himself and the drone. But it was going to be tight. He couldn't fly up the middle of the road, as lampposts lined the central reservation. He'd have to confine himself to the westbound carriageway. As he powered down towards the tarmac, he realised that the four lanes of the carriageway measured no more than forty feet, which gave him less than five feet of clearance at each wingtip. But by that point, he'd already committed himself. He couldn't pull out, and he couldn't afford the slightest wobble.

Unfortunately, he was flying into the teeth of the oncoming traffic. Being early on a Sunday morning, there were thankfully few cars on the road; but, as the first bridge rushed at him, he saw a big, eighteen-wheeler bearing down on the junction from the opposite side. There wouldn't be room for both of them under the second bridge; so, unable to manoeuvre, he took the only course open to him. His thumbs mashed down on the firing control, and the plane shook as all eight machine guns cut loose.

Bullets hammered the front of the truck. The radiator grille and front bumper flew apart, tyres burst, and the vehicle slewed to the side. Its front fender hit and crumpled against the metal barriers at the edge of the hard shoulder. It was still moving forward, but it was slowing.

Ack-Ack Macaque's Spitfire cleared the second bridge and he hauled the stick back into his groin, dragging the nose up. For a second, he thought he wasn't going to make it. The eighteen-wheeler filled his windscreen. He locked eyes with the terrified trucker at its wheel. And then it was gone, snatched away beneath him, and he was airborne, wheeling up into the sky over Wiltshire.

Behind him, the drone's second missile hit the side of the first bridge. He didn't stop to watch. Instead, he was pulling his plane around in the tightest possible circle, crushing himself into his seat with the g-force, and lining up on the junction again, this time from the other side.

As he bore down on the bridges, the underside of his fuselage almost scraped the roadway.

"Well," he muttered, "this has to be the stupidest fucking thing I've done all day." To have cleared both bridges once was a miracle; to attempt the same feat again was madness. He saw the drone ahead, moving uphill towards him, framed by the chalk sides of the cutting. For the moment, he was hidden. The drone's computer couldn't make him out; he was lost in the background noise, obscured by cars and bridges and smoke. He might remain hidden only a few seconds, but, with his opponent exposed and blind, a few seconds were all he needed.

The Spitfire boomed under the first bridge, wingtips inches from disaster. The noise of the engine bounced back at him from the concrete overhead. The wind snatched at the hair on his cheeks, and threw sparks from the cherry-red tip of his cigar. Grinning, he squeezed the firing control. Eight lines of glittering tracer converged on the drone's bulbous, sensor-packed nose. He flashed into sunlight, then into shadow again. Passing under the second bridge, he kept the control depressed, knuckles white, pouring everything he had at the oncoming machine. A wild screech ripped from his throat.

"Die, motherfucker, die!"

# CHAPTER NINETEEN
## NO MORE MISTER NICE MONKEY

ACK-ACK MACAQUE NURSED the damaged Spitfire back to the *Tereshkova*, and pancaked her down on the airship's runway. He had nowhere else to go. By the time he'd finished with the drone, the helicopter had gone, having disappeared into the countryside at treetop height. He hadn't even known in which direction it had gone, and his plane had been too shot-up to go searching for it, so he'd come limping home instead, seething all the way.

As he climbed out of the splintered cockpit, he saw Victoria waiting for him, along with Paul's hologram, the American writer and the orange-haired woman.

"What the hell do you lot want?" He wasn't in the mood to talk. All he wanted was to wring the necks of the Gestalt clowns who'd snatched K8; to choke the life out of them with his bare hands, watch their tongues loll and their eyeballs bulge. Especially Reynolds. Oh, how he'd love to get his fingers around the throat of that smug prick. Without breaking stride, he stalked past Victoria, heading for one of the hangars. He was going take a helicopter and start trying to pick up K8's trail. She could be a hundred miles away by now, in any direction, but he had to try. He knew the odds were against him, and that his chances of finding her were miniscule; he just didn't know what else to do.

"Wait up." Victoria ran to keep up with him. "Where are you going?"

"I'm going after her."

"I know. I want to help." She caught his shoulder, but he shrugged her off.

"Then stay the fuck out of my way."

"No." With surprising strength, Victoria took hold of his arm and spun him to face her. Her eyes were narrow and her nostrils wide. "This isn't just about you. This was an attack on all of us. Somebody waltzed onto my skyliner and kidnapped a member of my crew. Not even the CIA would be stupid enough to do something like that. As far as I'm concerned, it's a declaration of war against you, me, and the *Tereshkova* herself."

He glared at her through the cracked lens of his flying goggles.

"Then get out of my way, and let me find them."

"You don't have any idea where they are."

He flapped his arms in exasperation.

"Then I'll go down to the city and pick one of the bastards off the streets. They're all linked, aren't they? So it doesn't matter which one we get. I'll just beat the shit out of him until he tells me where they are."

Victoria pursed her lips as if considering this. Then, regretfully, she shook her head.

"We're in enough trouble already, thanks to your stunt on the motorway. If we're going to strike against the Gestalt, we have to do it directly, without civilians getting in the way."

"If they hurt her…"

"My guess is she'll be safe for now. We have two things the Gestalt want. They want to kill Cole and, for some reason, they want to recruit you. God knows why, but I'm betting they'll use K8 as leverage to achieve at least one of those goals."

The wind blew across the runway. Ack-Ack Macaque felt it prickle the fur on his cheeks and the backs of his hands. He looked towards Cole.

"Do we know why they want to kill the American?"

Victoria raised an eyebrow. "You wouldn't believe me if I told you."

"Fine, then. Don't bother." He turned towards the helicopter sheds. "It's not like I give a shit anyway."

"They have his daughter."

"They have my friend."

"Then, let's work together." Victoria put a hand on his sleeve. "To get them both back."

The wind jostled them. Ack-Ack Macaque bared his teeth into it. "Since when do you care about Cole's daughter?"

"Since those bastards attacked my ship. And besides, there's a hell of a lot more at stake here than you realise."

Ack-Ack Macaque gave a snort. There usually was.

"End of the world again?"

"Something along those lines."

He let his shoulders droop. "Okay, fine. We'll work together." He flapped a leathery hand at the sunlit horizon. "But where do you suggest we start? That helicopter could be halfway to anywhere by now."

With a whine, Paul's image wheeled up to them.

In full daylight, he looked faint and translucent, barely more substantial than a heat haze. Ack-Ack Macaque could see right through him—see the little car at his feet, and the blue skies and white clouds behind him.

"Perhaps I can help?" He was the only one in shirtsleeves, the only one unmolested by the wind.

"What have you got?"

"Carry me down to Victoria's office, and I'll show you."

"Carry?" Ack-Ack Macaque passed a hand through the image. It was no more tangible than moonlight.

"He means the car," Victoria said. She crouched down and scooped the little vehicle into her hands. As she straightened back up, Paul's image shimmered, broke apart, and disappeared. "It won't go up or down steps."

WHEN THEY GOT to the office and Paul had been reactivated, the five of them clustered around Victoria's desk. The screen inlaid into its surface had been switched on, and showed a satellite image of the surrounding countryside: a chequered bedspread of green, brown and yellow fields, grey towns, and dark, winding rivers.

"We're here," Paul said, peering down, over the top of his rimless spectacles. He indicated the landing strip at Filton, on the northwest tip of the city. "Now, when you last saw it, the Gestalt helicopter was *here*." He moved his hand along the ribbon of the M4 motorway. "And you lost it *here*, at this junction."

Beside him, Ack-Ack Macaque struggled to contain his impatience. His fingers squeezed the metal edge of the desk.

"Yeah, so?"

Paul smiled. His finger traced a route southwards, following the road that led from the motorway junction to a sprawl of streets and buildings clustered around the lazy curves of a wide river.

"Now, this is Bath," he said. "It's an old Roman city famous for the hot springs which give it its name."

Ack-Ack Macaque suppressed a moan. *Geeks*, he thought bitterly. *They can never just get to the motherfucking point.*

"What about it?" He bent over the picture, trying to squint out likely places where they could have landed a helicopter. "You think they're there?"

"No." Paul pushed his glasses back up, onto the bridge of his nose. "But, according to what I've been able to dig up online, Legion Haulage has a corporate retreat on the outskirts. It's an old stately home on the hill, just about here." His finger tapped a building on a green hill overlooking the River Avon where it meandered between two hills, forming a grassy floodplain crossed by both the A4 and the Great Western mainline to London. It was a sprawling country house, with outbuildings and several acres of land. According to the map, it was called Larkin Hall.

"They have to be there," Victoria said. Beside her, William and Marie Cole leaned over the display with interest. Cole looked rough: his hair stuck up more than usual, and his eyes drooped, still carrying the weight of the sedatives he'd been given. A week's worth of bristles peppered his jowls.

"They'll have security systems and armed guards," Marie said, sounding worried. "We can't just walk in through the front gate."

Ack-Ack Macaque wrinkled his nose.

"Like hell we can't." He fixed her with his one good eye. "Listen, lady; breaking into places and busting stuff up is kind of what I do."

Victoria gave him a look.

"What do you have in mind?"

His flight jacket hung open. He straightened up and scratched at the hair on his chest.

"Helicopter assault. Don't bother with the front door; just blow a hole in the roof and abseil in. Find the girls, kick as many arses as possible, and then get the hell outta there before those Gestalt twats know what's hit 'em."

Marie gave him a long, thoughtful look.

"Is that possible?"

"Sure it's possible. It's just your basic smash and grab. Used to do it all the time, in the war."

Paul raised a hand.

"I don't want to be the voice of sanity in this little group; but shouldn't we go to the police?"

"And do what?" Victoria stepped away from the desk. The medals on her chest clanked together as she moved. She went to stand by the floor-to-ceiling picture window, and stood with her hands clasped behind her, looking out at the aerodrome below. "The Gestalt have money, and lawyers like you wouldn't believe. By the time the police get a warrant to search the place, there won't be a trace of the girls." She took a deep breath in through her nose. "Besides, I wouldn't be surprised if the Gestalt already have a few of the local gendarmes in their pockets. Maybe even a few converts on the force." She leaned forward, so that her forehead kissed the cold glass. "Macaque? If I let you do this, who will you take?"

Ack-Ack Macaque pulled out a cigar and sniffed it.

"A small team of two, maybe three people. All the guns."

William Cole stood by the desk, blinking. He shuffled his weight from one foot to the other.

"I want to come."

Ack-Ack Macaque shook his head.

"No way, José. Not if you're going to flake out like you did last night."

Cole smoothed down the hair on one side of his head.

"I'm serious. I feel a lot better now."

"You look like shit, and you're a fucking liability."

Marie stepped forward, shouldering her way between them.

"That's his daughter in there."

"And that gives him the right to get himself, and the rest of us, killed?"

"It gives him the right to try."

Ack-Ack Macaque curled his lip. "No, it doesn't. I'm not taking him."

"Then take me instead." She stuck her chin forward. "She's my daughter too."

He looked her up and down. She stood with her weight on the balls of her feet, like a dancer. Her fists hung at her sides, but her shoulders were loose and relaxed, ready for anything.

"Think you can handle yourself?"

"I've been in worse places, and I know how the Gestalt work. I've fought them before. I could be useful."

"Okay, then." He couldn't be bothered to argue. He turned to Victoria. "I'll take her. Do you think you can get us there?"

Victoria turned away from the window, and pulled herself up. The overhead light shone on the bald skin of her scalp. The gold braid twinkled on her shoulders.

"We cast off in an hour."

Now it was Ack-Ack Macaque's turn to be surprised. He fought down the urge to grin.

"You're taking the whole ship?"

"K8's a member of its crew." Victoria's voice hardened. She ran a hand across the top of her head. "And if there's one thing the Commodore taught me, it's that nobody gets left behind."

He rolled the cigar in his fingers. K8 had stuck by him for the past year, and he'd done nothing but take her for granted and treat her like a lackey. The thought was an uncomfortable one. He wasn't used to thinking in those terms. Humans were humans; sometimes they were useful; sometimes they were friends. Being obligated to one of them, actually *caring* about them, was something he hadn't experienced before. He'd always had a healthy respect for Victoria Valois, and he enjoyed bantering with Paul, but he'd never felt responsible for either of them. K8 was something else. He'd known her in the game, and she'd helped him when he escaped from it. She was the one constant linking his old life with this one, his longest-serving friend and most stalwart of colleagues, and the thought of losing her filled him with a hot, helpless fury.

"Take me to the armoury," he said. "Those Gestalt wankers are going to be sorry. They'll rue the day they messed with us."

Marie leant on the desk with her fists.

"Do you think we can get them back?"

He sneered at her.

"Of course we'll get them back. Trust me, they've pissed off the wrong primate this time. No more Mister Nice Monkey. By the time I've finished with them, they'll be begging to give us the girls."

Marie narrowed her eyes.

"I hope you're right."

"Of course I'm fucking right." Ack-Ack Macaque drew one of his Colts. In the crowded confines of the office, the gun looked about the size of a cannon. "Take it from me, lady, those arseholes are going to wish they'd never been born."

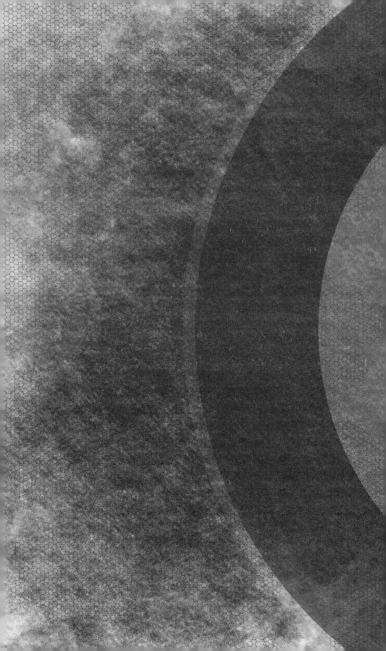

# PART TWO

## WHAT ROUGH BEAST

I was thinking this globe enough till there sprang
out so noiseless around me myriads of other globes.

(Walt Whitman, Night On The Prairies)

# CHAPTER TWENTY
## TOOLING UP

THE *TERESHKOVA*'S ARMOURY: Victoria Valois stood in the corridor and watched as Ack-Ack Macaque worked his way around the walk-in cupboard, pulling weapons from the shelves. There were few guns, but he already had his Colts on his hips. He added grenades, knives, and a couple of rusty throwing stars that he found in an old shoebox on one of the higher shelves. Beside him, Marie did the same, tooling herself up with the calm efficiency of an experienced soldier preparing for an operation.

"So, you say you've done this before?" he asked, pulling a wicked-looking machete from a rack of blades.

Marie reached for a coil gun: a magnetic projectile accelerator in the shape of a machine gun, capable of punching a titanium slug through a concrete wall. With practised efficiency, she hefted it in one hand, braced the stock against her hip, and clicked a magazine into place.

"I can look after myself." She had her orange hair tied back in a severe ponytail, and Victoria had given her a bulletproof vest from her own personal stash. Watching her, Victoria couldn't help but be impressed by the way the woman stood up to the monkey.

"Take whatever you need," she said, reaching down to touch the retractable fighting stick tucked into her own belt. Ack-Ack Macaque saw her doing it.

"Wishing you were coming with us, boss?"

She smiled, but there was little humour in it. They were the assault team, and she was the skyliner captain.

"I'll have more than enough to do here." She had no doubt that, after the events of last year, every move the *Tereshkova* made would be closely scrutinised by both the authorities and the media. Larkin Hall was close to the skyliner's scheduled route to London, so they could approach it without raising undue suspicion; but once there, she'd have to do some pretty fast talking to justify a helicopter assault on a stately home. If worse came to worst, she supposed, it would help that they had a friend in Buckingham Palace. Not that she'd presume on that friendship except in the direst of emergencies.

Briefly, she wondered how Merovech was adjusting to life on the throne. She hadn't seen him since the aftermath of the battle in the Channel, and still remembered him as he was when she first met him: a troubled young man in ratty jeans and a smelly red hoodie, struggling to come to terms with the death of his father. Now, he was king of the United Kingdom of Great Britain, France, Northern Ireland and Norway, and Head of the United European Commonwealth. He was preparing for his forthcoming marriage to Julie Girard, the digital activist who'd first drawn him into the intrigue that freed Ack-Ack Macaque from his virtual world and exposed the conspiracy at the heart of Céleste Technologies. The boy was a head of state, and still only barely out of his teens. He had quite enough on his plate without her turning up like Banquo's ghost.

If she could get along without involving him, she would. She had no wish to embarrass him, but she had no illusions that what they were about to do was illegal and could be construed as a terrorist act. The Gestalt might be a dangerous cult bent on global domination but, as far as the world at large was concerned, they were simply a group of technological eccentrics—a bit creepy, yes, but entitled to the same protections as everybody else. Launching an attack on one of the organisation's properties was an action bound to provoke a response from the UK authorities and, if it came to a standoff with the Royal Air Force, she wouldn't hesitate to pick up the phone.

"Besides," she said, "the two of you are carrying enough ordnance to level the place by yourselves; you don't need me tagging along."

"Are you sure about that, boss?" The monkey picked up a crossbow. "You can be pretty handy in a scrap." The crossbow had been made of some sort of carbon fibre, which made it light as well as tough.

Victoria turned to look up the corridor, in the direction of the airship's bridge.

"I'll have your backs from up here. If anything goes wrong, I'll have a chopper snatch you out in seconds."

Marie pulled a webbing harness over her shoulders and fastened it at the front. It had loops and pockets for weapons and equipment.

"How long will it take to get there?"

"About half an hour from when we cast off."

"That seems a long time."

"We have to fly slowly over the city."

"Can't we go around?"

"We could, but it wouldn't save any time." She checked her watch. "Now, I've got to get to the bridge so we can get under way. Monkey Man, are you going to fly us out?"

Ack-Ack Macaque stood in the centre of the armoury, festooned with weaponry and ammunition.

"You think I'd trust any of you idiots to do it?"

FIVE MINUTES LATER, Victoria sat in her command chair, looking forward through the curved windshield of the *Tereshkova*'s bridge. She wore an insulated cap with fur earflaps. The temperature in here was colder than in the rest of the gondola. The heat leached out through the glass of the big window and the metal of the walls and floor. The monkey sat at the pilot's workstation to her right, and the Russian navigator to her left. The touchscreens set into the arms of her chair displayed graphical summaries of the airship's systems. She couldn't read the numbers, of course, but was reassured to see that everything that should be green appeared to be green, and nothing glowed red or amber. The engines were all online, and she fancied she could almost feel their vibration through the deck.

Paul stood by her shoulder. He'd been tinkering with his image again, and now appeared to be clad in a black polo neck and slate grey chinos.

"You know," he whispered, "I could do this."

"What?"

"Fly the ship."

Victoria turned to look at him.

"Are you serious?"

"Perfectly. After all, it's just another computer system, isn't it? I don't see any reason I couldn't learn it, given enough time."

"Don't let the monkey hear you say that."

Paul gave Ack-Ack Macaque's back a guilty glance. "Of course not." He adjusted his glasses. "I don't want to undermine him or anything. It's just that if things go badly and we ever lost him, I'd want you to know that you had another pilot on standby. Potentially. If you needed me." He wouldn't meet her eyes, and Victoria felt a prickle at the back of her throat. This was, she realised, his way of trying to be useful.

"I'll always need you," she said.

At the helm, Ack-Ack Macaque cleared his throat.

"Will you two stop yapping? I'm trying to concentrate." He spoke without taking his eye from the controls, and Victoria knew he was busily aligning the engines to propel the airship's kilometre-long bulk eastward. She watched his hairy hands dance on his workstation's screen.

"All right, Mister Macaque." She sat up straight, and tugged the hem of her tunic into place. "In your own time."

The monkey hit a switch. A warning bell chimed over the intercom, followed by an announcement recorded in both Franglais and Russian. Down below, the delivery trucks, tenders and other vehicles had scattered from the runway to avoid the downdraught of the skyliner's fifteen giant impellers.

"Here we go." He dragged a fingertip down one side of the screen, and the bow tipped upward by twenty degrees. The airframe gave a series of creaks.

A pen rolled from the navigator's console and skittered across the deck until it clanged into the bridge's rear wall. Victoria winced. She knew that in the gondola behind her—and in those hanging from the other four hulls—drinks would be spilling, plates would be sliding off tables, and people would be stumbling and tripping into each other.

*Needs must*, she thought. One of their crew was in trouble, and that took priority over a few spilled gin and tonics.

The thrust kicked in, pushing her backwards in her seat. She'd never felt anything like it in all her time on the *Tereshkova*, and hadn't thought the old airship capable of such acceleration. The monkey must have pushed all fifteen engines into the red. The whole ship seemed to judder, and she gripped the arms of her chair as the airfield fell away.

"Watch your speed," Paul said nervously. Ack-Ack Macaque didn't bother turning around.

"Screw the limits. What are they going to do, shoot us down over the city?" He touched a control and increased the thrust even further. Around them, the bulkheads moaned in protest, like the timbers of a galleon caught in a storm. The old airship rose, as if hoisted on the crest of a wave, and Victoria's communication display lit up. The airfield's control tower wanted to talk to her. She smiled, and dismissed their call. Inside, she felt a wild surge of pride. The *Tereshkova* was hers, and it was doing something unsuspected and spectacular—something that would further cement its reputation as a maverick in the skyliner community; a true individual in a company of rogues.

Silently, she offered up a prayer of thanks to the Commodore. Losing her ability to write, her career in journalism, and her husband had left her lost and rudderless, and it had taken the *Tereshkova* to rekindle her sense of purpose. She hoped that in whatever vodka-soaked afterlife the old man now found himself, he knew how thoroughly he'd saved her.

Beside her, Paul's hologram stood stroking his chin, unaffected by the tilt of the deck. She poked a finger at him.

"You'd be able to fly like this, would you?"

His eyes were locked on the forward view, and she saw his Adam's apple bob in his throat as he swallowed nervously.

"I don't know. Maybe. If I really had to."

"You think so?"

Wide eyes met her gaze over the tops of his spectacles.

"Perhaps."

"Are you monitoring the internal cameras?"

"Yes. It's a mess back there."

"Any serious damage?"

"Nothing dreadful; mostly crockery and furniture falling over. A few bumps and bruises. Everything else is secured against turbulence. Except—" He bit his lower lip. "Oh dear, oh dear. Our furry friend's going to be very upset."

"Why, what is it?"

He glanced at the back of the monkey's head, and then leant in close to whisper in her ear.

"It's his Spitfire."

"What about it?"

"It's fallen off."

# CHAPTER TWENTY-ONE
## IN THE CELLAR

THE DRUGS THEY'D given K8 hadn't knocked her completely out, just rendered her queasy and muddled. A whole bottle of vodka would have had a similar effect. She had vague, blurred impressions of being bundled out onto the *Tereshkova*'s flight deck and stuffed into a helicopter. Her legs hadn't been working properly, and so the men in white had to support her by the elbows. Then it was all blue sky, white clouds and green countryside until they landed in a garden somewhere, and they led her into the cellar of a big old house, and threw her down onto a bare and filthy mattress.

She lay there for a long time, staring at the ceiling, trying to stop the room from spinning. Then she felt small, tentative hands shaking her by the shoulder, and turned her head (making the walls of the room swoop and sway even more sickeningly) to find herself looking into the concerned eyes of a girl about her own age.

"What...?"

The girl shrank back. A bruise darkened her cheek. Her eyes were wary.

"Are you okay?" she asked.

K8 tried to sit up; then put a hand to her head and groaned, waiting for the pain behind her eyes to recede.

"I've been drugged," was all she could manage. The girl didn't reply. Instead, she shambled over to a workbench by the door and came back clutching a metal canteen. She held it out and K8 took it, unstopped the lid, and sniffed.

"Water?"

The girl gave a nod. She had brown hair tied back in a long plait, and wore a grey t-shirt and a pair of combat trousers done out in the black, white and grey splodges of urban camouflage.

K8 took a sip from the canteen. The water inside was cool and tasted of aluminium. She rinsed it around the inside of her cheeks, and spat onto the floor.

"Who are you?" She wiped her mouth on her sleeve. "Where are we?"

The girl hugged herself.

"My name's Lila."

K8 frowned, and rubbed her forehead.

"You're Marie's daughter, right?"

"You know my mother?"

"Yeah, sort of. I heard her mention your name. Just now, before those freaks grabbed me." With great effort, K8 pushed herself up into a sitting position and placed her feet on the floor. The room dipped and shuddered, but then seemed to steady itself, and she decided she'd better remain upright for the foreseeable future—at least, until she felt better. Tipping the canteen to her lips again, she swallowed a mouthful of water, and tried to take stock of her surroundings.

The cellar was about the same size as the passenger lounge on the *Tereshkova*, and illuminated by a single strip of light in the centre of the ceiling. It had obviously been used as a storeroom for many decades. Sagging, cobwebby boxes sat stacked against the back wall. She saw the handle of a tennis racquet protruding from one, and the moth-eaten arm of an old teddy bear sticking from the flap of another. Piles of decades-old newspapers sat clumped in string-tied bundles. Small screws and chips of wood littered the floor where they'd fallen. The air smelled of wood and mildew, and reminded her of the smell of the lock-up garage where her grandpa had kept his old car.

"Where are we?"

Lila took the canteen from her hands and refastened the stopper.

"I'm not sure." She nervously brushed a strand of hair behind her ear. "I mean, I'm pretty certain we're still in England. All those newspapers are English, for a start. I'm just not sure *exactly* where in England we are."

K8 thought about trying to stand, and decided against it. She wasn't convinced her legs were ready to bear her weight.

"Have you been here long?"

"A couple of days."

"Any idea what they want with us?"

"They're using me as a hostage, to get to my father. Why they'd want you, I have no idea." Lila crossed her arms. "I don't even know who you are."

'Oh, sorry." K8 rubbed her eyes, trying to force herself to feel more awake. "I'm K8."

"Kate?"

"Aye, close enough. I'm from the *Tereshkova*. I've been looking after your father."

Lila tensed.

"My father?"

"William Cole, the writer."

"Oh." The girl squeezed her hands together. She turned her head away. "He's not really my father. It's complicated. The last time I saw my real father, he was on his way to the *Tereshkova*, to intercept Cole."

K8 felt a chill. "If you're talking about 'Bill', he did."

"How is he?"

She swallowed. She wasn't in any fit state to be breaking bad news to a stranger. "I'm afraid he was shot."

Lila's hand flew to her throat. "He's dead?"

"I'm afraid so."

Lila's gaze dropped to the floor. Her chest rose and fell. K8 looked away. She didn't know what to do or say. She'd never been in this situation before.

Eventually, Lila looked up, and wiped her eyes with the back of her hand.

"You said you'd seen my mother?"

"Your mother came aboard last night. She asked Captain Valois for help in finding you."

"And now you've found me."

"Yeah, and a fat lot of good it does either of us." K8 put her head in her hands and glared down at her feet. Her stomach made sharp complaining noises.

Lila was silent for a minute or so. Then, quietly, she said, "The Gestalt must have grabbed you because you were helping my mum."

From somewhere far beyond the cellar walls, they heard a car approach and pull to a stop. Doors opened and slammed, and silence returned.

"No," K8 said. "I don't think that was it. They weren't waiting for me; they were waiting for my friend. I think they were after him."

"And they grabbed you by mistake?" Lila looked sceptical.

"He'd already refused to join their cult. He even slapped one of them around a bit. I think they were waiting for him, but when I arrived, I guess they improvised."

"And now you think they're using you as bait, the same way they're using me?"

"Who knows?" She shrugged. "Maybe."

"Do you think it will work?"

"Oh yes. He'll come looking for me. You can bet your life on that."

"And then you'll both be caught."

K8 smiled through the nausea. "You don't know what he's capable of."

Lila rubbed her hands and blew into them. "Do you really think he'll try to rescue you?"

"If anyone can, he will."

"And he's working with my mother?"

"I think we're all on the same side now."

Lila turned away. Her face was pale and drawn, and K8 could see that she didn't want to let herself hope too much, or put too much faith in a rescue that might never come. After two days in this cellar, and who knew what mistreatment at the hands of the Gestalt, she must have given up all hope at least once; and so it was little wonder if she seemed wary of rekindling it—especially now, in the wake of K8's devastating news.

"Well," she said, her tone flat, "your friend had better be something special, because you have no idea what he's up against." She walked over to the door and absently rattled the handle, as if checking it was still locked.

K8 hawked and spat, trying to get the bitter, coppery taste of indigestion out of her mouth.

She said, "I don't think a houseful of lunatics in white suits are going to put up much of a fight."

Lila turned to face her, leaning her back against the door.

"You haven't a clue, have you?" She shook her head pityingly. "You don't know what you're fighting."

"Why don't you enlighten me?"

"Those people out there aren't the local Gestalt. They intercepted me when I tried to contact Cole. They were waiting for me, and they knew who I was."

"So?"

"So, I don't exist on this timeline. The only way they could know who I was would be if they came here from somewhere else. These aren't your local converts, these are the Gestalt's advance guard, its elite troops."

"And they followed you here?"

"No, they came here to kill Cole, and a number of others. They're laying the groundwork for a full-scale incursion."

K8 rubbed her forehead, trying to massage some life back into her slothful synapses.

"They're preparing an *invasion*?"

"I told you, these are the advance guard. They even have their Leader with them."

"The Gestalt has a leader?"

Lila shivered, and wrapped her arms tightly across her chest. "They took me to see him."

"I thought the Gestalt were all supposed to be the same?"

"They are. But the Leader's something else. He's... different. Not hooked into the web like the rest of them."

"And he's here? I mean, right here in this house?"

"He was yesterday, when they took me to him." She shuddered and looked at the black mould dappling the cellar's back wall.

K8 clenched and unclenched her fingers and toes. She had pins and needles in her feet, but her legs were feeling less and less unsteady with every minute that passed. She wouldn't be sprinting anywhere for a while, but felt confident that, if she had to, she'd soon be able to get up and walk—at least, as far as the door.

"But how are they going to invade the whole world?" She said. "The idea's daft."

Lila didn't turn her head. "They'll do it the same way they invaded my world. And we've been fighting them ever since."

"But if we can warn people, if we can get the word out, we can be ready for them."

"You don't understand. They're relentless. If you shoot one, another one takes his or her place. And they just keep coming. You can't outthink them, because they all think as one. You can't surprise them, because if you kill one of them, all the others immediately know about it—unless you can do it so quickly they don't have time to register the attack, but even then, the others know *something's* wrong."

"So, what do you do?"

"You stay quiet. You hide. And when you strike, you do it quickly, and then you run." She took a long, shuddering breath. "And we've been running for five years. Until—"

"Until what?"

Lila swallowed. "They developed this plague. It's like a virus. It gets into your soul-catcher and changes it. Makes you one of them."

K8 rubbed the back of her neck, where her own device had been implanted on her sixteenth birthday—a present from her employers at the time, Céleste Tech.

"What if you don't have a soul-catcher?"

"It builds one." Lila rubbed her eyes. "It converts flesh and bone into gelware, and burrows into your head."

K8 swirled the water around in the canteen. Her thoughts felt heavy and tired.

"So, why didn't it infect you?"

"We saw what was happening, and we left. We crept into one of their machines and used it to get away while they were still in the process of spreading the infection. We didn't know where we'd end up, but anything seemed better than staying. But now, they're going to use their plague against this world, too."

"Unless we can stop them."

A sigh. "We can't stop them."

"If we could get to the Leader somehow, and make him—"

"Forget it." Lila waved a hand. "You'd never get past his bodyguards. And if you did, you still wouldn't stand a chance. He'd never surrender."

K8 said, "Tough, is he?"

Lila took a long, raggedy breath.

"You have no idea."

From above, they heard footfalls echoing on stone steps, descending in their direction. Keys jangled, and Lila backed away from the door.

"They're coming!"

K8 tried to push herself up, but her knees were still unsteady.

"Help me."

"I can't." Lila shook her head and backed away further. "I think they're coming for you this time. I think they're coming to take you to *him*."

# CHAPTER TWENTY-TWO
## STINGER

THE *TERESHKOVA* THUNDERED across the city at full power, startling pedestrians and shaking windows in their frames. From his seat on the bridge, Ack-Ack Macaque saw the shadow thrown by its five hulls—a great rectangular eclipse darkening office blocks and church spires. He made a few final adjustments and then, satisfied the airship was headed in the right direction, unclipped himself from the pilot's chair and turned to Victoria.

"Nobody touches that throttle," he said. "We'll get there faster if we accelerate all the way. When we get close, I'll jump out, and I'll take the woman with me. When we're gone, I've set the autopilot to bring the ship around in a wide loop. By the time you get back to the target, you'll be at rest, and it should all be over on the ground, one way or another."

Victoria watched him carefully.

"You missed a part."

"Which part?"

"The part where I'm the captain and you're the pilot, and I give the orders."

He glowered at her. He was still furious that they'd lost his plane—which now lay smashed and concertinaed in a supermarket car park—and this wasn't the time for her to be playing hierarchy games.

"Would you do anything differently?"

She stroked her chin with finger and thumb, considering.

"Well," she said after a moment, "no."

"Then please, get out of my way, *Captain*."

Victoria narrowed her eyes, and there was a glimmer in them that told him her objections weren't entirely serious, that she was just making a point.

"Make sure you get them both back, okay?"

"Yes, boss."

"And *that's* an order."

"Yes, boss." He threw a floppy, long-armed salute and scampered aft, to where Marie Cole awaited him. She looked bulky with the bulletproof jacket that Victoria had given her, and bug-eyed with the goggles she'd put on over her face; but nevertheless, she exuded a fierce, furious determination that matched his own, and he had no doubt she'd do okay when the fighting got dirty and personal.

"Ready?" he asked.

"Lead on, monkey."

He led her up through the *Tereshkova*'s corridors and companionways to the helipad on top of the airship, and one of the sleeker passenger choppers. The pilot was already on board, warming the engine, and Ack-Ack Macaque hopped in beside him.

"Have you got the box stowed?"

"In the back, sir."

"Then take us up, as soon as you're ready."

"Aye, sir."

As the five-pronged shadow of the *Tereshkova*'s nose cleared the final suburb of Bristol, the helicopter rose from the flight deck. It hovered in the air for a moment, allowing the behemoth to move away ahead of it, and then dropped, coming down in a swooping curve that brought it down past the giant fins and rudders at the stern, and forward, under the speeding airship.

"Keep low," Ack-Ack Macaque told the pilot, "and follow the river. Watch out for bridges."

He scrambled into the back, where Marie sat strapped into her seat, coil gun resting across her knees. A large metal case sat on the deck by her feet, held in place by bungee cords. He crouched beside it, bracing himself against the seat in the cramped space, and began to unfasten it.

"What's that?" Marie leant forward for a better look.

Ack-Ack Macaque gave her a grin.

"This is our way in."

From the front, the pilot called, "Two minutes to target."

They were winding along the course of the River Avon. Ahead, they could see hills and main roads, Georgian terraces and the tower of Bath Cathedral.

The London mainline lay to their left, and they drew level with an eastbound train.

"Keep pace with the train," Ack-Ack Macaque ordered. The land was opening out into a wide river valley, down the middle of which the track ran, side-by-side with the river. Larkin House stood on a hill to the north, and he hoped that by staying low, concealed visually and audibly by the train, they might be able to approach without raising an alarm.

Looking out of the side window, he saw faces looking back at him from the train's carriages, and gave them the finger.

When they drew level with their target, the pilot pulled up and over the train.

"Thirty seconds," he reported.

Ack-Ack Macaque exchanged looks with Marie. Then he flipped the fastening on the box and opened it, revealing a long, fat tube with a gun sight and a pistol grip. It had been painted olive green, with bright red, black and yellow warning decals. It was one of the Commodore's hidden treasures, but there was no time to sit and admire the thing. He pulled it from the case and slung its strap over his shoulder, kicked his boots off, stuck a cigar into his mouth, and shuffled to the side hatch.

"Sit tight," he told Marie. He slid the door open and climbed through, onto the helicopter's landing strut. Cold winds tore at him but he gripped the strut with his toes. Ahead, the hillside came at them like a rising green wave and he could see the pale sandstone frontage of Larkin House in the centre of a tidy arrangement of fir trees, gravel paths and ornamental hedges.

Crouching, he wrapped his tail around the strut, and let go with his hands. Gripping hard with his toes, he swung around until he hung upside down by his feet. The helicopter rocked at this, but stayed on course. Below, white-suited figures emerged from the house and pointed guns at him. He saw muzzle flashes but, if any of the bullets hit the chopper, he didn't see or feel them. Instead, he concentrated on getting the tube—which now swung from his arm on the end of its strap—onto his shoulder, where he was forced to hold it in position with both hands.

*Come on,* he thought, *this isn't any harder than hanging from a tree branch. Travelling at a hundred miles an hour. Through a cyclone.*

The tube housed one of the Commodore's most prized souvenirs, taken from a cupboard in his cabin. It was a portable ground-to-air missile picked up off a battlefield somewhere in the Middle East thirty years ago.

Steadying the launcher, Ack-Ack Macaque lined the sight up on the eaves of the old house

"Okay," he muttered to himself around the cigar, "time to blow shit up."

He pulled the trigger. There was a sharp *whoosh*, and the tube bucked in his hands so hard he almost lost his grip on the strut. The missile leapt forward on a candle of flame, and the helicopter dipped its nose to follow.

Squirming around, Ack-Ack Macaque managed to pull himself back up to the helicopter's open hatch. He let the empty launcher fall away into the fields below, and drew one of his big, shiny Colts. Marie looked at him, and he gave her a big thumbs-up.

"Everything's okay!" he hollered above the engine noise. Ahead, the missile hit the roof and blew apart in a huge fireball. Tiles and bits of wooden joist flew into the air, and black smoke mushroomed over the house. "Okay, as long as they weren't keeping your kid in the attic."

They passed over the front gates of the house, and he dropped a grenade, to make the clowns with guns keep their heads down. Then the helicopter was over the hole in the roof, its downdraught whipping the smoke and flames. The drop was somewhere between fifteen to twenty feet.

"Okay, lets go." Cigar clamped securely in his teeth, he leaned out of the helicopter, and dropped.

The wind tore at him. His jacket flapped. He fell into the fire, and through, into the space beneath the roof. His bare feet hit wooden planks hard enough to jar his spine, and he rolled onto his shoulder, just getting out of the way in time before Marie crashed through the smoke and hit the deck beside him.

By the time she'd picked herself up, he was on his feet, both Colts at the ready, as the helicopter peeled away, heading back towards the *Tereshkova*, which was hammering past a couple of kilometres to the south.

Black smoke filled the attic. He coughed and pulled his scarf up to cover his nose and mouth. There wasn't time to waste looking for a hatch leading down, so he yanked the pin from a grenade, sang, "Have a banana," and rolled it as far along the floorboards as it would go.

A second explosion rocked the house. When it had cleared, the floor had a ragged, burning hole in it.

Marie brushed dust and splinters from her clothes. She looked at him with an expression of respect, astonishment, and irritation.

"Please," she said, "warn me the next time you're going to do that."

He grinned at her, scooped up a smouldering stick of wood, and lit his cigar.

"There's something you need to know about me, lady—"

"That you're dangerously irresponsible with explosives?"

He frowned, pulled out his cigar, and exhaled smoke.

"Uh, yeah," he said. "That's near enough."

DROPPING DOWN THROUGH the hole in the floorboards, they found themselves in a dormitory. The room had probably once been a grand bedroom; now it contained three rows of triple bunk beds. Chunks of shattered plaster lay on the blankets and floor, and the bunk closest to the hole was alight.

"Well," Ack-Ack Macaque said, "I told you I'd get us into the house, didn't I?"

Marie cradled the coil gun, keeping its barrel pointed at the door.

"You certainly did. I can't fault you on that. But it's lucky the girls weren't in this room."

Ack-Ack Macaque gave a shrug.

"Ah, they'd have been okay. I needed a grenade to get through those ceiling beams."

From the landing beyond, they heard the sound of shoes running on a polished wooden floor. Holding his Colts at arm's length, Ack-Ack Macaque drew a bead on the door. Marie waved him away.

"No, you'll give away our position," she said. "We need to kill them quickly, before they know what's hit them, otherwise they'll alert the rest of the hive. Leave this to me."

He glanced at her gun. It was a slim metal tube wrapped in electromagnets, with batteries in the stock, and a foot-long magazine protruding from the bottom of the barrel, just in front of the trigger. It looked like something knocked up in somebody's garden shed. Christ alone knew where the Commodore had found it.

"Really?"

She took up a firing stance.

"Have you ever seen one of these at work?"

He waggled his head.

"Nah."

"Then you might want to stand back."

The footsteps reached the door, and the handle rattled as somebody seized it. Marie clicked the coil gun's trigger, and moved the barrel back and forth. Firing without sound or recoil, the gun peppered the door, punching dozens of pencil-thin holes through the wooden panels, the frame, and the walls to either side.

The effect was as if she'd taken a chainsaw to it. As the stream of tungsten darts crossed and re-crossed the door, chunks of wood were cut away and blown out into the corridor. By the time she clicked the trigger off again, only one large piece remained, attached to the lower hinge, and even that had a few holes through it. Outside in the corridor, two Neanderthals lay slumped against the far wall, their white suits ragged and soaked in bright red blood.

Ack-Ack Macaque walked forward carefully, keeping his guns trained on them, but he needn't have bothered—when he got closer, he saw they were both quite definitively dead. Bits of their massive jaws and swollen craniums were missing, torn away by the deadly rain of miniature projectiles, and their chests and stomachs had been minced to hamburger.

He poked one in the shoulder with the barrel of his gun, and the man's arm fell off, severed in three or four places, as if it had been hacked apart with a meat cleaver.

"Man," Ack-Ack Macaque muttered, "I have *got* to get me one of those guns."

The walls of the landing had been painted red; the floors were dark, varnished wood, and heavily framed paintings adorned the walls. Ack-Ack Macaque ran a finger across one of the paintings, and it came away covered in dust. Other doors led off from the landing, presumably into other bedrooms, and a wide stone staircase swept down to an entrance hall. Crouching by the wrought iron rail, he peeped over. The entrance hall had a bulbous, black metal chandelier hanging from a chain above its diamond-patterned flagstone floor, and a reception desk installed just inside the main doors of the house, at the foot of the stairs. A white-suited man and woman stood behind the desk, consulting a fire alarm console, on which several red lights were illuminated. As he watched, they stopped what they were doing, and both turned to look at the stairs. He ducked back.

*Damn,* he thought, *they're all linked, aren't they?* Marie had done her best, but it made no difference; as soon as you killed one of the Gestalt, the others all knew something had happened. They might not know the cause, but they sensed the loss. Now, they'd all be converging on this landing to find out what was going on, and he wasn't sure he could hold them all off.

*Well,* he thought, *so much for stealth. If I wanted a sneak attack, I wouldn't have blown up the roof.*

He picked another grenade from his belt, and tossed it over the rail. He heard a shout, then a satisfying *crump*, and the clatter of broken glass.

"Maybe that'll make them more cautious," he muttered, standing up and dusting himself down. The two by the reception desk were either unconscious or dead. He kept one gun trained on them and the other on the front door as he made his way down, step by step. The back of his leather jacket squeaked as he pressed it against the painted wall. His cigar left a descending trail of grey smoke.

Marie said, "They don't know there are two of us. You keep them distracted, and I'll stay up here and check the other rooms."

"Knock yourself out."

They had only seconds, and a staircase was no place for a shootout. Three doors led off the hallway, deeper into the rest of the house, and he knew he had to choose one. Rather than cross the hallway, he chose to slip around to the door beneath the stairs. His caution wasn't the result of fear; at this point, he had no regard for own his physical safety, he just wanted to make sure he survived long enough to find K8, and get her out of this madhouse.

The door opened to his touch and he stepped inside, guns at the ready. If one Gestalt member saw him, the rest would be on his trail instantly, so he had no time for subtlety. The rule for today was to kill or be killed; and he couldn't afford to die before he freed K8. She might be a brat, but she was a damn clever brat, and a dependable friend. She'd been there for him in reality and in the game and now she was his only remaining link to the game world, and the person he used to be.

She was his colleague and his comrade, and he couldn't imagine life without her. She'd saved his life in the past; now it was his turn to repay the favour. Monkeys were instinctively social creatures, yet he was the only one of his kind. She was the closest thing he had to a member of his troupe, and those primate loyalties ran deep. He knew he'd get her back even if—*especially if*—he had to kill every last motherfucker in the building.

The door brought him into a long corridor, which seemed to run the length of the house, with doors leading off to either side. As he stood there, three of the doors opened, and men and women in white suits stepped out, blocking the way. They were of all ages and nationalities, but their faces all carried the same eerie smile. Some clutched guns, but most were armed with whatever they'd had to hand: knives, letter openers, chair legs…

"You cannot win," they said in unison, standing shoulder-to-shoulder, not attacking. "You are one, we are legion. You will join us."

"Go suck an egg."

"You will join us willingly." The crowd took a pace forwards. "Or otherwise…"

Ack-Ack Macaque glanced at his Colts. Both were fully loaded, which meant he had twelve shots—not nearly enough to deal with the mob in front of him. He might get the first few rows, but he wouldn't have time to reload before the others were upon him. He'd have to drop the revolvers and switch to the automatic pistol tucked into the waistband of his trousers, under his jacket. That would give him another ten shots. Then there was the knife at his belt and, if all else failed, his bare hands and fangs.

He fixed the closest two with a glare, and rolled the cigar from one side of his mouth to the other.

"Fuck you," he said.

As one, they took another step towards him, and raised their weapons. That was all he needed. He opened his mouth with a shriek, and leapt to the attack.

# CHAPTER TWENTY-THREE
## DIALLING OUT

WILLIAM COLE STOOD on the *Tereshkova*'s bridge, watching the countryside wheel around as the old airship slowed and turned, ready to begin its run back to Larkin Hall and the scene of the battle. From where he stood, he could see a black column of smoke rising into the autumn air. Most of the building's roof was ablaze. And, somewhere down there, beneath that inferno, his wife and child were fighting for their lives.

He scratched fitfully at his wild hair.

"How could I have let her go like that?"

Behind him, Victoria Valois glanced up from her instruments.

"I don't recall you having a choice."

He turned on her.

"But I could have insisted! I could have gone in her place."

"No, you couldn't. What use would you have been, eh?" She looked back down at her console. "At least Marie's fought the Gestalt before. She knows what to expect."

William shook his head. He had a pain in the back of his throat.

"I am such a coward."

He turned back to the window. The smoke and flames looked thicker than before.

Had he lost her again?

THREE CAVEMEN CAME into the cellar. One of them held Lila at bay while the other two grabbed K8. She tried to fight them off but they were solidly built and seemingly impervious to the kicks and blows she aimed their way. She tried to gouge their eyes and knee their groins, but they simply held her tighter, and twisted her arms up behind her back until she cried out and stopped squirming. Her strength had been sapped by the drugs in her system.

"You come with us," the Neanderthals said together. It was the first time she'd heard them speak, and she was surprised. Somehow, she'd been expecting a crude grunt rather than fully formed words.

Moving in perfect step, they pulled her out of the cellar and up a set of stone steps, into a white-tiled kitchen equipped with a wood-burning range, a walk-in larder, and a porcelain sink as big as a bathtub. As they led her through the room, the house rocked to the sound of an explosion. She heard a helicopter overhead, very low and very loud, and small arms fire coming from the front of the building.

"Are we under attack?"

The hands on her arms didn't loosen. Without breaking stride or showing even the slightest curiosity, the three Neanderthals carried her through the kitchen and out, through a series of utility rooms, to a wooden door, which led out into a well-tended kitchen garden, with rows of herbs and vegetables and ornamental bay trees. After the dry, dust-laden air of the cellar, the bright sunshine and chill November breeze hit her like a double handful of cold water, and she sneezed. The fresh air helped her head to clear, and she struggled anew, to test their grip.

"Where are you taking me?"

From within the house behind, she heard the muffled thump of another explosion. Her heart surged. That *had* to be the Skipper. He'd come for her, as she'd known he would. Who else would be tossing grenades around inside a stately home? She stopped wriggling and laughed.

"You idiots are for it now."

The Neanderthals weren't listening; or, if they were, they were doing a very good job of ignoring her and everything else around them. Still marching in perfect synchronisation, they marched her out onto the lawn, and stopped in the centre of a circular patch of dead grass maybe two metres in diameter.

Behind them, the roof of Larkin Hall was ablaze. Smoke billowed up into the blue sky, chased by orange tongues of flame. Gunshots went off like firecrackers.

The Neanderthals seemed to be in no hurry to get away. In fact, they could hardly have chosen a more exposed spot on which to stand. If the Skipper were in the house, all it would take for her to be rescued would be for him to look out of a window...

"Skip!" she hollered. "Skip, I'm out here!" But all that earned her was a cuff across the top of the head from one of her captors.

The caveman who'd whacked her pulled a device from the pocket of his white jacket. It was black and shiny, and resembled a fat SincPhone. The casing looked to be tough rubber, worn in places but designed to take abuse. She watched him tap the touchscreen with a fat, hairy-knuckled finger. Was he making a call?

Far beyond the conifers at the far end of the lawn, she caught sight of the *Tereshkova*. Impeller blades glittering in the sunlight, the old airship banked sharply, and came around to face the house. She felt the urge to wave her arms and shriek. It might be old and, with its black and white paint job, somewhat ugly, but the elderly skyliner was her home; the first permanent one she'd had since the offer of work with Céleste Tech had enabled her to escape the disintegration of her parents' marriage.

The Neanderthal with the handset paused with his finger over the touchscreen, and muttered something in a language she didn't understand.

"What?"

He grinned at her, exposing flat, shovel-like teeth in a too-wide jaw.

"I said, 'hold on to yourself.'" He brought his hand down and stabbed the 'phone'. K8 felt a quiver move through her entire body. Every muscle and membrane shook. Her eyes trembled in their sockets, blurring her vision, and the sky went dark.

When her sight cleared, she found they were still in the garden, standing in their circle of dead grass, but everything around them had changed. The house wasn't on fire; in fact, it was larger than it had been a moment ago, with a couple of turrets that hadn't been there before, and a whole extra wing that seemed to have materialised out of nowhere. The sounds of fighting had gone, and the *Tereshkova* had disappeared from the sky. In its place hung another airship—bigger, armoured, and unmistakably decked-out for war. Cannon poked from turrets along its length, and its upper surfaces bristled with radar emplacements and anti-aircraft batteries. Its impellers were much larger than the *Tereshkova*'s, and every inch of its hull had been painted black.

A VTOL passenger jet sat on the grass nearby, engines idling, and the Neanderthals carried her towards it. K8 had never flown in a plane before. To her, this one looked kind of like a helicopter without rotors, and she didn't like it. Planes were rare in her world, and she didn't trust them. The idea that a slim metal tube could be held aloft by the difference in speed between the air passing over and under its wing seemed ludicrous.

"Come along," her captors said, bustling her forwards, "the Leader will see you now."

# CHAPTER TWENTY-FOUR
## THE LEADER

BRUISED AND BLOODIED, Ack-Ack Macaque limped down the steps from the kitchen to the cellar. His cigar, guns and flying cap were all missing, lost in the fight. His jacket had been cut and torn in a dozen places, and his skin slashed and scratched. In his left hand he held a machete, in his right, an antique samurai sword. Both blades were slick with the blood of their former owners.

"K8, are you down here?" He thought he could smell traces of that scent she liked to wear. "Hello?" He reached the bottom of the stairs and leant against the wall, trying to get his breath back. He'd had to fight his way through the corridor, and now his arms hurt and his legs were tired and shaky. Things had been so much easier back in the game. In those days, he could fight forever without getting tired or injured, and always have enough breath left over for a witty quip or scathing putdown.

Here in reality, things were somewhat different. Leaning against the wall, listening to the breath wheeze in and out of his heaving chest, he regretted every single cigar, every shot of rum and litre of beer. Compared to the character he'd been in the game, he was hopelessly out of shape.

And the Gestalt drones were really hard to fight. Usually, when facing overwhelming odds, he went for shock and awe, using battle cries and ferocity to scatter and panic his opponents. A few bites and screeches would usually shatter their discipline and strike fear into the stoutest of hearts. The ranks would collapse and he'd be able pick off his adversaries individually. That hadn't worked with the Gestalt in the corridor. He couldn't break them up. Whatever he did, they were still a perfectly coordinated group, able to attack and parry as one. Taking them on had been like tangling with a multi-headed, multi-limbed hydra, and he'd had to fight hard for every centimetre he'd advanced.

Looking back into the kitchen, he saw Marie appear in the doorway. She had the coil gun cradled in her right arm. Her left hung at her side, slathered in blood, and her right leg dragged behind her as she moved. Drops of blood dripped from her fingertips, onto the white tiles. The sleeve of her jacket had been torn away and used as a makeshift bandage. Warily, she looked at the weapons in his hands.

"Have you found Lila?"

Ack-Ack Macaque waved the point of his stolen katana at the door at the foot of the stairs.

"I think she's in here."

Marie limped towards him. "Is it locked?"

"I don't know, I haven't tried." He could feel his arms and back stiffening, and was sure he'd torn at least one muscle, if not more. "Help yourself."

He stood aside, and she brushed past him. The handle rattled in her hand, and she swore under her breath.

"Lila, honey? It's me. Are you in there?"

"Mum?" It was a girl's voice.

"Lila, I'm coming in. Stand away from the door." She stepped back and braced herself against the wall, keeping the weight off her bad leg. She reached into her pocket and pulled out a gun identical to the one Ack-Ack Macaque had seen in Bill's apartment. Keeping the barrel angled downwards, she pointed it at the door and squeezed the trigger. He couldn't see the beam, but a spot began to smoulder midway between the handle and the frame.

Within seconds, the door had a thin hole burned through it. Marie moved the gun around in a semi-circle, severing the section of door that held the lock. When she had finished, the rest of the door swung open, leaving the handle and lock in place. Ack-Ack Macaque closed his eye, and sank down onto the lower step. The stone was cold on his ass. He heard Lila crying and Marie fussing over her, checking her for injuries and evidence of torture.

"Hey, K8?" he said tiredly. "Are you in there?"

No reply.

He re-opened his eye to find Marie and her daughter standing in the doorway. Lila took one look at him and shrank away behind her mother, plainly terrified by his wild, bloodied appearance.

"She's not here." Marie limped forward, staying firmly between him and Lila.

Ack-Ack Macaque felt a flush of anger. All that fighting and killing, and he still wasn't done.

"Well, where the hell is she?"

"Lila says they took her to see the Leader."

"And where's he?"

"Somewhere else."

"Another hideout?"

Marie shook her head.

"Another *world*."

The walls of the cellar seemed to close in around him. Ack-Ack Macaque put his blades on the step and rubbed his eye patch. His chest felt tight, and sweat broke out on his back. Up until this moment all his missions had been successful. He'd never lost before, never come home empty-handed.

"Another world?" He tugged at his right ear. His mind raced, retracing his steps, trying to figure out where he'd gone wrong. Marie and Lila were still looking at him, and he wanted to scream at them, fling his shit around and frighten them away. How could this have happened? How could K8 not be here, after all the trouble he'd endured to rescue her? It didn't seem fair. He'd lost comrades in the past, in the game, but this was new and different. He actually cared about K8, even though he would have been loath to admit it under normal circumstances, and someone had known that, and used his feelings for her against him. She'd suffered because of his friendship, and now she was gone, spirited away to another plane of existence—lost in a sea of probability, on an unknown and unreachable world.

He looked down at his bare feet. They were chilly on the stone floor.

"What am I supposed to do now?"

His phone rang but he made no move to answer it. On the fourth ring, Marie said, "Hadn't you better get that?"

He curled his lip at her.

"Get lost."

On the sixth ring, still glowering at the woman and her daughter, he reached into his pocket, pulled out the phone, and clamped it to his ear.

*Hey, Ack-ster. It's Paul. You've got to get back up here, man.*

"Why should I?"

*Just get up here, right now.*

"But, K8—"

*This is about K8. We're sending a chopper. Just get up here as fast as you can.*

WHEN ACK-ACK MACAQUE arrived back on board the *Tereshkova*, a Russian steward met him at the helipad and escorted him to the captain's cabin, where he found Victoria and Paul waiting. As he walked in, Paul flinched, and Victoria's hand went to the handle of the cutlass at her hip.

"Okay, what's going on?" The chopper ride hadn't helped his frustration. "If you people don't start giving me some answers, I'm going to start banging heads together."

Victoria waved him to silence with her free hand.

"There's a call for you." They were both looking at him very strangely.

"But—"

She shook her head, unable to explain. "Just take it." She motioned to one of the large SincPad screens on the wall. The screen brightened into life, and Ack-Ack Macaque found himself staring into a mirror.

"What the—?" The face on the screen was his, only it wasn't. Whoever this monkey was, he'd been groomed and washed, and the sleek black hair around his face shone with cleanliness. Instead of a ripped and battered old aviator jacket, he wore a white suit with a white shirt and tie, and an eye patch that covered his right eye instead of his left. Looking at him, Ack-Ack Macaque felt his hackles rise.

"Who, the hell, are you?" He turned to Victoria. "What fuckery is this?"

The other monkey regarded him with a baleful glare.

"Who do you *think* I am?" He brushed the lapel of his suit jacket. "Check out the threads. Consider the context."

"You're *me*?"

"You seem surprised." The stranger sat back, away from the camera. He appeared to be seated in a cabin similar to the one in which Ack-Ack Macaque now stood, but the walls of *his* cabin were draped with tapestries and other expensive ornaments. Statues stood on plinths in front of bookshelves lined with the spines of ancient hardbacks. Having made himself comfortable, he waved a regal hand. "Before you say anything, let me first express what a genuine pleasure it is for me to touch base with you. As we're both iterations of the same basic individual, I hope we can find a way to collaborate together towards mutual understanding and profit."

"Huh?" Ack-Ack Macaque flexed his fists. "Look, pal. How about you just tell me what you want, and why you're here."

The monkey on the screen adjusted his tie with manicured fingers.

"Oh dear," he said. "You're one of the thick ones, aren't you? Well, you can call me 'Leader'. Everybody else does. I created the Gestalt out of nothing, and I've led them to dominance on half a dozen worlds. I'm the CEO, the king and the president, all rolled into one. I'm a pharaoh in three different Egypts; I'm the place where the buck most definitely stops; '*le grand fromage*'; and 'a jungle VIP'. In short, I'm the *boss*, and you'd do very well to bear that in mind. Capeesh?"

Ack-Ack Macaque's hands twitched, longing for his trusty Colts. He glanced across at his companions. Victoria was leaning on her desk, arms folded, watching the confrontation through narrowed eyes. Paul stood, hands in pockets and mouth agape, obviously delighted by the sight of two identical monkeys arguing between themselves.

"Don't try that alpha monkey shit on me," Ack-Ack Macaque said to the face on the screen. "I invented that."

The Leader just smiled and made a finger steeple in front of his lips. Shiny white cufflinks flashed in the light of the screen.

"I know you came here to reclaim your pet human, the little one who thinks it's clever to spell her name with numbers as well as letters," he said, "but you should really take a moment to reassess my earlier proposition. There's still a place for you on my team. I know how lonely you are. I used to be just like you. But now, think what we can achieve *together*. Think of the synergies. You and me, maestro, we'd be unstoppable: the dream team."

"If you've hurt her…"

The Leader shook his head.

"Your concern does you credit, but can we park that issue for a minute, and concentrate instead on what I'm offering?" He rubbed his covered right eye, and Ack-Ack Macaque had to make an effort to refrain from copying the gesture. "In a couple of hours, my fleet will arrive in your world, and I'll have an airship over every major town and city."

"Airships can be shot down."

"Not enough of them, and not quickly enough. You don't have enough planes or missiles, and my assets are packing some serious hardware of their own."

"We'll fight you."

"No, you won't. You see, as soon as I've given the fleet a short window in which to demonstrate their superior firepower, I'll broadcast my terms. This isn't some nineteenth century pirate raid, you know. We know what we're doing because we've done it before, on six worlds, and the outcome's always been the same. This is a takeover, plain and simple. Anybody who wants to come over to my side beforehand will be welcomed with open arms. But those who refuse—" he lowered his chin, and his yellow eye burned through the screen, "—will be subject to extreme measures."

"What sort of measures?"

"Let's just say, I have the means to make conversion automatic and mandatory. I have recently acquired an airborne agent that is capable of germinating inside the human body. It converts messy, rebellious neurons into clean, obedient gelware." He interlaced his fingers. "All I have to do is give my fleet the signal to release it and, within hours, every human on the planet's either dead or a functioning member of the Gestalt." He fiddled with his cuff, looking casual as hell. "So, it's time for you to choose, my brother. Come willingly, or come as a slave. Rule with me, or be ruled *by* me."

"You're mad."

"No, companero, I'm *winning*." He glanced at the white hands on his platinum wristwatch. "Now, you have less than four hours. My fleet's going to rock up at eighteen hundred hours, GMT. I'll be on my flagship, over London, drinking a cup of Earl Grey with your little friend. In fact, I'll pour an extra cup for you, just in case. If you'd care to join us, be there, and don't be late."

# CHAPTER TWENTY-FIVE
## ZEPPELINS FROM THE GREAT BEYOND

WITH A FLICK of his hand, the Leader cut the connection and the wall screen went blank. From where she leant against her desk, Victoria Valois saw Ack-Ack Macaque's posture slump. He'd been holding himself upright for the confrontation; now, he looked half dead.

"Are you all right?"

The macaque swivelled his face towards her, too tired to move his feet.

"Verbose motherfucker, wasn't he?"

She smiled.

"Do you think he was serious?"

"Do you have any reason to think he wasn't?" Ack-Ack Macaque put a hand to the side of his jaw, and pushed his chin up and to the side. Something crackled in his neck.

"You look like merde," she said. His knuckles were battered and raw. One of the sleeves of his flying jacket had torn at the shoulder seam, and now hung down almost to his elbow. His fur stuck out in clumps, caked in dark and sticky blood. She wondered how much of the blood was his, and how much had come from other people.

"What can I say? It's been a long day."

She pushed off from the desk and stood upright. Tapped the fingertips of her right hand against the palm of her left.

"I'm almost afraid to ask what you want to do."

"About what?" He jerked a thumb at the dead screen. "About that arsehole?"

"He's you."

"He most certainly is not."

"A version of you."

"So what? He's still an arsehole, and we're still going to kick his fucking head in." He turned his body to face her, his movements stiff and laborious. "Right?"

Victoria let out a breath she hadn't realised she'd been holding.

"If you say so."

The monkey's eye narrowed.

"You didn't think I'd be *tempted*, did you?"

Victoria shrugged.

"Stranger things have happened."

"Not to me, they haven't." He reached into his inside pocket and pulled out a cigar. About a third of it hung at an angle, having been damaged during the fight at Larkin Hall. He snapped off the short end and dropped it into her wastepaper basket.

"You can't deny you've been lonely."

He reached into the pocket on the other side of his jacket, and extracted his Zippo. "No, I can't." A quick flick of the little wheel, and a flame sparked. "But that doesn't mean I'm going to get gooey-eyed about the first talking monkey that comes along." He held the flame to the end of the cigar and huffed clouds of blue smoke into the room. "Especially as he's planning to fuck the planet."

The air-conditioning kicked in. It sucked most of the smoke up into vents on the ceiling, but couldn't completely obliterate the pungent and lingering whiff. Victoria wrinkled her nose, and mentally recited the code words that let her access the command menus for her cranial implant. Once in, she quickly deactivated her sense of smell. Fond of the monkey as she was, the aroma of cigar smoke always made her feel ill.

"So you do care about us?"

"Of course I do. I already saved the world once, didn't I?" He took a mouthful of smoke, rolled it around, and blew it at the ceiling. "Besides, I'm not really alone, am I?" He coughed, and looked away, wiping his mouth on the back of his hand. "I've got you two, and K8."

Victoria exchanged a look with Paul, and they both raised their eyebrows. This was the first time they'd heard him talk this way; the first crack they'd seen in his habitually gruff exterior.

"Yes," she said, "of course you do."

The monkey scuffed a foot against the deck. He looked supremely uncomfortable.

"That's okay then."

Victoria tried to suppress her smile. It appeared that, despite his coarseness, Ack-Ack Macaque had the same insecurities and needs as everyone else, including the need to belong; and it seemed losing K8 had finally driven home to him who his friends really were, and made him appreciate everything he had, and everything he stood to lose.

"You should get checked out," she said, wanting to spare him further embarrassment. "Get Sergei to patch you up."

Ack-Ack Macaque looked down at himself. He tried to straighten his torn sleeve.

"But K8—"

"You're not going to be any use to her in that state. Get down to the infirmary and get Sergei to see to you. That's an order."

He took the cigar from his lips and rubbed his brow.

"Yes, boss."


AFTER HE'D GONE, Victoria walked around her desk and sat in the chair.

"Jesus Christ," she said.

In the bright noon light from the picture window, Paul's image was an insubstantial ghost haunting the corner of her office: the murder victim who wouldn't lie down, the ex-husband who never left.

"What are you going to do?"

Victoria pulled the cutlass from her belt and dropped it into the umbrella stand.

"You said you could fly this thing?"

Paul took off his glasses and rubbed them on the hem of his shirt. "Well, yes, if I had to. All the connections are in place."

"You have to."

"Right now?"

Victoria drew herself up. "Make course for central London, best speed."

"Aye, aye." Paul's brow screwed in concentration as he devoted more and more of his processing time to the business of running the airship's systems. His image grew tenuous, and then finally disappeared, as he focused his attention elsewhere. Moments later, Victoria felt a tremble through the deck as the skyliner's engines powered up and the *Tereshkova*'s nose swung eastwards again, towards the capital.

Ahead, the windscreen showed a bright blue sky growing paler all the way to the far horizon. A single vapour train caught the sun like a comet trail, and she found herself wondering what the world would have been like had jet travel really taken off in the latter half of the twentieth century. With the first skyliners entering commercial service in the early 1960s, and the subsequent oil blockades and price wars of the 1970s, jet air travel had never become an economical option, and now only the richest and most extravagant used it as a means of crossing oceans. Skyliners might be slower, but they were dependable and cheap, and their nuclear-electric engines had none of the economic and environmental disadvantages of oil.

But how would things have been, she asked herself, had the skyliners not come along when they did—if the post-war British and French shipyards had been allowed to wither and die instead of being turned over to airship production? What would the globe look like with everybody rushing around at nine hundred kilometres per hour, and the skies streaked by hundreds of shining white trails?

Paul's voice came over the intercom.

"We can't fight them all," he said. "Not by ourselves."

Victoria glanced up at the security camera in the corner of the ceiling.

"We'll alert the authorities."

"Will they believe us? Because, quite frankly, I'm in the middle of this, and I'm not even sure *I* believe it."

Victoria knew he was right. Even among skyliner captains, most of whom were considered pretty eccentric in their own right, she had a reputation as a maverick. Putting the world on a war footing in three hours would take more than just her word.

"In that case," she said, "I'm going to have to make a call."

"Not—?"

"Who else? Besides, he owes us a favour."


THE FACE LOOKING back at her from the screen was that of a young man, but his eyes seemed more mature and weary than one might have expected from his apparent age. They were the eyes of a boy who'd served in the South Atlantic; who'd lost comrades in a helicopter crash; lost his father at an impressionable age; and fought his mother in order to prevent a holocaust.

"Hello, Victoria. What can I do for you?" This was Merovech I, King of the United Kingdom of France, Great Britain, Northern Ireland and Norway, and head of the European Commonwealth. In the time she'd known him, he'd played many roles—a soldier, a criminal and a runaway, to name three— but this was the first time she'd spoken to him since his coronation, and the first time she'd seen him actually looking like a king. Gone were the ripped jeans and red hoodie she remembered; in their place, a tailored suit, crisp white shirt and regimental tie.

"Your majesty." Victoria tipped her head forward. "I'm afraid this isn't a social call."

Merovech leant towards the camera.

"I should say not. I saw what our monkey friend did on the M4, and how much damage he caused."

"I can explain."

"I think you'd better."

Hands clasped behind her back, Victoria rocked back on her heels. The young king had become a man. Every gesture and tone conveyed authority and patience. She wasn't sure how much of that came naturally, and how much had been taught.

"Merovech, listen." She put a splayed hand to her chest. By addressing him informally, she hoped to break through the façade, and reach the young man she'd once fought alongside. "You remember last year?"

"I'm hardly likely to forget."

"Well, this is worse."

Merovech raised an eyebrow. "Worse than all-out nuclear war?"

"Yes. At least in a nuclear war there's the possibility of a few survivors."

"What are we talking about?"

"An invasion. Several hundred armed skyliners, one over every major city, and each one packed with some sort of hideous plague."

"Where are they coming from?"

"From thin air."

The young king sat back in his chair, and his image blurred for half a second as the camera refocused.

"I beg your pardon?"

Victoria rubbed her forehead. "Look, it's an invasion from another dimension, from a parallel world. I can't explain more than that because, quite frankly, I don't understand it all myself."

"Is this for real?"

"I keep asking myself the same question."

He looked at her for what seemed like a very long time, and she could see that he was weighing their friendship, deciding how far he could trust her. Finally, he cleared his throat and said, "When?"

"Three hours." She felt a surge of relief. "You'll need everything you have in the air, and you'll need to alert the other countries. But be careful. If these things unload their cargo, it's game over, and we're all as good as dead."

Merovech frowned, suddenly doubtful. He tipped his head to one side and tapped a finger against his lips.

"How can I ring the President of the United States and tell him we're being invaded by Zeppelins from the Great Beyond?"

Victoria took a step closer to her screen.

"You're the Head of the European Commonwealth, he'll have to listen to you."

"But will he believe me?"

"Does it matter? If one country scrambles every fighter plane it has, the rest will have to follow suit. They might not know the reason, but they won't want to be caught napping. You get every European plane in the air, and I can guarantee the Russians, Chinese and Americans will do likewise."

Merovech made a clicking sound with his tongue.

"After last year's unpleasantness with China, putting that many planes in the air could be dangerous."

"It'll be a lot more dangerous for you to do nothing."

"You don't know what you're asking."

"Yes I do. I've got the monkey with me. Twelve months ago, the three of us saved the world. Now, we're asking you to help us save it again."

# CHAPTER TWENTY-SIX
## FAMILIAR STRANGERS

IN A PASSENGER lounge on board one of the *Tereshkova*'s starboard gondolas, William Cole sat on a bar stool with his elbows resting on the copper counter top. The lounge had been decorated in the style of a Zeppelin from the 1930s, with lots of bare rivets and brass fittings, and lazily revolving ceiling fans carved to resemble wooden propellers. Behind the bar, a painting hung over the cash register. It depicted a young man in a white Russian dress uniform with a red sash. William didn't know who the young soldier was, but he recognised the jacket, and some of its medals, as being identical to the one worn by Captain Valois.

*I guess that must be the Commodore*, he thought to himself.

Opposite the painting, on the other side of the lounge, a row of portholes showed him the green countryside of southern England. The undulating landscape rolled past beneath the ship like the hide of some tremendous dragon.

He was waiting for Marie, and Lila. In his hands he held an old photograph. It was a printout from a digital file, and he'd been carrying it around in his pocket ever since the day of his wife's funeral. It was a shot he'd taken in New York, not long after they'd first met. He'd taken it on the observation deck of the Empire State Building, and it showed her laughing, leaning back against the railings with the whole of Manhattan spread out behind her. She was wearing a black 'I ♥ New York' t-shirt. Her orange hair had been cropped short and tucked behind one ear, and the sun picked out the freckles on her nose. It was the one photograph of her that he'd included in his bug-out bag; the one picture he wanted to keep, as a reminder of everything they'd had, and everything they'd lost. It was a picture of her taken when they were both young and in the first passionate throes of love, when the world seemed filled with excitement and hope, and all their dreams seemed attainable. At the moment the shutter clicked, neither of them had known that she would shortly fall pregnant, that the baby would die, and that, unable to comfort each other, they'd separate and spend so many years living apart, married to the wrong people, only to reunite a decade later, a short time before her untimely death.

A glass of soda water stood on the counter beside his left wrist, fizzing quietly. It was all he wanted. Once, he might have ordered a glass of bourbon to steady his nerves; now, he no longer felt the need. He'd taken a hot shower and changed his clothes and, for the first time in months, felt clean inside and out.

What would Marie—his Marie—have said if she'd known that, one day, he'd find another version of her, and get to meet the daughter they'd lost? Would she have felt betrayed, or would she have been pleased for him, wanting only for him to be happy?

He smoothed out the edges of the photo with his thumbs, hoping her answer would have been the latter, because, whatever she might have thought, he couldn't afford to pass up this second chance.

After all, he told himself, he wouldn't be cheating as such. This *was* Marie. She had many of the same memories as his Marie. She'd even remember this photograph being taken. At the point the camera clicked, they'd been the same person. It was only later, when the baby died—or in her case, lived— that their lives had diverged. The last sixteen years may have panned out differently for her, but she was still, essentially, the same girl he'd taken up to the eighty-sixth floor of the Empire State; and the picture he held was as much a photograph of her as it was of the woman he'd said goobye to just over two years ago. He thought of the closing lines of *War Of The Worlds* by H.G. Wells: *And strangest of all is it to hold my wife's hand again, and to think that I have counted her, and that she has counted me, among the dead.*

How many people had ever been given such an opportunity? He placed the picture on the counter, and took a sip of water. The ice cubes clonked and jangled against his moustache and upper lip. How many, indeed?

He turned to the portholes and watched a wisp of white cloud drift past. They were making good time towards London but he didn't know how high they were. Were they higher than the observation deck on the Empire State? Perhaps he should have arranged to meet Marie and Lila on the helipad at the top of the *Tereshkova*'s central hull. Perhaps that would have been somehow more fitting than arranging to meet in a bar? He'd spent far too much of his life in bars. If they all came through this alive, and if the world escaped assimilation by the Gestalt, he promised himself that things would change; *he* would change. He'd stop taking drugs and start getting regular exercise. If it took every last scrap of his strength, he'd make the woman in the photograph proud of him. He'd even start writing again, and do it properly this time.

A girl walked into the lounge. She had glossy, shoulder-length brown hair tied back in a loose ponytail, and she was dressed in the white jacket and black trousers of a borrowed steward's uniform. It took him a moment to realise who she was, but when he did, the realisation hit him like an electric shock that sparked from the sensitive pit of his stomach to the prickling skin at the back of his neck. This was Lila, the daughter who never was, the daughter who'd died in the womb. And now here she stood, as large as life, and twice as beautiful.

His mouth went dry, and he sucked his bottom lip. What could he say to her, what could anyone possibly say in this situation? The only words that came into his head were either far too pompous, or impossibly trite. In the end, he settled for, "Hello."

She smiled at him.

"Hello." She held out her hand. Her accent was pure cut glass. "Mother's resting at the moment, but I thought you and I should probably meet."

William rubbed his palm against his trouser leg before taking her hand. Her skin was cool and unexpectedly rough, and her grip was strong.

"Pleasure to meet you," he stammered as they shook formally.

She really did have his eyes; but on her, they looked much better.

After a moment of awkwardness, he realised he was still holding her hand, and hurriedly let go.

"Would you like a drink?"

She shook her head and pursed her lips. She seemed as nervous as he was. After a moment's hesitation, she slid onto the bar stool next to his, crossed her legs at the ankle, and clasped her hands in her lap.

"How are you?" she said. She had a wine-coloured bruise on her right cheek.

William straightened his back, and unconsciously reached up to flatten the hair at the side of his head.

"I'm okay," he said, meaning it. "The past twenty-four hours have been kind of rough, but I'm getting there."

"You don't find this peculiar, meeting me like this?"

He gave a snort of not-quite laughter.

"Yeah, of course I do. It's all extremely, majorly, fundamentally *weird*. But you don't know what my life was like up until yesterday." He looked into her eyes, fighting down the sudden urge to confess, to drag up his dust ball of a life and lay it all out in front of her, so she could see how miserable and alone he'd been. "Compared to that, weird is kind of good." He pulled back slightly. "Listen, I don't pretend to understand half of what's happened. All I know is that right now, you and your mother are here, alive and breathing, and that's all that really matters."

Lila tugged at the hem of her borrowed jacket, and glanced around the room. She seemed to be grappling with something.

"I don't know what to call you." Her brow furrowed. "I don't even know what you should call me."

William blinked. "What would you like me to call you? You're my daughter."

She shrugged, clearly uncomfortable.

"I don't know. I just lost my father."

William felt an odd, fluttering sensation in his chest. He gripped the edge of the copper counter.

"You weren't even *born* when I lost you."

Her eyes were like perfect jewels set into the marble of her face. They filled him with a strange mourning for his own lost youth—for the gawky Ohio farm boy he'd misplaced somewhere along the way. How different his life would have been if he'd had a girl like this to care for and raise. How much better a man he'd have had to be.

"So..." His voice wavered. "What do we do now?"

Lila bit her lower lip, and brushed her hair behind her ear. The gesture was one she'd picked up from her mother, and it brought a lump to his throat.

"I don't know about you, Dad," she said hesitantly, trying out the word, "but there's a fight coming, and I'm going to be part of it."

**BREAKING NEWS**

From *The European Sentinel*, online edition:

**Jets Scramble as Europe
Put on Military Alert**

PARIS 16/11/2060 – Official sources remain tight-lipped about unconfirmed reports of frenzied activity at RAF and Commonwealth airbases across Europe, and speculation that this could be part of a massive, Europe-wide mobilisation of air defence forces. All that is known for certain is that all leave has been cancelled for service men and women from all branches of the armed forces, and that the aircraft carriers HMS *Shakespeare* and HMS *Jules Verne*, which had both been en route to Oslo for a special visit to mark the centenary of Norway's integration into the United Kingdom, have instead been diverted, and are now believed to be steaming for the mouth of the Thames Estuary.

Are these measures a prelude to hostilities with another country, and if so, which one? Or could they be somehow related to last year's attempted royal coup d'etat?

So far, official sources have refused to comment, saying only that Commonwealth citizens should remain calm, and monitor news channels for further updates.

Read more | Like | Comment | Share

**Related Stories**

Witnesses report 'caveman' suspect in Greek police chief murder

Gestalt 'embassies' close their doors

Dead millionaire's back-up personality wins legal right to inherit wealth

'Miracle' taco contains likeness of Elvis

Car bomb explodes in Zurich, killing fitness instructor

Feature: As the Martian probe enters the final stages of its approach to the red planet, we assess the possible threats posed by its soon-to-be revived occupants.

# CHAPTER TWENTY-SEVEN
## WELCOME TO THE JUNGLE

THE VTOL PLANE took K8 and her three minders to the armoured airship. As soon as it touched down, they went to seize her again, but she slapped their hands away.

"Hey, I can walk by myself, okay?" She straightened her jumper, tired of being manhandled. "We're on an airship, remember? You've got me. Where am I going to go?"

The Neanderthals frowned at each other, then the one who'd spoken before said, "Okay, you walk. But don't try anything stupid."

K8 pulled herself up out of her seat, and moved along the aisle to the aircraft's cabin door. The plane had come down on the upper surface of the armoured airship, in a gap between gun emplacements and sensor pods. Carefully, K8 climbed down the steps, followed by the three cavemen in white. When they were at the bottom, she put her fists on her hips.

"Okay, Ug, which way?"

The one with the voice raised his arm.

"That way, through the hatch," he said. "Down the ladder. No funny stuff."

K8 turned in the direction he pointed.

"Oh, don't worry, sunshine. I'll leave the jokes to you."

She went over to the open hatch. Pleated metal stairs led down into the bowels of the ship. She paused to take a last look at the boundless sky, and to draw a last lungful of clear, untainted air. Then she started down. As she clumped towards the bottom rung, she took note of the thickness of the armour plate on the hull to either side of her. It was at least ten centimetres deep. That was enough to stop all but the most powerful machine guns. If the thickness remained consistent all over the hull, the airship would be nigh-on bulletproof, not to mention weighing about the same as a small mountain. Most of its interior would have to be given over to gasbags, she thought, just to support that immensity.

At the bottom of the stairs, the Neanderthals led her forwards, through the airship's interior, towards the bows. She saw racks holding automatic rifles and submachine guns, piles of ammo boxes, and heaps of white-painted body armour. The walls had been decorated in a deep, sumptuous olive, and the door handles and other fittings had been fashioned from brightly polished brass.

Several times, they passed human members of the Gestalt. All were dressed in identical white suits, and all were silent. Even groups who appeared to be clustered together for discussion stood without speaking or smiling. Nobody on the airship spoke a word, and yet they were working and cooperating seamlessly. Some of them turned to watch her as she walked past, their eyes flat and passive and their expressions unreadable. On the *Tereshkova*, you could always hear voices—stewards making their rounds; passengers coming and going; mechanics changing light strips or unblocking sinks, whistling as they worked—but here, she heard only the distant thrum of turbines and the gentle whir of air in the vents.

She didn't like it. The mute, emotionless Gestalt made her think of an old black and white horror film she'd seen once, about a group of white-haired children in a small English village. She'd been twelve years old when it came on the TV one evening, and it had given her nightmares for a week.

At one point, the corridor turned into a metal walkway suspended over a chamber with the appearance and approximate dimensions of a drained swimming pool. Four black boxes stood spaced along its bottom, each the size of an upended coffin. Frost glittered on their shiny sides, and K8 slowed to take a look.

"What are they?" She leaned over the railing. She thought they might be computer servers of some kind. Thick power cables and a variety of coloured data leads plugged into ports on the deck. The air in the chamber felt itchy with static.

"Engines." One of the Neanderthals poked her between the shoulder blades. "Now, move."

Reluctantly, she let them shepherd her onwards, until they reached an armoured door plated entirely in brass.

"Wait."

K8 crossed her arms. "Why? What's—?"

"Shush." The Neanderthal tapped a thick finger against his temple. "Am talking to Leader."

All three of them were motionless for a few seconds, just long enough for K8 to start feeling fidgety, before the vocal one gave a grunt and motioned at the door.

"You can go in now."

"In here?" She eyed the door dubiously, remembering Lila's fear of the Gestalt Leader, and the bruise on the girl's cheek.

The Neanderthal gave her an insistent shove.

"Leader will see you now."


K8 PUSHED OPEN the brass door and stepped through into warmth and steam, and an overpowering greenhouse smell of dank compost and ripe vegetation. Trees stood in large pots, seemingly placed at random, with vines and creepers trailing between them. Smaller pots held ferns and sprays of bamboo, and butterflies flickered hither and thither like animated scraps of colourful cloth. Reed mats covered the floor, strewn with fallen leaves, and, from somewhere nearby, she heard the lazy trickle of a fountain.

Pushing through the dangling branches, she emerged onto a wooden veranda. Surrounded by trees on three sides, the veranda looked forward, through the blunt nose of the airship's prow, which was transparent, having been constructed from thick panes of glass.

"Ah, there you are." The Leader sat at a wrought iron patio table, one leg crossed over the other, and a china teacup halfway to his lips. Looking at him, K8 felt herself go cold inside and, for a second, stopped breathing.

"You—" She couldn't get the words out. "You're—"

The Leader placed his cup and saucer on the table. Black monkey hair stuck out from his white cuffs. A furry tail snaked from the back of his sharply creased trousers.

"Please," he said, "have a seat. Can I offer you something to drink?"

Feeling suddenly faint, K8 tottered forward and sat on the closest of the three iron chairs set around the table.

"No," she said. "No, thank you."

"As you wish." He brushed his knee with fastidious fingers, and straightened his posture. "Now, you may be wondering why I wanted to touch base with you?"

K8 took a deep breath. She couldn't stop staring.

"I was wondering, ayc."

The monkey glanced at his fingernails, and then interlaced his fingers. "I believe that you and I have an acquaintance in common."

"The Skipper?"

"If by that you mean the primate going by the ridiculous moniker of 'Ack-Ack Macaque', then yes."

"What about him?"

The Leader smiled. His teeth were impossibly white. "I've just been negotiating with him. He's a bit rough at the edges, but I think he's got definite potential. If we could find a way to optimise his temper management, and thereby redirect his physicality towards more profitable goals, he and I could collaborate together very well."

"He'd rather die."

"Yes, his lively exchange of views with Mister Reynolds rather gave me that impression. Still, nobody's perfect."

He picked up his teacup between leathery fingers and K8 fidgeted in her chair. She couldn't take her eyes off him. He looked so much like the Skipper, yet spoke and acted so, so differently.

Glancing back into the ersatz jungle, she said, "Those black boxes…"

His single eye looked at her over the rim of his cup.

"The engines."

"Are they what moves you between parallels?"

He took a sip of tea, rolled it around the inside of his cheeks, and swallowed.

"Indeed they do. I call them my 'probability engines', but I won't bore you with their technical specifications." He put the cup back onto the table and wiped his palms on a white silk handkerchief from his top pocket. "Suffice to say, moving between worlds takes a lot of power, both in terms of energy input and in the amount of processing power needed to make the requisite calculations."

"What do they run on?"

The Leader dabbed his lips, and pushed the hankie back into his jacket. "They draw power from the airship's fusion plant."

"You have fusion?" The idea sent a shiver the length of her spine. In her world, fusion had been one of a number of advances that always seemed to be about ten years away, forever on the horizon—like cheap space travel or a cure for AIDs—but never quite materialising. The idea that the inhabitants of another world had found a way to make it work, and a way to make it portable, filled her with unease, and an unreasonable stab of jealousy. And then, for the first time, she began to understand the reality of her situation. Wherever she was, she surely wasn't in Kansas anymore.

"How else could we generate enough energy to rip a hole between worlds?" The Leader uncrossed his legs. "But enough questions. There'll be plenty of time later, after you've been inducted into our fellowship. In the meantime, I have some enquiries of my own."

K8's unease blossomed into alarm. She had no intention of joining his 'fellowship'. Her heart beat so hard she was sure he could hear it, and she spoke to cover the noise.

"You know," she said, "you're the first member of the Gestalt I've met who says 'I' instead of 'we'."

The monkey gave an airy wave. "Well, I *am* the leader."

"No, it's more than that." K8 swallowed. "You're not fully connected, are you?"

In one fluid motion, the monkey rose to his feet. He stood over her, drawn up to his full height, clutching his lapels.

"Every society needs to be governed."

Any moment now, K8 was sure he'd order some thugs to drag her away, to be converted into one of his white-suited drones. She spoke to stall him. "But I thought the Gestalt were supposed to be a democracy?"

The Leader gave a snort. "Whatever gave you that idea, child? Just because they have their minds webbed together, that doesn't mean they're capable of self-determination. Mob rule never works; it just brings everything down to the level of the lowest common denominator. You need someone set apart from the herd, someone with vision, who knows what's best and can take the tough decisions."

"And that's you, I suppose?"

"If you like." He huffed a breath in through his cavernous nose. "Think of it in terms of an ant colony. Every member of the colony has his or her place and task and, to outsiders, the whole thing appears to move with a common will and purpose. But, behind the scenes, there's always a superior being pulling the strings."

K8 forced a smile.

"So, you're the queen, are you?"

His yellow eye frowned down at her and, for the first time, she caught a glimpse of the incisors behind his smile.

"That isn't the phrasing I would have chosen," he said quietly. Then, abruptly, he turned and walked over to the bamboo rail at the edge of the veranda, where he stood looking out through the airship's glass nose cone. Unsure what to do, K8 remained seated. Had she touched a nerve, or was this just his way of changing the subject? When uncomfortable or bored with a conversation, Ack-Ack Macaque had a tendency to get up and walk out; maybe his doppelganger shared that characteristic. Or maybe he just heard things in his head to which she had no access.

Without any real sense of hope, she said, "What do I have to say to get you to let me out of here?"

The Leader didn't turn around. He gripped the bamboo rail and kept his eye on the sky and clouds.

"They made him a cartoon character."

K8 blinked.

"Who, the Skipper?"

The Leader lowered his head, looking down at the landscape below.

"They created an intelligent monkey, and then plugged him into a video game." He drummed his fingers. "They never gave him a chance."

"He's doing all right."

"All right?" He turned to face her. "All that talent, and what is he? He's a pilot on an airship. *An* airship, and it's not even *his*." He held his hands behind his back, gripping his left wrist with his right hand. "Do you know how many vessels I have at my command?"

K8 shrugged, but the Leader ignored her. The question had been rhetorical.

"I was created in a lab," he said, "the same way as your friend. Like him, I was a simple macaque raised to sentience by the addition of artificial neurons, created by scientists trying to devise a new kind of weapons guidance system. But we became very different monkeys. When they'd finished with me, they didn't plug me into a video game. They didn't turn me into 'Ack-Ack Macaque'. Instead, they gave me to a different team, on a different floor. That's where our timelines diverged. I was given to a team studying direct mind-to-mind communication."

He held out his hand, inspecting his tidy, clipped nails. "They already had plans to spread their work beyond the confines of the laboratory. Within a month, I was part of the team. Within two months, I was running it." He looked at her as if peering, like a disappointed professor, over a pair of invisible spectacles. "We broke out of the lab and seized our first warship. And then, within six months, we'd acquired enough weapons and personnel to forcibly convert the remaining human population to our cause. Since then, we've spread ourselves to a dozen worlds, and assimilated them all."

K8 felt her ears burning, her cheeks growing hot.

"But... why? Why would you do that?"

The Leader sniffed.

"Progress, child."

"Progress?" She slammed her palms on the table, rattling the china tea set. "Turning everybody into mindless drones is 'progress'?"

The monkey shook his coiffured head.

"Au contraire, child. Mindlessness is the last thing I'm trying to achieve. Quite the reverse, in fact." He lifted an elegant cigarette holder from the table; lit the cigarette in it with a white platinum lighter. "How do you think I came here? How do you think I developed the means to cross dimensions, to achieve—" he waved the cigarette holder in a circle that encompassed the jungle, the forward window, and the entire airship in which they were held, "—all of this?"

K8 shook her head. She didn't want to know but, somehow, couldn't stop listening.

The Leader's eye narrowed.

"Have you ever heard of 'parallel computing'?"

"Yes, of course." K8 frowned. It was a way of breaking large problems down into smaller ones, and then solving all those small ones simultaneously using multiple processing elements—whether within the same machine, or across a network of distributed computers. "Oh!"

He saw her understanding, and gave a nod.

"Yes, I created the largest virtual computer ever devised, running on the cranial wetware of seven billion people. Then I spread it to another world, and another." He took a drag of the cigarette and blew a thin line of lazy smoke from the side of his mouth. "And with all that at my disposal, I can solve anything: war, starvation... mortality." He mashed the half-smoked cigarette into an ashtray, and laid the holder aside. "Compared to that, what has *your* monkey achieved?"

K8 blinked at him.

"Hey," she said, nettled. "He saved the world."

The Leader looked down his nose at her, and his face curdled with disgust.

"He should be *ruling* it." He smacked a fist to his breast. "Look at me. I started out the same way he did, and I've conquered world after world."

"Well, maybe he doesn't have your lust for power."

"Nonsense." The Leader turned back to the sky beyond the windows. "Everybody wants dominion over his or her fellow beings. Everybody secretly wants to be the top of the heap, king of the hill. Everybody wants to rule the world. The question is whether or not they have the balls to take it."

K8 twisted her mouth into a sceptical sneer.

"And you do?"

The monkey laughed, and his tail twitched.

"Of course. I know what I want to achieve, and I'm prepared to take proactive steps to actuate that outcome. That's why, as soon as we make the transfer to your timeline, I'm going to launch all the missiles we have. No negotiation, no time wasting, just decisive action." He clamped the cigarette holder between his teeth. "In order to give our virus time to work, we need to throw the enemy into disarray. So, as soon as we appear, we strike."

# CHAPTER TWENTY-EIGHT
## SOMEBODY ELSE'S APOCALYPSE

VICTORIA VALOIS LAY on her bunk, unable to sleep. The *Tereshkova* would arrive over the outskirts of London within the hour, but Paul had persuaded her to try to rest. She'd been awake for almost two days straight, and there was a limit to the amount of fatigue for which her gelware could compensate. But, try as she might, she couldn't relax. How could she, knowing what they were about to face?

She rubbed her eyes, and then ran her hand back, across her bare scalp, to the pillow.

How had she found herself in this situation again? Since saving the world last year with Ack-Ack Macaque and Prince Merovech, she'd kept as far from politics as she could, done her damnedest to stay away from international disputes and diplomatic intrigues. Cocooned within the safety of her gondola, she'd all but fallen off the grid. And yet here she was again, sailing into the crucible, ready once more to throw herself into battle against superior forces in order to avert apocalypse. Why did it have to be her? Who'd appointed her world saviour? She wasn't anything special, merely a brain-damaged ex-journalist with a knack for being in the wrong place at the wrong time.

All she'd wanted had been a nice, juicy mystery to alleviate the boredom.

She should have known better.

Irritably, she rolled onto her side, and found herself looking at her desk, and the window beyond. How could she sleep in daylight?

If she wanted to, she supposed she could slip into command mode and use her gelware to force her body to sleep—but that was something she'd never tried, and she didn't like the idea of artificially snuffing out her consciousness. It was a line she was reluctant to cross. Sleeping tablets were one thing, but she balked at the notion of turning off a switch in her brain in order to put herself under. The idea made her feel like a machine; and besides, what if she botched the instructions? She'd rather be shaky and exhausted than risk permanently shutting off the very gelware processors that kept her alive.

But maybe dying would be preferable to becoming one of the Gestalt?

She couldn't imagine what it would be like to share her skull with the thoughts of others; to have the echoing spaces of her mind filled with the ceaseless din of other voices; to submit her will to that of the majority and become little more than a synapse in something else's brain; a walking, talking logic gate in an unknowably vast super-organism. The idea filled her with revulsion. She already felt like a half-human cyborg; she wouldn't live as a zombie in somebody else's apocalypse. If the worst happened, and conversion became inevitable, she'd turn her gelware off and slide into unknowing, insensate oblivion.

Or perhaps, she thought grimly, she'd ask Paul to blow the skyliner's engines.

Would that even work?

Each of the *Tereshkova*'s fifteen impellers drew its power from its own nuclear-electric engine. If she asked him, could he find some way to detonate them all simultaneously, destroying the airship and all on board? Could he, in effect, turn the old skyliner into a flying bomb? Victoria didn't know enough about the physics involved, but she made a mental note to find out. Who knew what she might be called upon to do, and what she might be expected to sacrifice, in the coming hours?

For a few minutes more, she lay and listened to the familiar sounds of the gondola. She heard the wind buffeting against the walls; the flex and creak of the hull; and the almost subliminal hum of the motors. She heard people moving around in the corridors, opening and closing doors; the occasional scrape of a chair or shoe on the metal deck; and the clang and rattle of pans in the kitchen. It all sounded so peaceful and comforting that she could hardly bring herself to believe that it might soon be destroyed; that this flight might be the *Tereshkova*'s last.

With a sigh, she climbed off the bunk and walked over to the window. With luck, Merovech would be able to scramble enough planes to deal with the airships over Commonwealth territories; but what about the rest of the world? How many airships would it take to conquer the globe?

Paul's voice came over the intercom speakers.

"Vic?"

She blew out a long breath, and massaged her forehead with her fingertips.

"What do you want?"

"We've got a problem."

Victoria raised her eyes to the heavens. *Another one?*

"Please God, what now?"

"Can you let me in?"

For a second, she didn't understand what he meant. Then, with a sigh, she crossed to the cabin door and pulled it open. The remote control car waited in the corridor. She stood aside to let it in.

The car sped to the centre of the room and slithered to a halt on the Persian rug. Paul's hologram rose from its projectors. He'd altered his look again, and now appeared to be wearing a droopy khaki bush hat, a white t-shirt, and crisp urban camouflage combat trousers. Silver dog tags hung around his neck, and his clear frameless spectacles had transformed into mirror shades with round, purple-tinted lenses.

"What's going on?" She tried to keep her tone businesslike.

Paul scratched his chest.

"It's the monkey."

"What about him?"

"He's gone. He's taken off, literally. As soon as Sergei had him patched up, he went to the kitchen and ate a jar of instant coffee. Then he stole a helicopter from one of the hangars. He even bit a mechanic when she tried to stop him."

"Merde."

"You can say that again."

"Where's he heading?" She didn't think for a second that Ack-Ack Macaque would run out on a fight. But what if he'd decided to defect? What if he'd decided the best way to save K8 was to hand himself over to the Leader? The thought made her feel crawly inside.

"We're tracking him via the chopper's built-in GPS transponder," Paul said.

"And?"

He shrugged. "He seems to be heading south, into Somerset."

Victoria frowned. "What's in Somerset?" All the action was ahead of them, in the Capital.

"He could be heading for France, or—" Paul stopped. He took his shades off. "Oh," he said.

Victoria restrained a futile urge to grab him by the lapels.

"*What*?"

"I'm picking up a transmission. He's making a call."

"Can you patch it through?"

"Yeah, hold on a sec." Paul's eyes rolled back in his head, and the room's speakers hissed into life. They let out a nerve-jangling blast of static, and then she heard the monkey's yawp, his voice shaky from vibration and backed by the *thud, thud, thud* of a helicopter rotor.

"...fuelled and ready to go," he was saying, "I'll be with you in fifteen minutes, and I'll need pilots for all of 'em."

"Who's he talking to?" Victoria asked, raising her voice over the noise.

Paul lowered the volume.

"The control tower at the Fleet Air Arm Museum," he said.

Victoria frowned. "Don't tell me..."

"Yeah," Paul couldn't keep still. "You remember those Spitfires they dug up in Burma a few years back?"

"Yes, I bought him one."

"Well, they have a dozen currently under restoration at the museum and, according to its website, at least half of those are airworthy."

"Holy crap."

"Quite." Paul slid his glasses back into place, and shook his head. A smile tickled his lips. "It seems our friend's rounding up a posse."

# CHAPTER TWENTY-NINE
## UTTERLY FUCKED

SAT ON THE wooden veranda, surrounded by the fetid air of the potted jungle, K8 began to feel feverish. At first, she put the sudden clamminess down to fear, but the warmth kept spreading. At the small of her back, sweat pooled and ran like condensation on a cold beer glass. Seeing her growing discomfort, the Leader grinned, and his sharp canines caught the light from the armoured windows at the airship's nose.

"Are you quite sure you wouldn't like a cup of tea?"

K8's hands were trembling. She screwed them into little balls.

"Go to hell."

The monkey rose to his feet and tugged at his cufflinks, first one, then the other.

"I can see," he said, "that you're going to prove an interesting addition to the group dynamic."

K8 swallowed hard.

"I'd rather die."

He looked down at her, head slightly to one side.

"Would you?" He sounded surprised, and almost disappointed. "Would you really?"

The shaking in her hands spread to her forearms and shoulders.

"You're damn right I would."

The monkey touched his chin with leathery fingers.

"Well, that won't be necessary, I assure you." Leaving her seated at the wrought iron table, he walked back over to the veranda's rail and stood, looking out at the sky. Parrots and budgerigars flapped among the upper branches of the trees, little flits of colour against the drab battleship grey of the chamber's roof. The Leader was a silhouette against the windows. K8's nose itched and her eyes hurt. All of a sudden, the light from outside seemed uncomfortably bright.

"I'll never join you."

The Leader turned to her, but she couldn't make out his features against the glare. She held up a hand to shade her eyes.

"It seems," he said, "that you're labouring under a misapprehension."

"Dream on, pal."

He smiled and shook his head, ran a paw back through his coiffured mane.

"Allow me to speak plainly." He jabbed his index finger in her direction. "You have no choice in the matter. You will join us. You will become part of the collective."

K8 coughed. Her eyes were watering, and her nose had begun to stream. She dug in her pocket for a screwed-up tissue.

"How can you be so sure?"

The Leader leant back against the rail. He tapped a finger to his lips.

"Because we've already ticked that box."

K8 sniffed and hugged herself. The shakes were getting worse.

"You what?"

The monkey came back to the table and picked up the silver teapot.

"Do you recall the injection on the *Tereshkova*?" He opened the lid and sloshed the contents around. "Well, I'm very much afraid it contained more than simple sedatives." He refilled his cup, but didn't sit.

Through watery eyes, K8 glowered up at him.

"How long have I got?"

He looked at his watch. "You'll feel under par for another few minutes, like you're coming down with the flu."

"And then?" K8's fingers and toes felt cold. Her stomach growled like a frightened dog.

"Then all your questions will be answered."

She felt a lump welling in her throat. She couldn't attack the monkey; in her weakened state, he was far stronger than she was. Neither could she run. He'd catch her before she found her way through the potted trees; and, even if he didn't, she'd never get past the guards waiting outside the brass door. If she wanted to escape, her only choice would be to throw herself over the edge of the veranda, into the depths of the airship, and hope the fall broke her neck.

It wasn't much of a choice.

"Why me?"

The Leader reached for the milk jug, and stirred a little of the contents into his tea. Then he placed the teaspoon on the saucer beside his cup, and set the jug back where it had been.

"I'm sure you know the answer to that one."

She closed her eyes. Of course she knew. He wasn't the slightest bit interested in her as a person; she had no value to him beyond her worth as bait. She was simply a lure to entrap the Skipper. But, by the time Ack-Ack Macaque came for her—and she had no doubt whatsoever that he *would* come for her— she'd already be gone, claimed by the hive mind and sentenced to a zombified half-life as one of its drones. Even if by some miracle he got to her before the transformation was complete, he had no cure, no antidote with which to save her; and anyway, who knew what would be left of the world by then? If the Leader succeeded in dumping his plague, there'd be nowhere for them to go, nowhere to run. No way out.

She was, she admitted to herself with a sinking heart, utterly fucked.

"But, I thought—"

"I need you on board for this one, K8. It's all about intelligence gathering; market research, if you like. If I'm going to persuade our mutual associate to join the winning team, I'm going to need to get a handle on his worldview. I need to find out what makes him tick, and so I'm going to need access to your memories and knowledge of him." The Leader raised his drink. In his hairy, simian hands, the teacup looked absurdly dainty. "If he refuses to play ball, and it comes down to a fight, well then, who knows his weaknesses better that you, eh?"

K8 couldn't reply. Her right eye socket felt as if a rusted spike had been driven into it. It was all she could do to stop herself from crying out. She ground her knuckles against her burning forehead, trying to rub away the pain.

"Don't think of it as losing," he said, looking down his nose at her. "Think of it as upgrading early, to avoid the rush."

# CHAPTER THIRTY
## WHAT WOULD MENDELBLATT DO?

WILLIAM COLE LINGERED in the doorway of the *Tereshkova*'s infirmary, watching the woman in the bed. She hadn't seen him yet. Her eyes were resting, and her auburn hair tumbled across the pillow like copper filigree. Her left arm and right ankle had both been plastered, and now hung suspended from a traction rig. Beneath the covers, her chest rose and fell, and its gentle rhythm brought tears to his eyes. As long as he could see it, he knew she lived.

Was there a word, he wondered, for what he felt? He'd never been so happy or so terrified; never felt so vulnerable or powerless. Over the past two days, he'd had his dead wife returned to him, and then almost lost her again. He'd become a husband and father on the brink of Armageddon, allowed only a fleeting moment of ephemeral happiness before the world fell apart.

It all seemed so damn unfair.

He thought of the old saying, that it was better to have loved and lost than never to have loved at all. Whoever came up with that had been an idiot. Two days ago, William would have probably welcomed the coming catastrophe, welcomed an end to loneliness and grief, and have quite happily thrown himself off the end of Portishead pier, into the sea with heavy rocks in his pockets, in order to escape the coming plague. But, as things stood now, he suddenly had something worth protecting, something worth living for. He had a family: two people he loved more dearly than he loved life itself, and no way to shield them from the coming horrors. He'd always known fate could play tricks, but he'd never expected it to be downright cruel. Losing his wife and daughter once nearly killed him. To lose them twice would be surely more than any man could be expected to bear.

Above the bed was a porthole, with blue November sky beyond. Leaning against the doorframe, he found himself remembering bright autumn days from his childhood: the front lawn of his parent's house in Dayton; his father sorting Christmas lights in the garage, or tinkering with the petrol mower; his mother upstairs, running her stock trading business on a laptop in the spare bedroom, making video calls to New York, Tokyo and London. He remembered playing with the other kids in the neighbourhood; the sandpaper roughness of his father's cheek, and the smell of oil and old cologne on his shirt; the clatter of his mother's heels on the parquet floor; and the aroma of meatloaf from the kitchen.

Where, he wondered, had all that gone, and how could he have let something so precious slip away from him? That had been his family, his support, and his *home*. Right now, he'd give anything to hear his father's voice, to lose himself in one of the old man's bear hugs; but his father was dead, and his mother in a nursing home in Dayton, her mind already lost to the twisting confusions of advanced senility. However much he longed to go back, he never could, and never would. He wasn't a child any more. He was a father himself, with a teenage daughter of his own, whom he'd only known for a few brief moments, and to whom he couldn't offer anything like the stability or security shown to him by his own father.

The thought brought an irrational stab of shame, as if he'd failed in a sacred duty—failed Lila, Marie, and himself.

His cheeks burned, and he didn't seem to know what to do with his hands. They fidgeted like spiders, moving from beard to pockets, and back again.

When he opened his eyes, he found Marie watching him from the bed.

"William, what's the matter? Is Lila—?"

"Lila's fine." He swallowed hard, and brushed his hair flat with his left hand.

"You saw her?"

"We talked."

"And?"

He cleared his throat, wiped a hand across his eyes. "She's incredible."

Marie smiled. "Yes, she is, isn't she?"

He walked over to the bed and stood uncertainly. Should he pat her shoulder, or bend down and kiss her cheek? After a moment's dithering, he settled for taking her hand.

"She wants to fight," he said.

"So do I." Marie looked at her suspended arm and leg. "But I can't."

"Shouldn't we try to stop her?"

Marie shook her head. "No. Absolutely not. This is her choice."

"But, aren't you worried she might be killed?"

Her eyes widened in anger. "Of course I'm worried. But look what we're up against. If we lose, that'll be it, game over for good, and it won't matter whether she was on the front lines or back here hiding under your bed." She kicked at the covers with her good leg. "Personally, I'd rather see her dead than become one of them."

William was aghast.

"How can you even say that?"

"Because I've seen what happens, okay? I've seen what they do to people. Men, women and children turned into drones, all traces of individuality banished by the machines in their heads." She took a breath. "And so has Lila. She's seen it all, and she knows exactly what we're up against. She knows the odds and she knows the stakes, and if she wants to fight, there's nothing you or I can do to stop her."

"But the danger—"

"Danger's relative. Sometimes it's more dangerous to do nothing." Frustrated, she tugged at the wires holding her damaged limbs in position. "And if it weren't for these, I'd be right out there with her."

"What about me?"

"If you want to help her, go with her."

"What good would I be?"

Marie looked up at him.

"The Bill Cole I knew was a guerrilla fighter. What kind of man are you?"

"I don't know."

"Then don't you think it's time you found out?"

"I wouldn't know where to start."

"Of course you would. Seriously, William, don't you remember your dreams, the ones you wrote down as stories? They weren't dreams, they were memories. I don't know how or why, but you've always been close to your alternate selves."

"No, I don't think—"

She slapped her palm against the covers.

"What was the name of that detective in your books?"

"Lincoln Mendelblatt."

"Well, he's you. Or at least, he's a version of you. When you're writing all that stuff about him, you're really writing about yourself."

William turned away from the bed. He could feel his cheeks going red.

"Bullshit."

Marie caught his hand, and squeezed.

"It's time to ask yourself," she said, "what would Mendelblatt do?"

# CHAPTER THIRTY-ONE
## STAY FROSTY

VICTORIA VALOIS STOOD on the *Tereshkova*'s bridge, at the front of the airship's main gondola. She stood with her legs slightly apart and her hands clasped behind her back, at the edge of the windscreen, which sloped down from the ceiling and curved into the floor. It had been designed to afford the pilot and navigator an uninterrupted view of the sky and terrain ahead. The toes of her boots overlapped the join between glass and deck, and, looking down between them, she could see the ribbon of the motorway cutting through the countryside between Reading and Slough. Ahead, London lay beneath a towering mound of cumulus, the cloud's shadow falling across the city's glass towers and sprawling streets like the footprint of an alien mothership.

As they were riding into battle, she'd chosen to wear one of the Commodore's more resplendent jackets: a red one with gold buttons and a silver scabbard on a white silk sash. She'd decided to leave her head bare, presenting her scars as an unashamed 'fuck you' to the world. Earned in combat, they were her medals—badges of suffering and survival, displayed now as an act of defiance, a warning to others and a reminder to herself.

Merovech had assured her that she wasn't needed, that the RAF could handle things without the help of an unarmed and elderly skyliner; but she'd told him she was coming anyway, and he hadn't tried to stop her. He knew as well as she did that there was nowhere else for her to be. Having come this far, she had to see the story through to its conclusion, even if it meant pitting herself against overwhelming odds; even if it meant dying in the attempt. With the whole world under threat, she had little to lose. She wouldn't wait on the sidelines, passive and cowering. Better to go out kicking and screaming, she thought. If she had to die, she'd make sure the bastards remembered her.

*Do not go gentle into that good night...*

Well, duh.

The only thing that frightened her was the thought she might fall before the battle's end, that she might never know the outcome—never know if her death had done more than simply buy the world a few moments of grace.

Behind her, the bridge lay deserted. With Ack-Ack Macaque currently AWOL, Paul was running the ship. All remaining passengers and non-essential members of the crew—including the navigator—had been put ashore, ferried down to the ground on the *Tereshkova*'s remaining helicopters. As far as she knew, the only flesh-and-blood people left aboard were a couple of engineers; half a dozen of her most trusted stewards; the writer, William Cole; his wife; and their daughter. With her arms and legs in traction, Marie couldn't be moved, and Cole had nowhere else to go, refusing to leave her side.

At least the girl, Lila, might be of some use. She'd fought the Gestalt before, on other parallels, and had some insights into their methods and tactics.

But how could Victoria best apply the girl's expertise? Officially, the *Tereshkova* carried no ship-to-ship armaments. The 1978 Treaty of Bergerac, which enshrined the autonomy of skyliners in international law, expressly forbade them from carrying anything but the most defensive of weapons. She had half a dozen anti-aircraft missiles, a few flares, and that was about it. The monkey had taken the Commodore's handheld missile launcher, and now only a few antique submachine guns remained in the airship's armoury—enough to equip the six remaining stewards, but hardly enough to hold off a full-scale global invasion.

Gloomily, she contemplated the suburbs unrolling beneath her. The sun, now dipping towards late afternoon, threw the *Tereshkova*'s rectangular shadow ahead of it, and she watched it ripple across ring roads and roundabouts, tower blocks, industrial parks, and flooded gravel pits. Several kilometres to the southeast, she saw Heathrow. A few elderly jets lumbered around like pollen-drunk bees, staggering off on international runs to New York, Tokyo and Sydney. Above the cargo terminal, a couple of skyliners hung in the air like whale sharks looming over the surface of a reef, their torpedo-shaped bodies grey with distance and cloud-shadow. She thought she recognised one, but it was difficult to tell.

She could have used her neural implants to check their identities, but couldn't be bothered. Some people obsessively collected sightings of individual skyliners, and each craft had its own online fan communities; but Victoria had never been one of them. She was happy enough to exchange pleasantries with a fellow captain if they passed each other during an ocean crossing, or found themselves in port at the same time, but she'd never really fallen for the whole 'romance of the skies' that so captivated the glorified train spotters posting photographs of the various ships on their forums. For her, the *Tereshkova* was a refuge. The Commodore had taken her aboard when her marriage to Paul collapsed, and the old gondolas, with their creaking walls and cramped cabins, had become her home. She liked the feeling of remoteness she got when looking down at the world from her porthole. Always moving, always in the same place. The scenery changed, but her immediate surroundings stayed comfortingly the same.

She heard a hiss as the intercom speakers switched themselves on.

"Uh, Vicky?" It was Paul's voice. "We've got an intruder in the cargo area."

"An intruder?" That was impossible. While she'd been resting, the stewards had searched the ship to ensure no one remained save those who were supposed to be aboard.

"It's like they appeared from nowhere."

"From another world, perhaps?"

"Exactly."

She gripped the sword protruding from the scabbard at her hip.

"Where are they now?"

"Main forward cargo hold."

Victoria glanced up at the ceiling. The main forward hold lay inside the central hull's envelope, almost directly above the bridge.

"I'm on my way."


SWORD DRAWN, SHE made her way aft to the companionway that led up into the body of the skyliner. With so few people on board, the ship felt echoing and empty, and somehow colder than usual. Her boots seemed to clang deafeningly on the cleated metal steps, and she became aware of the sound of her own breathing, and the insistent knocking of her heart.

At the top of the steps, she stepped off onto the walkway that ran the length of the central hull's keel. Overhead, gasbags, platforms, and storage bays filled the vast space contained within the hull's lightly armoured cylinder. After the warmth of the gondola, the unheated air felt sharp and fresh, tangy with the smells of cold metal and rubber, and alive with metallic squeaks and screeches, and the ever-present vibration of the engines. Sepia, mote-flecked sunlight filtered down from panels set into the airship's upper surface, high above.

The forward cargo hold was a large room at the end of the walkway: an aluminium-walled compartment wadded into the point of the tapering bow, and accessed through a pair of double doors— one of which now hung ajar. It was mainly used for storage of passengers' luggage. Larger items of cargo were accommodated in special bays in the outer hulls.

Although she could feel the chill around her, Victoria's palm, where it gripped the sword, felt damp. She thought about using her gelware to squirt a mild sedative into her bloodstream to calm her nerves, but decided against it. As she didn't know who or what she might be facing, it would probably be best to 'stay frosty', as the monkey often put it.

Sword held out in front, she crept her way forwards. She knew the stewards would be on their way, but couldn't bring herself to wait. It was up to her to lead. She was the captain, after all, and this was her ship and her home, and therefore her responsibility. She cleared her throat.

"Okay," she said. "I know you're in there. Come on out."

She tensed, but nothing happened. She heard something that might have been the deck creaking beneath the weight of someone moving, but no one replied, and nobody appeared in the doorway.

Carefully, she inched closer. The sword's point wavered before her, ready to impale anyone who startled her.

"I know you're there," she said.

More sounds of movement came from within. Victoria stopped edging forwards, and dropped into a fighting stance. In the doorway, a middle-aged man stepped into the light. She saw thin grey hair and the ubiquitous white suit of a Gestalt drone.

"Hello, Captain."

Victoria drew herself up.

"Mister Reynolds."

Where Ack-Ack Macaque had hit him, the man had a split lip and a dark bruise around his mouth.

"How agreeable to see you again," he said, smiling awkwardly around his injuries.

Victoria thrust her chin forward.

"How did you get back aboard?"

Slowly, Reynolds reached into the inside pocket of his suit jacket and pulled out something that looked like a SincPhone.

"We walk between worlds."

Victoria held out her hand.

"Pass that to me."

Reynolds shook his head.

"No, we don't think so."

She waggled the sword.

"May I remind you that I'm the one holding the big, pointy weapon?"

Reynolds's hands enfolded the device. His smile remained unwavering.

"Even so, Captain, we will have to decline."

Victoria thought about insisting that he hand it over, but then decided to switch tactics. From her years working as a journalist for *Le Monde*, she knew that a sudden change of subject could wrong-foot the tight-lipped, and get them to reveal more than they were intending.

"So, what were you doing in there?" She looked over his shoulder, into the darkness of the cargo hold.

Reynolds, who was still clutching his transport device, turned his head slightly, following her gaze. For a second, he hesitated, and she saw his smile falter; but by the time he turned back to face her, it had returned to full strength.

"I'm afraid we are the bearers of bad news," he said, his voice dripping with false, honeyed regret.

"What have you done?" Victoria took a step closer, bringing the tip of the sword to within a foot of his face. He didn't flinch. In fact, his blue eyes seemed to twinkle in the light sieving down from above.

"We have placed a bomb in your hold," he said. "A very sophisticated bomb."

Victoria drew back, her breathing fast and shallow.

"Get out of my way."

Reynolds shook his head, and held up a hand.

"Some rules, Captain." He brushed a speck of dust from his sleeve. "Our Leader is very keen to meet your macaque."

"He's not here."

"We know. We also know that you still have the writer, William Cole." The man's smile broadened. "Hence, the bomb."

Victoria ran her tongue across her lower lip. Her mouth was dry.

"You mentioned some rules?"

"Ah, yes." He raised a finger. "Rule one. If this airship drops below three thousand feet, the bomb will go off." Another finger. "If anyone tries to move the bomb or otherwise tamper with it, it will go off." He raised a third and final finger. "And if Cole and the monkey aren't delivered to us within the hour, it will most definitely go off."

Victoria took a deep breath through her nose.

"And what if I keep you here? Are you going to set it off while you're still on board?"

Still smiling, Reynolds shook his head.

"We're afraid you can't keep us, Captain."

He thumbed a button on the device. Blue sparks crackled along his arm and played across his body. "You are defeated, and now, we go to meet our Leader."

"Yeah?" Victoria drew back her arm. "Then give him this message from me."

Enveloped in flickering light, Reynolds raised a supercilious eyebrow. He thought he had all the winning cards.

"What message?"

"This one." Victoria stabbed the sword forward, putting her entire weight behind it. The blade caught Reynolds in the waistcoat, midway between navel and ribcage. His mouth and eyes opened in outrage and surprise, and she rammed it home, up to the hilt. The fabric at the back of his jacket stuck out like a tent. Red blood soaked into white cloth like spilled wine on a restaurant table. Sparks crackled. Victoria snatched her hand back, leaving the sword in place.

Mouth gaping, hands pawing at the pommel, Reynolds shimmered once. His knees buckled. There was a bright blue flash, a burst of ozone, and he vanished.

# CHAPTER THIRTY-TWO
## THIS TOWN AIN'T BIG ENOUGH

THE FIVE SPITFIRES came in from the southwest, in a v-shaped formation. In the lead plane, hand wrapped around the throttle, Ack-Ack Macaque chewed nervously at an unlit cigar. The Fleet Air Arm Museum had been hosting five airworthy Spits in their hangars but, although he'd been able to scare up four pilots at short notice, none of them had any combat experience.

Ahead, through the armoured glass pane at the front of the cockpit's perspex canopy, he saw the black and white zigzags painted on the *Tereshkova*'s five hulls. Annoyingly, his hopes that the museum kept a stock of live ammunition had been dashed, so his makeshift squadron would have to land on the old airship in order to load up with bullets from his personal stash. Between the five of them, they'd use up his entire stock.

*That's if the fucking guns even work,* he thought to himself with a snarl. He'd been assured that each and every one of the Browning machine guns on each of the Spitfires had been faithfully restored, and were therefore all in good working order; at least, theoretically. Whether they'd stand up to being fired in anger was another matter, and he half expected them all to either jam or explode as soon as their firing controls were depressed.

*Still*, he thought, *I've done the best I can. They may be five museum pieces, and inexperienced pilots might be flying four of them, but surely they're better than nothing?*

Over a hundred years ago, the British had used these antique fighters to halt the Nazi advance and keep the Luftwaffe at bay. He gave the dashboard an affectionate pat. With a bit of luck, maybe the kites could work their magic a second time.

And anyway, what was there to lose?

He brought his plane around, lining up with the runway that ran diagonally across the backs of the airship's hulls.

"It's me," he said into the radio. "I'm coming in."

*Who else would it be?* Paul's voice spoke in his headphones. *Welcome home, monkey boy.*

Beyond the *Tereshkova*'s bow, Ack-Ack Macaque saw the suburbs of London: leafy streets laid out in rows and crescents; red brick tower blocks; billboards; railway cuttings and embankments. From up here, it looked peaceful.

"Any sign of attack?"

*Not yet. And no word from your evil self, either.*

Strapped into his seat, Ack-Ack Macaque bristled.

"Hey, I thought I was my evil self."

Paul laughed.

*Sorry, dude. I guess you're just going to have to face it. Like it or not, you're one of the good guys now.*

"Goddammit."

He had the nose of his plane aligned with the runway. Because the *Tereshkova* was ploughing forwards at a respectable rate of knots, he would have to come in at an angle, using the rudder to keep himself on target. With his right hand, he toggled the lever that lowered the undercarriage. Behind him, the other four planes lined up like ducklings, ready to follow him down—ready to transform the *Tereshkova* from a passenger liner to an aircraft carrier.

ACK-ACK MACAQUE LEFT his plane with one of the mechanics and, without stopping to watch the others land, made his way down through the airship to the bridge.

Stepping into the room, he pulled out his lighter and lit the damp cigar in his mouth, huffing great clouds of blue smoke into the room.

"Hey, Boss. What's shaking?"

Alone in front of the main window, Victoria wrinkled her nose and flapped a hand in front of her face.

"We had a visit from your old friend, Mister Reynolds."

"And how is the old bastard?"

Her hand went to the empty scabbard at her side.

"Dead."

"Good." Ack-Ack Macaque looked around at the unmanned workstations. "So, who's flying this thing?"

"Paul."

"Seriously?"

"He seems to be doing a reasonable job of it."

Ack-Ack Macaque loped over to the window.

"Then I'm out of work?"

"Not at all, just redeployed." Victoria crossed her arms over her chest. Medals jangled. "We need you on the front line."

He looked at the distant towers of Central London, and tried to imagine them in flames, pillars of smoke reaching up into the clouds—a new Blitz to wipe away everything rebuilt since the last one.

"Who's coordinating the defence?"

"Merovech's enlisted some high-ups in the RAF. They're trying to liaise with the Russians and the Yanks, but everybody's talking at the same time, and no-one's listening."

Ack-Ack Macaque curled his lip. He had some strong opinions on the subject of commanding officers and top brass. When he tried to express them, words such as 'arse' and 'elbow' came to mind.

"So, we're on our own?"

"No, we'll have fighter support. There are two aircraft carriers steaming up the Thames, and we can call in planes from Air Command in High Wycombe."

"What about the other cities?"

"From what I can gather, Edinburgh, Manchester, Paris and Belfast are covered. The rest will have to take their chances."

"That's a bit harsh."

"There simply aren't enough planes."

Ack-Ack Macaque blew a smoke ring at the ceiling. "Well, I brought another five."

Victoria turned away from the view. Looking down, he saw the capital opening up before them like an unfolding map.

"Listen," she said, walking over to a cabinet set into the wall. Inside were half a dozen swords. She selected one and slid it into her scabbard. "There's something else you can do, right now, that might just give us an edge."

Ack-Ack Macaque removed the cigar from his mouth and held it between the fingers of his left hand.

"What's that?"

"The leader of the Gestalt."

He felt his lips draw back from his teeth.

"What about him?"

"He's a version of you. He might talk differently, but deep down, you're the same."

"He's a lunatic."

"Exactly." She came over and stood beside his chair. "Can you put yourself in his position? Can you think like him? You're the best chance we have of second-guessing his tactics."

Ack-Ack Macaque rolled the cigar thoughtfully.

"I thought he made his tactics pretty bloody clear."

"Yes, but if we're going to have any hope of defending ourselves, if we're going to fight him, we need to know how his mind works." She turned to a screen on the wall of the bridge, and it blinked into life, displaying a strategic satellite view of the city, with red and green icons marking the positions of known forces, and yellow arrows indicating major targets. "If you were him, what would you do?"

Ack-Ack Macaque gave the map a wary squint. Then he kicked himself to his feet and shuffled over to it.

"If it was me, I'd materialise here." He tapped a point on the screen where the river snaked through the heart of the city, just downstream from Westminster Bridge. "And launch everything I had. Take it all out in the first few seconds: government, monarchy, civil service, everything. Wipe out every one of the bastards, and the battle's over. There's nobody left to give orders."

Victoria stroked her chin. "Decapitate the state, you mean?"

"Yeah." Ack-Ack Macaque couldn't help grinning. "Knock out the high command, and you can mop up the foot soldiers later."

"You wouldn't just nuke the place?"

His grin spread. "I can't lie, that would be very tempting; but I don't think that's his game. He doesn't want everybody dead. He wants converts for his religion. He wants fresh brains for the hive, and he can't have them if they've all been vaporised." He took a draught of smoke, and then blew it out the side of his mouth. "If he can throw us into disarray, even temporarily, it gives his virus thingy space to work. By the time we've regrouped, we'll already have been infected."

Victoria leant close to the map, eyeing the Commonwealth Parliament—the seat of power for most of a continent.

"A single, overwhelming attack," she mused, "and then all he has to do is sit back and wait for us to come to him."

"Unless we nuke him first."

She straightened up, eyebrows raised, her hand on the pommel of her replacement sword.

"Non! We cannot! This is London, for heaven's sake. Eight million people!"

The monkey shrugged.

"Then all we can do is wait until he appears, and then hit him as hard as we can." He scratched his cheek. "What does the girl say?"

"Lila? Pretty much the same." Victoria let her shoulders drop. She ran a hand back across the dome of her scalp.

"There's something else," she said. "Reynolds left us a present before he died. It's in the cargo hold directly above this room. If we're not there waiting for the Leader when he arrives, ready to hand you over to him, it'll go off."

Ack-Ack Macaque gave a snort.

"That stupid fuck."

Victoria frowned. "Reynolds?"

"No, the Leader. He's just made his first mistake."

"How so?"

"Because I *want* to get onto his ship." He curled his hands, picturing his thumbs digging into the other monkey's larynx, choking off his air supply. "He's got K8. If I'm going to get her back in one piece, I'm going to need to meet him, face-to-face. And if that happens, I can kill him."

"But he'll know you want that, won't he?"

Ack-Ack Macaque shrugged. "Yeah, I'm sure he does."

"So, why does he—?"

"Because he wants to recruit me." Ack-Ack Macaque tapped his temple. "And because he's fucking nuts. He probably wants to fight me as badly as I want to fight him. There's only room for one alpha monkey, and neither of us will stop until we find out which of us it is."

"This town ain't big enough for the both of you?"

He stuck the cigar in his mouth and grinned around it.

"It's a primate thing."

Abruptly, the map vanished and the wall screen cleared to a picture of Paul's face.

"Heads up," he said. "Something's happening."

The display changed again, to a BBC News feed. The volume was off, but the pictures spoke for themselves. They were being relayed from a camera in Trafalgar Square, on the steps of the National Gallery, looking south down Whitehall towards the tower of Big Ben. Above the roofs, the sky crackled with blue and white sparks. People were standing and pointing, or running for cover. Police vans tore past, lights flashing. A cloud of pigeons flew in front of the lens.

And then, *blam!* Something vast, black and impossible snapped into solidity above the city, blocking out the daylight. The picture went dark, and then came back up as the camera adjusted to the sudden shadow.

Ack-Ack Macaque scowled at the screen and swore under his breath. They were looking at the underside of an airship so large he couldn't see its edges—just row upon row of gun emplacements; a scattering of engine nacelles; and more than a dozen large, armoured gondolas, each bristling with missile tubes and machine gun turrets. The thing had appeared partially inside the low cloud layer, and rivulets of displaced grey fluff rippled away to either side.

Turning away from the screen, he looked to the front window, and whistled. Ahead, the Leader's flagship filled the skies. It must have been at least two kilometres long, more than twice the size of the *Tereshkova*. Its footprint stretched from Green Park to Waterloo, and every inch of it radiated a brutal menace.

And then, even as he watched, he saw the first missiles streaking down from the giant warship, hitting the self-same targets he'd just selected on the map, turning the skyline into a series of fireballs.

# CHAPTER THIRTY-THREE
## THE COMMONWEALTH EXPECTS

As THE FIRST explosions still shook the capital, Ack-Ack Macaque dropped to all fours and scampered from the bridge. He threw himself up the nearest companionway. He had to get airborne. It was his default response, a reflex written into the software of his mind. He'd been created to re-fight a fictionalised Battle of Britain, and had scrapped his way through countless simulated air raids and scrambles. This was what he did, and what he knew. When the bell rang, you ran for your plane. It was as simple as that. In some ways, it was a comfort to find himself back in such a familiar situation.

Using his arms to haul himself upward, he charged up flight after flight of metal stairs, until he reached the top of the *Tereshkova*. By the time he got there, he was wheezing for breath, and coughing up globs of brown tobacco-tasting mucus. All five of the planes were waiting at the end of the runway. There wasn't much room for them, but somehow they'd managed to cram themselves together. The pilots and solitary mechanic had been in the process of loading ammo belts into the machine guns built into the wings of the lead plane when the attack began, and had stopped to stare at the carnage, hands shading their eyes as they peered ahead.

"Hey!" He did his best parade ground yelp. "No time for gawping. I need these babies in the air, right now. How are we doing?"

The nearest pilot turned to him. Like the rest of this ad hoc squadron, he wasn't military. He was a retired airline pilot, a volunteer at the Fleet Air Arm Museum, and his face dripped fear and bafflement.

"Have you seen—?"

"Of course I've fucking seen it. Why do you think we need the bullets?" He pushed past, to where the mechanic knelt on the wing. The mechanic's name was Smithy. He wore oil-stained overalls and a battered, shapeless cap.

"It's okay, chief." Smithy closed the lid of the ammo compartment and wiped his hands on an old rag. "This is the last one. I can't swear they'll all work, mind, but they're loaded and ready to go."

Ack-Ack Macaque felt his teeth peel back from his gums. His pilots were looking to him, plainly shocked and badly frightened. None of them were warriors. He spoke loudly, to cut through their confusion.

"Okay, sweethearts, this is it. 'The Commonwealth expects', and all that crap." He strode to the leading plane, and hopped onto the wing beside the open cockpit canopy. He knew he had to say something to motivate and inspire them, but, "Follow me, and don't get yourselves killed," was the best he could come up with. In annoyance, he flung a hairy arm at the distant warship. "I'm going to land on that big bastard and try to rescue my friend. Your job is to keep it busy. Try to stop it deploying its doomsday weapon before the jets get here."

Cigar clamped in place, he glared around at their upturned faces. Like startled owlets, they blinked back at him. They were weekend hobbyists pitched into an unforeseeable war. When the firing started, they'd be lucky not to crash into each other, let alone take on the enemy. Still, they were all he had, and he knew he had to make the best of them. If this was going to be his final flight, his last battle, he was damned if he wasn't going to take it seriously.

He snapped his heels together and threw them a stiff salute. Then, with as much style as he could muster, he turned and dropped into the pilot's seat.

*Oh well*, he thought. *Here goes nothing.*


HE BARRELLED ACROSS the London sky with the other four planes arranged in a line behind him. This new Spitfire wasn't the same as his old one. Like horses, every plane had its own character and set of quirks. This was a Mark V, with wings clipped for greater manoeuvrability—a model he hadn't flown before. A few of the controls were in different places, and the stick felt jumpier than he was used to. Nevertheless, it was still a Spitfire, and he thrilled to the guttural growl of its engine. Like him, it was a relic from another time.

Ahead, the Gestalt warship loomed like a cliff face.

*Ack-ster, it's Paul.*

"What is it?"

*We've received a signal from the RAF. Planes are scrambling from the* Shakespeare *and* Verne. *They should be with you in five minutes, and suggest you hang back until they arrive.*

"Screw that, I'm going after K8."

A fresh volley of missiles burst from the underside of the behemoth, and he followed their white smoke trails down to the ground. That was Downing Street gone. The Parliament buildings and large areas of Whitehall already lay in ruins. The invasion seemed to be proceeding exactly the way he'd told Victoria it would, with a decisive first strike aimed at destroying the country's political and military leaders.

*Well, not on my watch, motherfuckers!*

With his left hand, he pushed the throttle forward as far as it would go. The Gestalt ship hung in his gun sights.

"Okay, spread out," he told his wingmen. "Concentrate your fire on the gun turrets and missile launchers. Try to knock out as many as you can."

He watched them peel away to either side, taking up attack positions, while he held his course, hurtling straight at the enemy. He couldn't afford to show fear or hesitation. Somewhere on board, the Leader would be watching. He would guess who was piloting the lead Spitfire, and be ready to attack at the first sign of weakness or hesitation.

This was a test of courage. They were sizing each other up.

Stabbing at the radio with a gloved hand, Ack-Ack Macaque changed the frequency.

"Okay," he said into his mike, "it's me. I'm coming aboard."

As if in reply, fire erupted from every turret he could see. Lines of tracer raked the sky. Anti-aircraft missiles streaked like sparks. And, one by one, his Spitfires fell. The first two disappeared in greasy fireballs. The third seemed to fall apart in mid-air, hacked to bits by bullets. The fourth pulled up sharply—a sure sign the pilot had been hit—and tipped over onto its back. He watched it dive on Lambeth, accelerating into the road just shy of the bridge. And, just like that, all four of his wingmen were gone, blown away before any of them had managed to fire even a single shot.

When he looked up, the airship's guns had all swivelled in his direction.

"Oh, bollocks."

His squadron hadn't stood a chance; and now, if he was at all mistaken about the Leader's desire for a face-to-face confrontation, neither did he. For a long, long moment, he kept driving forward, into the teeth of the arsenal arrayed against him, knowing it would be fatal to flinch now. If he was right, this was all still part of the pre-fight posturing. The Leader was demonstrating his superior firepower, and Ack-Ack Macaque his courage. Essentially, they were beating their chests and circling each other.

For tense seconds he continued to hurtle at the juggernaut. Then he heard a burst of static over his headphones, and a familiar voice hissed, "Welcome, my brother. I am flattered you have decided to accept my invitation."

Ack-Ack Macaque felt his hackles rise. His tail thrashed against the cockpit wall.

"Screw you."

"Crude as ever, I see." The Leader sounded weary, almost bored. "But it can't have escaped even your limited attention that I have you at something of a disadvantage."

Ack-Ack Macaque pushed his goggles up onto his forehead. The gun barrels twitched in unison as they tracked the movements of his plane. He was beaten, and he knew it.

"Just tell me one thing." He fumbled one-handed for a cigar. "What do you want with me? First you send Reynolds, now all this. Why've you got such a hard-on for my approval?"

The Leader didn't speak for a few moments. When his voice came back over the airwaves, his tiredness held an edge of disappointment.

"Don't you feel it too?"

"Feel what?"

"Haven't you ever wanted to meet another one of your kind? Haven't you ever been lonely?"

Ack-Ack Macaque jammed the cigar between his teeth. The black armour-plated flank of the airship filled his entire forward view. If he didn't pull up soon, he'd hit it dead centre, at three hundred miles per hour.

"So," he rolled the cigar from one side of his mouth to the other, "you're looking for a playmate?"

"No, my simple brother." The Leader gave a half-hearted chuckle. "I'm looking for a lieutenant. Now—" his voice hardened, "—I want you to come aboard."

Ack-Ack Macaque pulled back on his stick, and the Spit's nose rose towards the low grey clouds. He zoomed over the whale-like back of the airship and looked down. "You haven't got a runway." All he could see were a few helipads, with choppers and VTOL jets parked on them.

"You have a parachute."

"Fuck off."

"If you want to see your little friend again, you'll do it."

Ack-Ack Macaque snarled.

"If you've hurt her—"

"I'll give you thirty seconds."

Ack-Ack Macaque screeched, and hammered the Perspex canopy with his fists.

"Twenty-eight…"

He thought of K8 and took a long, shuddering breath through his teeth.

"Twenty-six…"

"Okay, okay." He wiped his right eye with the back of one hairy wrist. "I'll do it. But I'll need to gain some altitude, or the 'chute won't open properly."

The radio crackled.

"Understood. But we're still tracking you. Try anything idiotic, and I'll blow that balsawood kite out from under you before you can blink. Capeesh?"

Ack-Ack Macaque's shoulders hunched, and he drove his plane skyward.

"Yeah, I got you."

As the Spitfire's prop drilled into the rainclouds, he took a last look downwards, and saw a glint at the airship's bows. What was that?

Were they *windows*?

A wicked grin smeared itself across his face. His plane circled upward in a narrowing spiral, like a vulture riding thermals above a wounded buffalo, and then the clouds enveloped him and everything turned to fog.

\*     \*     \*

As SOON AS the monkey's plane vanished into the overcast, the Gestalt warship opened fire on the *Tereshkova*. Bullets punched through the black and white zigzags at its bows, piercing all five hulls. Propellers sparked and windows smashed. Radio aerials snapped and fell.

On the *Tereshkova*'s bridge, Victoria grabbed for support as the floor lurched. In the doorway behind her, William Cole yelped as he was thrown against the frame.

Slowly, the bow began to turn.

Clinging on to the arm of the pilot's chair, Victoria shouted, "What are you doing?"

"Turning away," Paul's voice quailed through the intercom speakers. Bullets rattled against the aluminium hull like hail clattering on a tin roof.

"No!" She pulled herself upright. "If you turn sideways, you'll just make us a bigger target."

"What, then?"

She glanced at the cloud layer.

"Take us up. Follow the monkey."

"I can't!"

The front windows shattered, and Victoria ducked.

"Why not?"

"We're losing gas from the port hull."

"Jettison it!" The *Tereshkova*'s five hulls were kept in place by lightweight steel girders. Up until last year, they could only be disengaged manually. Then, after damage to one of the outer hulls had almost cost the whole craft, one of Victoria's first acts as Captain had been to install explosive bolts at all the key junctures.

"It's losing buoyancy," Paul protested. "It'll crash."

"Better it than us."

She heard a detonation, and the deck shook. She couldn't tell if it had been the bolts, or a shot from the Gestalt.

"Separation complete," Paul reported.

The *Tereshkova*'s four remaining hulls quivered like a wet horse, and began to rise. The hail of bullets paused as the sudden change in altitude threw off the Gestalt's gunners.

Through the howling gap where the window glass had been, Victoria caught sight of the discarded section pitching down towards the city like a kilometre-long torpedo, trailing smoke and debris. Almost in slow motion, it dived into the shadow of the Gestalt craft and hit the brown waters of the Thames, throwing up a huge fan of spray. The nose smashed against the piers of Westminster Bridge, crumpling even as the bridge cracked and buckled before the weight of the impact. Clumps of masonry fell into the river. The fins at the stern rose into the air, hung there for an instant, impellers still spinning wildly, and then crumpled back with a splash.

"Jesus." William Cole joined her behind the pilot's chair.

"You said it."

"No, I mean those engines. They're nuclear-powered."

"They're designed to survive crashes."

"Will they?"

"Who knows?" Right now, irradiating half of London was among the least of her concerns.

She lost sight of the chaos on the ground as the *Tereshkova* reached the clouds. For a moment, the bombardment wavered, but quickly picked up again with equal ferocity.

*Damn*. For a minute there, she'd thought they might find cover in the overcast.

"They must have infrared tracking." Paul's voice held an edge of panic. The deck shuddered again. "We're taking damage to all sections. Venting gas in a dozen places."

Victoria turned to Cole, who was in the process of brushing glass and dust from his hair and beard.

"Take your family," she said, "and get out."

He looked at her, wild-eyed.

"Marie can't move."

"Then find a way to move her." She seized him by the shoulders, spun him around, and shoved him at the door. "Allez-y!"

He ran off unsteadily into the corridor, heading aft.

She heard the *blang, blang, blang* of bullets punching through metal and flinched. Her hand went to the sword at her side.

"What do we do?" Paul cried.

"How the hell would I know?" With the *Tereshkova* literally falling apart around them, her options were shrinking by the second. "How much longer can we stay airborne?"

"Assuming they don't hit the airbags again, another ten minutes. Twelve at the outside."

"Not good."

"And we're losing manoeuvrability."

She shook her head.

"Putain de merde." She climbed into the pilot's chair and pressed the ship-wide intercom. "Attention all hands," she barked. "This is the Captain. Assume crash positions. We are going down. Repeat. We are going down."

AT THE TOP of its climb, the Spitfire emerged from the clouds into sunlight, and stalled. As it hung vertically in the clear air, with its prop spinning at the cobalt sky, Ack-Ack Macaque pulled the goggles back over his face, and dragged open the canopy. He had only seconds before gravity's fingers brought the nose down and the plane began the long fall earthwards. Bracing himself against the lip of the cockpit, he used his knife to hack a strip from his safety harness. Then he stood up, and gripped the control stick with his prehensile toes.

"Think you've got me, fuck-knuckle? Think again."

The plane began to slip backwards and he clung on with his feet until the nose snapped earthwards and he had it aimed where he wanted. With all the cloud and murk between him and his target, he had to line it up from memory, and then use the strip of harness to lash the stick in place. It was trickier than he'd thought it would be, but he did the best he could do in the few seconds available to him, and hoped it would be enough.

Falling nose first, the plane began to pick up speed. The wind flapped at the collar of his jacket. He crouched on the seat and leapt, arms and legs stretched out as if hurling himself from one jungle branch to another.

"Geronimo!"

He fell spread-eagled for a few seconds, towards the undulating carpet of cloud. Air rushed past his face, pulled at his hands and feet. Then, just as he reached the tops of the mashed potato-like peaks, the 'chute sprang open, jerking him back with a snap.

Swinging from its straps, he fell into the white and grey void, one hand on the lines, the other pulling a pistol from the holster at his thigh. He knew the enemy airship lurked only a few metres below the base of the clouds, so he wouldn't get much warning before he hit it. But that also meant her defenders wouldn't get a lot of time to shoot at him, either. He'd only be vulnerable for a few seconds. And, if he came down where he hoped, they'd already have better things to worry about.


THE MIST LIGHTENED around his feet and he fell into clear air, just in time to see the ruined Spitfire whirling away from the airship's bows, slipping from the toughened glass like a crushed butterfly falling from a car windscreen.

"Hell and damnation!" He'd hoped that by crashing it into the ironclad from above, the plane might have sheared the front of the ship's nose right off—but it seemed to have done little beyond smashing half a dozen panes, and cracking a handful of others.

The deck rushed at him. As he'd expected, there were people waiting for him. Members of the Gestalt stood at intervals along the two-thousand metre-long craft, each dressed in an identical white suit, and each cradling an identical machine pistol. He put bullets in the nearest two, but then had to haul at the parachute and brace for collision. His feet struck the armoured surface with a shock that rattled his skeleton like a maraca, and he went limp, rolling with the impact.

He came to rest on the edge of one of the broken panes of glass, where the bow joined the body of the airship, his torso and legs on the metal hull, his boots dangling over the edge of the jagged hole. Flapping in the wind, the parachute tugged at him, and he flicked the release and wriggled out of the harness before it could inflate and drag him off the ship, dumping him onto the buildings below.

Weapons raised, the remaining Gestalt drones walked in his direction. They didn't seem hurried. He heaved himself to his feet and plugged one. The man crumpled soundlessly, only to be replaced moments later by another emerging from a hatch. All along the airship's length, Neanderthals in white suits were clambering from ladders and companionways. If he shot one, three more appeared to take their place. With their thicker bones, they were tougher than ordinary humans, and he knew he simply didn't have the ammunition or strength to fight them all.

Behind him the splintered hole led down into a cavernous interior. He saw more glass far below. The entire nose was glazed, like the cockpit of a World War II German Heinkel. He glimpsed leaves and vines further back, in the body of the airship. The nearest treetop was maybe thirty feet below. With the heel of his boot, he kicked away the remaining glass splinters around the window's frame. Shots were fired at him, and he paused to return the compliment, felling a white-clad woman with a silver beehive. Behind her, maybe fifty others shuffled forwards, their movements eerily synchronised. Treading as carefully as he dared, he balanced around the edge of the broken pane until he was at the lower edge, closer to the pointed bow. From here, he could see the trees more easily, and also some sort of wooden platform set with tables and chairs.

Thirty feet seemed suddenly more like forty. Still, there was no way to back out now. Muttering to himself, he re-holstered his pistol and backed off a few paces. The guys and gals in white opened fire again. Ducking, he made a dash for the hole, and threw himself headlong through it, aiming for the nearest trees.

His jacket fluttered around him as he fell into the comparative gloom of the airship's interior. He saw the wooden platform—some kind of balcony—beneath him; but, before he could make out any more detail, he crashed into the upper branches of a coconut tree. The thick fronds snapped and tangled around him, catching his arms and legs, slowing him; and the trunk bowed, absorbing some of his momentum. Then he broke through, and fell, in a shower of twigs and leaf fragments, into a web of vines and creepers. He fell from one branch to another, until he ended up swinging from one leg, his right knee hooked over the lower branch of a potted cedar. His goggles hung down on their strap, almost touching the floor. The cigar remained clamped firmly in his teeth, but it had snapped midway along its length, and the loose end dangled in front of his eye.

Debris settled around him.

\* \* \*

FOR A FEW MOMENTS, he was content to remain there, letting his shaken brain catch up with his precipitous descent. Then he heard clapping, and the Leader emerged from the trees.

"My dear fellow," the monkey said, "that was quite an entrance. But then, I guess I shouldn't have expected anything less."

Ack-Ack Macaque spat out the remains of his cigar. Painfully, he reached up to grab the branch supporting him, and unhooked his leg. At this point, he felt more bruise than monkey, and every abused limb griped with its own chorus of aches and pains. He lowered his feet to the floor, brushed down his aviator jacket, and readjusted his eye patch.

"That's nothing," he rumbled. "Wait 'til I tell you about the time I made a jetpack out of fire extinguishers."

The Leader bowed his head and made a welcoming gesture.

"Please," he said, "we've been waiting for you. Won't you join us?"

He turned and led the way through the trees, onto the veranda, and Ack-Ack Macaque trailed after him, rolling and stretching his stiff shoulders beneath his jacket. His boots crunched over shards of glass from the broken panes high above.

The veranda overlooked the interior of the airship's conical nose. And there, silhouetted against the blue sky, a wrought iron table with three chairs, one of which was occupied.

"K8?" Her posture looked wrong. Instead of her usual teenage slump, she sat with her back straight and her hands resting on her knees. A half-finished

cup of tea sat on the table before her, gentle wisps of
steam curling upward past her unseeing eyes. "What
have you done to her?"

"Oh, her, she's fine." The Leader dismissed the
matter with a flick of his hand. "It's you I want to
talk about, my brother."

"Stop calling me that."

"Then how should I address you?"

Ack-Ack Macaque curled his lip. "Most people
use my given name."

The Leader pulled back a chair, scraping the metal
legs on the veranda's wooden planks, and gestured
for him to sit.

"But that's just the point," he said, "Somebody
*gave* you that name, and the identity that goes
with it. They made you, just as they made me. The
difference between us is that I had the wherewithal
to think outside the box, to reject the paradigm
handed to me by those damn dirty apes, and forge
my own identity. Create my own brand, if you like."

Ack-Ack Macaque remained standing. His fingers
curled and uncurled. He'd been primed for a fight,
but this clown seemed intent on talking him to death.

"Look at you," the other monkey continued,
walking around to stand behind K8. "A monkey
in a flying suit? You're a joke to them. A living
cartoon character; a plaything created for a game,
still playing out that game in real life."

"And what are you?"

The Leader's eye narrowed.

"I'm a self-made monkey. I'm a king on many
worlds, a pharaoh on three. I'm practically a god."

"Because you turn everybody into mindless puppets?"

"On the contrary, my brother." He placed his hands on K8's shoulders. "They are not mindless, quite the reverse. They retain their thoughts and memories, but share them with the wider consciousness. They become part of a giant web of humanity that stretches across the timelines, linked by transmitters like the ones on this ship. A multi-global harmony of thought and reason."

K8 hadn't reacted to his touch.

"They're still zombies."

"Not at all." The Leader shook his head. "They've simply surrendered their initiative to that of the consensus. Their individual identities remain, and are preserved as essential parts of the whole, rather than isolated sparks of awareness. The things which make them unique human beings are the things about them we cherish most." He patted K8's shoulder proprietarily. "Take your little friend here, for instance."

Ack-Ack Macaque looked down into her face. Her features were smooth and untroubled, her eyes focused on the middle distance.

"She has become one with the collective." The Leader bent around and spoke into her ear. "Isn't that right, Katie?"

"Yes, Leader." Her voice was a calm monotone that seemed to come from somewhere far behind her face. Hearing her speak, Ack-Ack Macaque felt a hollow open in his stomach. It was an upturned, empty, impotent sensation.

"You still remember everything, don't you, Katie?"

"Yes, Leader."

"Even this reprobate here?"

Her eyes swivelled up to focus on Ack-Ack Macaque, and he felt a wild surge of hope.

"Yes, Leader." Her tone remained flat, her gaze cool and dispassionate, accepting his presence without reaction.

Rage burned like a flare in his chest.

"No..."

He drew himself up and glared: a direct physical challenge.

The Leader stepped back from K8's chair and straightened his tie.

"Really?" He looked sceptical. "We're the only two of our kind in the world, closer than brothers, closer than twins. And you want to *fight*?"

Ack-Ack Macaque squeezed his aching hands into fists.

"You're damn right I want to fight."

The other monkey gave a snort.

"Then I'm sorry, but you leave me no other choice. Katie, if you please?"

Without changing expression, the girl reached under the tea cosy on the table and produced a pistol, which she pressed to her own temple.

"Make another move," the Leader growled, "and she's dead."

# CHAPTER THIRTY-FOUR
## OPTIMISED PEOPLE

VICTORIA STAYED IN the pilot's chair. She had nowhere else to go. Around her, the old skyliner moaned and squealed its torment. Wet air barged through the shattered windshield, hurling debris and loose sheets of paper around the bridge.

"Nine thousand feet," Paul intoned over the speakers.

Victoria gripped the console in front of her, trying to make sense of the readouts and winking lights. Her mind kept flashing back to the helicopter crash, the one in the South Atlantic more than two years ago; the one she should never have survived; the one that had left her a half-human cyborg.

How much of her would be left after this one?

"Can we steer?" She spoke to stave off the panic that thrashed inside her. Most of the screens on the bridge were dead. A small one set into the console lit with a projection of her ex-husband's face. He still wore his round spectacles, but he'd somehow found the time to add a red and white Kamikaze headband to his image. Spikes of peroxide yellow hair stuck up above it like the bristles of an unwashed paintbrush.

"Barely." He bit his lip. "Eight and a half thousand. Best guess is we'll be coming down somewhere between Victoria Embankment and St. Paul's."

"Can we turn?"

"What difference does it make?" He waved his arms. "Wherever we hit, we're going to be hitting buildings."

"Not if we land *on* the airship."

He looked at her open mouthed. He took his glasses off, and then put them on again.

"Come on," she said. "If we discard the other three hulls, we'll be small enough. He's bigger and wider than us."

He pushed the glasses into place with an index finger. "But, what if we glance off?"

"Who cares?" She felt a dizzying sense of freedom, and knew the gelware in her head had cut in, suppressing her fear in a blast of clear-thinking machine clarity. "We're going down anyway."

"But the Ack-ster—?"

"He'd do the same."

Paul thought about it. The wind howled through the bridge.

"Okay," he said after a few seconds. The deck heaved to port as he used the ship's remaining rudders to bring her about. "What choice do we have?" He swallowed. "Seven thousand…"

Victoria couldn't see anything ahead but cloud. They were still in the murk, but the number of shots hitting them had dwindled.

"Get the stewards up here," she said. "As soon as we hit, I want them out, ready to fight."

"What about Cole and his daughter?"

"Everybody fights."

She watched the interior of the cloud slide past the window. Heading set, the *Tereshkova* lurched forward again, every last drop of engine power being used to propel it forward, and down.

Almost immediately, the Gestalt's bullets resumed their clatter. Victoria ducked.

Paul said, "I think they're onto us."

"Then let's give them something else to shoot at." She leant close to his image. "Jettison the hulls."

A series of bangs rattled the length of the skyliner, and the deck surged under her as the weight of the other sections fell away. They were on their own now, just one airship in a crowd of four. To the Gestalt gunners, reliant on infrared images, they must look like a sudden fleet of ships—or a gigantic wreck. But this obfuscation came with a price. Most of the engine nacelles and rudder fins were on the outer hulls. Losing them left the central section almost helpless. In effect, they were riding a kilometre-long balloon with only a single impeller to push it along. Now that they were locked on course for a collision, there was nothing they could do to alter their decision. They had lost the manoeuvrability needed to change course. Like it or not, they were going to hit the ironclad, and hit hard.

"I'm getting reports in from other skyliners around the globe." Paul flashed some images onto a sub-window behind his face, making him look like a newsreader. Over his shoulder she saw aerial battles over foreign cities; burning planes, exploding buildings.

"Are we winning?"

He bit his lip.

"Not even slightly. There are too many 'ships, and not enough cooperation."

"So we're losing?"

"We're getting annihilated."

The bridge bucked as the remains of the *Tereshkova* hit turbulence. Then they were out of the cloud, with the broad bulk of the enemy ship directly ahead, and their abandoned hulls falling around them like spent rockets. They were seconds from collision with the Gestalt. Tracer bullets hosed the sky, their lines of firefly sparks joining the two ships. With one finger, Victoria pulled back the attitude control and raised the nose, bringing up the bow.

She touched the image of Paul's face on the screen.

"I love you," she whispered.

He didn't hear her.

"Brace!" he yelled, his voice echoing through the ship. "Brace, brace!"

"WELL," THE LEADER said with a thin smile, "it seems we have a standoff."

He stepped backwards until he reached the veranda's bamboo rail. Teeth bared, Ack-Ack Macaque glowered at him. Between them, K8 sat impassively, the barrel of the gun she held making a slight indentation in the short-cropped ginger hair above her right ear.

"Let her go, shitweasel. You and I need to settle this, monkey to monkey."

The Leader shook his head.

"You still think you can fight me?" He seemed amused. "Look at the state of you." He leant his elbows on the rail. "I'm surprised you can even stand."

Ack-Ack Macaque gave him the finger.

"Spin on it."

The Leader laughed, and turned his face to the broken glass ceiling.

"Oh, my friend. Why must you think of me as 'the bad guy'? Surely even you can see the good I do?" He stretched out his arms. "There are entire worlds out there that know nothing of war or hunger. They have no crime or suffering, no murder or terrorism. No loneliness. Just world after world of happy, optimised people, working and striving together towards common goals." He interlaced his fingers. "Togetherness, mutual understanding and brotherhood. That's what it's all about." He checked his ornate wristwatch. "As your world will discover for itself, in a few short moments."

"Says you."

The Leader tugged his lapels, straightening his jacket.

"My fleet has begun to seed the skies with little machines, each with the dimensions of a single molecule. The process will take a few moments. After that, these little machines disperse themselves on the wind, adapting and assimilating every human with which they come into contact. Within hours, the world will be as your friend here." He drew back his lips in a smirk that was half smile, half challenge. "You can be as sceptical as you like, 'Ack-Ack', but I build utopias. Good ones. Better than anything you've currently got."

"We've got our freedom."

"And what good is that? Last year, you almost blew yourselves up in a thermonuclear war."

"We didn't though, did we?

The Leader flicked dismissive fingers. "Only by the unlikeliest of chances."

Suddenly, he frowned. He opened his mouth to speak again, but broke off before he'd uttered a complete syllable.

"That's strange," he said, tipping his head to one side. The frown grew deeper. He looked at Ack-Ack Macaque. "My connection..."

Ack-Ack Macaque heard a strangled noise and glanced down at K8. She was looking straight back at him. Her features were pale and strained, and her teeth were clamped together. A single bead of sweat ran down the side of her forehead. The hand holding the gun began to shake. Behind her, the Leader cried out in pain and put a hand to his brow.

Ack-Ack Macaque looked from one to the other, and realisation dawned.

"Holy shit!" He sprang forwards and seized K8's arm. It was her. She was fighting back. Somehow, she'd found a way to resist.

Twisted like wires around the pistol's grip, her fingers didn't want to relinquish the weapon, but he managed to pry them apart just as her knuckle whitened on the trigger. He jerked her hand free, and the gun went skittering across the wooden decking and clonked against a plant pot.

Spent with effort, K8 collapsed, arms and legs flopping down on either side of the chair. He took her by the shoulders.

"K8, can you hear me? Are you still in there?"

She gave him a look.

"You know me, Skip," she croaked. "I can hack anything. But it's hard. I don't know how much longer I can block his connection. Be quick, before the others notice."

Ack-Ack Macaque squeezed her shoulders. He didn't need telling twice. Separated from the hive and unable to summon reinforcements, the Leader was vulnerable. He lunged forward, covering the distance between them in a handful of steps. The other monkey saw him coming, and thrust out a hand.

"No, you imbecile!"

But it was too late.

They crashed together in a flurry of raking claws and snapping teeth, each intent on ripping out the other's throat. Ack-Ack Macaque was fast, and fought dirty, but he was carrying the injuries accumulated during the storming of the Gestalt headquarters, as well as the bumps and scrapes from his fall through the trees. The Leader was fresh and rested, and fought with such ferocity that Ack-Ack Macaque quickly found himself being pushed back. A manicured thumb tried to gouge his eye, and he bit it.

But then a blow caught the side of his head, and he staggered. His vision blurred for a second. Reaching out, his fingers grasped the Leader's lapels, but the other monkey had something in his fist. The Leader's arm pulled back and light flashed from a steel blade. Ack-Ack Macaque tried to block the blow, but only succeeded in deflecting it. Instead of puncturing his gut, the point of the knife caught him across the upper arm, slicing through leather, hair and skin.

"Aargh!"

Gripping the wound, he stumbled back. The Leader followed, a snarl of triumphant bloodlust on his leathery features, his hand drawn back for another thrust.

And then something hit the airship from above.

There was a cataclysmic crash and a great weight pressed on them. Something had hit the airship, and hit it hard. Ack-Ack Macaque felt his feet lift as the floor surged downwards, and, for an instant, everything went weightless. The Leader staggered and threw out a hand to steady himself against the veranda's rail. The distraction was all Ack-Ack macaque needed. With a bloodcurdling howl, he ducked under the knife and flung himself at the other monkey. His shoulder hit the Leader in the stomach and, caught off-balance, the other monkey fell back against the rail.

"No!" he cried.

Ack-Ack Macaque wrapped his arms around the Leader's waist.

"I'm taking you down, sweetheart."

He heaved with every ounce of remaining strength. Dry bamboo snapped and splintered, and they both crashed through and fell, still struggling, into empty space.

**BREAKING NEWS**

From *B&FBC NEWS ONLINE*:

**GLOBAL WAR!**

Reports are coming in of massive aerial attacks against cities in Europe, the Americas, and the Far East. Details are uncertain, but it seems that in the past few minutes, major bombardments have hit London, Paris, Berlin, New York, Tokyo and Beijing. There are also unconfirmed reports of further strikes in Madrid, Rome, Ankara, Los Angeles, Buenos Aires, and Athens.

So far, the bombings seem to be targeting government buildings and military installations, but explosions have hit some civilian areas. The source of these attacks is unknown, but it is feared thousands may already be dead.

Click here for amateur footage of the attacks

No official sources could be reached, but Commonwealth citizens are advised to seek shelter, and tune to the Emergency Broadcast System for updates.

In the meantime, all

-- CONNECTION LOST --
-- CONNECTION LOST --
-- CONNECTION LOST --
-- CONNECTION LOST --
-- CONNECTION LOST --

# CHAPTER THIRTY-FIVE
## THREADS

VICTORIA VALOIS MOANED, and tried to move. She was still seated in the pilot's chair, but the floor of the *Tereshkova*'s bridge had crumpled inwards, its metal walls concertinaed by the force of the collision, and she now found herself wedged between the seat and the curved metal ceiling, held in place by the remains of the instrument console.

And beyond the ceiling, she thought, the bomb. Had it survived intact? Obviously, it hadn't gone off, but that didn't mean the impact hadn't triggered some sort of malfunction. For all she knew, a countdown could be under way right now. And here she was, with her cheek pressed up against it.

She twisted around in her seat. The chair had been wedged sideways into the narrow gap between floor and ceiling—an uneven space filled with smashed furniture and broken sections of bulkhead. If she could get free from behind the console, she could probably crawl to the front of the bridge, and squeeze out through the remains of the front window; but the console's edge pressed uncomfortably into her abdomen, pinning her against the back of the chair, and she couldn't escape.

"Paul? Paul, are you there?"

Nothing. All the instruments were dead, and all the lights were off.

She tried pushing at the console but its metal stand had been bent in such a way that she couldn't move it.

"Captain?"

The voice came from somewhere aft, beyond a section of deck that had cantilevered up into the ceiling.

"I'm here."

"Captain, it's William. Are you okay?"

She squirmed her hips, trying to wriggle her way out, but to no avail. She tried twice, and then fell back with a curse, slapping the instrument panel that held her.

"I'm stuck," she said.

Cole didn't answer straight away, but she heard him banging around.

"I can't get to you," he said. "Not without equipment."

"How many of you are back there?"

"Four stewards, myself and Lila."

"Marie?"

He paused again. "I don't know. We can't get to the infirmary from in here."

"Can you get out?"

"We can climb through the main hatch behind the passenger lounge."

"Then go. Don't wait for me."

"Are you sure?"

"Just get out. Take guns, and do whatever you can. I'll join you later."

"Okay." He didn't sound convinced. "Good luck, Captain."

"And to you."

She listened to him work his way back into the interior of the gondola. Overhead, the main body of the *Tereshkova*'s central hull gave a loud, metallic groan as the wind caught it, and heeled it over slightly to the left.

It wouldn't take much, she thought, to completely dislodge the *Tereshkova*'s carcass from its precarious perch atop the Gestalt vessel. A decent gust of wind, or some gentle manoeuvring by the bigger craft, could be enough to tip it off, and send it falling, to dash itself to pieces on the roofs and spires of Westminster.

If she were going to get free, she'd have to do it herself.

Closing her eyes, she mouthed the series of passwords that allowed her access to the command mode of the gelware processors in her skull. These slimy artificial neurons handled the bulk of her brain's processing, regulating the physical functions that kept her body alive and working, as well as supplementing the damaged areas responsible for reasoning and memory. Stepping into command mode was a way of tinkering with their settings, and thereby changing the way her body behaved. Strictly speaking, it was cheating. It was not something the surgeons and technicians who'd installed the neural prostheses had bargained on her being able to do; but she'd pestered and cajoled them, using every trick in her reporter's tool kit, until they'd finally given her the access codes.

Now, as she shifted her focus, her mind was pulled up, out of the hormone-washed gunk of her biological cortex, and into the crisp, rarefied air of pure machine thought. In this heightened state, she saw everything with luminous summer clarity, unencumbered by fear or anxiety. Life-threatening situations, which would otherwise have left her biological cerebellum quaking, became abstract puzzles to be solved, and self-preservation a desired outcome rather than an overpowering physical imperative.

Coolly, she considered the console in front of her, assessing its weak points and comparing them to her body's capabilities, balancing necessity against acceptable levels of organic damage. It would be no good, for instance, to escape her present predicament only to find that, because she'd dislocated both hips in the process, she was unable to walk.

There.

Feeling under the console, her fingers found the point where the stand—basically, a steel tube sprouting from the floor—had been welded to its underside. That was the weak spot. If she could apply enough force, she could break the join and kick the stand free, thereby removing the thing that kept the console braced against her.

Pressing back in her chair, she brought her foot up so that it rested against the stand, just below the weld. Then, in her mind's eye, she summoned up the menus governing adrenaline production and pain tolerance, switched off the safeguards, and turned all the dials up to maximum.

Mentally exhausted, she dropped out of command mode and her awareness fell, like a released fish, back into the comforting shallows of her natural mind.

In response to the changes she'd made, her adrenal glands were dumping huge amounts of adrenaline into her bloodstream. She felt her heart quicken, and her breathing grow rapid, drawing oxygen to her muscles. It was the classic 'fight-or-flight' response, and she'd found a way to weaponise it. Butterflies fluttered in her chest, and she itched with a sudden, smothering feeling of claustrophobia. She had to get out, and get out now!

She heard the whine of an elcctric motor, and a toy car bumped and trundled through the gap where the forward window had once been.

"Paul?"

The car wobbled towards her on its thick, knobby tyres, and paused a few metres away. Her ex-husband's image flickered into the gloom of the wrecked bridge, crouched in the confined space.

"Hello, Vicky."

Gone was the Kamikaze headband. Now, he'd reverted to his default appearance: white lab coat over a garish green Hawaiian shirt, cargo pants, and ratty old trainers. His gold earring twinkled.

"Paul, you're alive."

He shook his head.

"No, I'm not. I've just downloaded myself into this car, but I'm still dead. And, unless you shift your butt, so will you be." He eyed the ceiling dubiously. "This whole thing's going to collapse."

"I'm trying."

"Try faster."

Gritting her teeth, she pushed with her foot. Engorged with blood, the muscles in her calf and thigh, already hard from regular training sessions with her fighting stick, bulged like steel cable.

"Come on," Paul urged.

She felt the sole of her boot flatten against the steel pole, and pressed harder. The chair creaked under her. The quadriceps at the front of her thigh felt ready to rip in half. The back edge of the console rasped against the ceiling. Something had to give; she just hoped it wouldn't be her leg or ankle.

She closed her eyes and kicked with every ounce of strength.

"Argh!"

With a crack, the weld split. The post clanged back, and the console came free. Victoria tumbled out of the chair, onto the uneven remains of the deck. Her foot throbbed, but she didn't have time to worry about that now. On hands and knees, she followed Paul's car forward, across the smashed glass and plastic littering the remains of the bridge, to the window.

As she emerged into daylight, she saw the *Tereshkova*'s prow rising above her, and gave the wall of the smashed gondola a final pat.

"Goodbye, old girl."

Following Paul, she rolled out from under the skyliner and got to her feet. Her right foot was sore, but the gelware kept the pain in check.

They were on the armoured upper surface of the Gestalt battleship. Further along the two-hundred-metre length of the *Tereshkova*'s pancaked gondola, she could see Cole and his daughter. They were heading in her direction. Behind them, four of the Commodore's stewards had taken positions behind air ducts and missile turrets, and were keeping at bay a group of armed Gestalt. Pillars of black smoke rose from the city below. Fighter jets screamed overhead, raking the ironclad with cannon fire.

"Come on," she called to Cole. "We need to get inside."

The writer carried a Kalashnikov. The wind blew his hair up like the wing of an injured bird.

"No," he said, looking over his shoulder. "I have to go back. My wife—"

"Leave her."

"But—"

Victoria put a hand to his cheek, turning his face to hers.

"She can't walk, and we can't carry her. And if we don't get down inside this thing and kill that monkey, she's as good as dead anyway."

Cole looked down at her with red-rimmed, haunted eyes.

"No," he said, his voice firmer and more decisive than she would ever have believed. "I lost her once, I can't lose her again." He stepped back. "I'm sorry Captain, but I have to do this. I can't leave her. I won't." And with that, he turned and walked back towards the stern.

Victoria let him go. In his position, she would have done the same.

Had done the same.

She glanced at Paul. He glanced back.

"Hell to it," she said.

Lila was still standing in front of her, an automatic pistol held to her chest. Victoria looked from her to her retreating father.

"Are you with us?"

"Yes, ma'am."

"Your mother—?"

The girl clenched her jaw. "She'll understand."

"Okay, then." Victoria drew her fighting stick. They'd wasted enough time already. "In that case, you go ahead, and shoot anything that moves."


VICTORIA AND LILA made their way to an anti-aircraft turret near the bows. Paul's car trundled after them. The installation had obviously been hit by one of the circling jets. The domed roof had been peppered with fist-sized holes, and the white-suited Neanderthal inside lay dead and mangled in his chair, thick blobs of glossy blood dripping onto the deck from the tips of his hairy fingers.

Behind his chair, a hatch opened onto a narrow companionway. The stairs led down into the interior of the airship. They were only wide enough for one of them to descend at a time, and were a lot steeper than those on the *Tereshkova*. As Victoria ducked under a low stanchion, she figured they must be have been designed to allow the gunner to reach his post, rather than as a means of general access to the roof.

With Lila in the lead, they crept down, ready to shoot or stab, and acutely aware that if only one member of the Gestalt caught sight of them, the whole of the hive mind would instantly know about it. Victoria had to carry Paul's car under her arm. She felt a bit bad about letting the girl go first, but Lila was much better armed than she was, and handled the weapon with a respectful nonchalance that spoke of training and experience.

The companionway wound down through the ship in a spiral, eventually ending in a heavy oval hatch that would have looked more at home on a submarine than an airship.

Lila peeped through the porthole in the door.

"Corridor," she whispered.

"Clear?"

"Two guards at the bow end."

"What are they guarding?"

"Big brass door."

"How are we going to get past without them seeing?"

"Can't."

"What, then?"

Lila pursed her lips. "Look, it's big and brass, it's at the bows and there are two guards. Whatever's behind it has got to be important."

With her left hand, Victoria gripped the handle of her fighting stick; with her right, she put the toy car down and reached into the pocket of her tunic.

"What's that?" Lila asked.

"A tracking device." Victoria thumbed the power button and waited for the screen to boot up. When it did, it showed a series of concentric green circles, which indicated distance in units of ten, fifty, and one hundred metres. A red direction arrow bobbled about. "I find it useful for keeping tabs on the monkey."

"Does he know?"

Victoria shook her head. "Are you kidding? I got a vet to insert the microchip while he was passed out drunk, after we lost him for two days in Las Vegas. He doesn't even know it's there. If he ever finds out, he's going to go berserk."

She held the little device flat in the palm of her hand. The arrow swung back and forth, and then settled.

"Alive or dead," she said, "he's behind that door."

"Right, then it's decided." Before Victoria could stop her, Lila pulled the hatch to the corridor open. Without stepping out, she leaned around the frame and fired twice, and then twice again. The shots echoed loudly in the steel-walled corridor. Victoria's nostrils twitched to the familiar tang of gun smoke, and she heard the thuds of bodies hitting the deck.

Lila raised the pistol to her lips and blew.

"Okay," she said, "the guards are down. But now every white suit on this ship knows we're here."

Victoria slipped the tracker back into her pocket, and grinned. She couldn't help herself. Right now, they had nothing to lose. She felt liberated, and dangerous. She reached down and picked up the toy car.

"Then we'd better make this quick," she said.

# CHAPTER THIRTY-SIX
## PRIVATE JUNGLE

STEPPING OVER THE bodies, they pushed through the brass door, into the potted forest. Victoria looked up at the overhanging fronds and the glass ceiling. The place had the warm compost smell of a greenhouse. A parakeet flapped from one tree to another, its plumage an impressionist dash of blue and yellow. Butterflies twitched hither and thither.

"C'est quoi?"

Lila was in the process of reloading her pistol, taking loose cartridges from her thigh pocket and snapping them into the magazine.

"Remember we're dealing with a monkey," she said. "This is probably his gym or something."

"A jungle gym? On a Zeppelin?" She gave the girl a sideways squint. "Have you been here before?"

"No." Lila touched the bruise on her cheek, and scowled. "I only saw the Leader once, but that was on the ground, at the mansion." She pushed the last bullet into the magazine with her thumb, and snapped the whole thing back into the butt of the pistol. "Now, let's be quiet. Those guards were protecting more than just a bunch of trees, you know."

She moved off between the pots, and Victoria took a second to marvel at her. She was only a teenager, yet she talked with the assurance of a combat veteran. What kind of upbringing, what kind of *life*, had that poor kid endured?

She placed Paul's car on the deck.

"Okay," she said, "you can come out now."

The car buzzed. The headlights flickered on and off, and it jumped forward half a wheel rotation. Then the projectors kicked in and Paul shimmered into apparent solidity amongst the ferns and creepers.

He used a finger and thumb to settle his glasses more firmly on his nose.

"Um," he said, looking around. "Where are we?"

"The boss monkey's private jungle."

"Ah."

Victoria shook her fighting stick out to its full length.

"Come on."

Holding the staff in both hands, she picked her way into the foliage, and Paul trundled after her, his image seeming to glide above the leaf-strewn matting that covered the deck. It was very quiet beneath the trees. Even the roar of the jets and the clatter of gunfire from above seemed somehow muted. The trees rose from their pots like the pillars of a cathedral, their branches forming archways and overhead vaults.

Ahead, through the low-hanging ivies and lianas, she saw Lila crouched beside a particularly large pot, her back resting against the curved ceramic, her gun at the ready. Beyond, the vegetation thinned out, and she caught a glimpse of an open area, with grey sky beyond it. Lila waved at her to get down.

"There's somebody out there," she hissed.

"Where?" Victoria craned her head for a look. She saw an iron patio table and accompanying chairs, one of which was occupied by a slumped, skinny figure in jeans, with arms hanging loose, and short, carrot-coloured hair.

Oh, *merde*.

"K8?" Victoria ran forward. "K8, what happened? Where's the Leader?"

The girl looked up at her and raised a trembling arm. Tea dripped from a spilled cup. A saucer lay in pieces on the floor.

"Over," she whispered. "They went over."

Victoria walked to the edge of the veranda. The entire nose cone of the airship had been glazed, like the cockpit of some art deco spaceship from a pulp magazine. A section of the bamboo rail had been broken. She stood at the edge and craned forward. Below, she could see the rooftops of central London, and, stretching back beneath the veranda, an unglazed area of shadow and machinery.

"Any sign?" Paul asked, wheeling up beside her.

Victoria shook her head.

"That has to be a fifty foot drop." If Ack-Ack and the Leader had fallen from here, they hadn't hit the glass, which meant they must be somewhere amongst the machinery. Victoria got down onto her hands and knees, and leant over as far as she dared. Far below, wires and cables covered the floor of the chamber. Computer servers stood like islands. Strange, archaic-looking pistons moved up and down. Fans turned. Lights blinked. Coolant steamed.

An iron ladder had been bolted to the far end of the veranda.

"You could climb down," Paul suggested. "And make sure they're dead."

"Maybe in a minute." Against such a drop, the ladder looked fragile and spindly. And besides, there were more important things to worry about first. Victoria turned back to K8. She walked over and crouched in front of her. "Are you hurt?"

Sweat glittered on K8's forehead. She put a hand to the back of her skull, where her soul-catcher nestled beneath the skin.

"I'm plugged into the hive."

"Shit." Lila brought her pistol to bear. "So, they already know we're here."

K8 shook her head. "No. I'm blocking them. For now." Her voice was hoarse. Her fists were hard little balls in her lap, the knuckles as white as bone. "But I don't know how much longer I can keep it up."

Victoria waved Lila's gun away, and put a hand to K8's freckled cheek.

"We'll get you out of this," she said.

The girl shook her head again, flinching away from the physical contact.

"I don't think so, boss." She gave the brittle, self-conscious smile of a little girl trying to be brave. "The stuff he put in my head's getting stronger all the time. I don't know how much longer I can fight it."

A jet screamed past outside, and something exploded aft. They felt the deck quiver.

"We don't have a lot of time," Lila said. "If the monkey's dead, we need to find the control room, and stop them dumping the agent."

"Oh, I'm not dead."

The voice came from the edge of the veranda. Victoria turned in time to see a hand appear at the top of the ladder, followed by a hairy head. A white-suited monkey clambered awkwardly over the bamboo rail and dropped to the wooden deck. Beneath the suit, he wore a bandolier across his chest, and a holster on each hip.

Lila raised her gun.

"No!" K8 lunged forward in her chair. "Don't shoot him. Look at his eyes."

Victoria frowned. His eyes?

Then realisation hit her.

"Mon dieu!" She lowered her sword, and put a hand on Lila's gun, gently pushing it downwards.

"But—"

"His eye patch. It's on the left."

"So?"

"The Leader wears his on the right." She turned to the monkey. "Isn't that right, Ack-Ack?"

The macaque threw a floppy salute.

"Howdy, boss." He straightened his tie.

"Nice threads." Paul looked him up and down. "What happened to their owner?"

"I used him to break my fall."

"He's dead?"

"Very."

"So, it's over?" Lila asked hopefully.

Ack-Ack Macaque shrugged. "Not yet. The attack's still under way."

"How do we stop it?"

"Leave that to me."

Victoria slid her sword into its scabbard.

"What are you going to do?"

Ack-Ack Macaque jabbed a leathery thumb in K8's direction.

"Well," he said. "First off, she and I need to convince the fuckwits in white that I'm their chief."

"No, YOU CAN'T do that." Victoria was horrified. "I won't let you."

They had been arguing for several minutes.

"It's the only way," Ack-Ack Macaque assured her. "K8 can broadcast to the entire hive."

"But it'll destroy her."

He reached into a silk-lined jacket pocket and pulled out a rather battered-looking cigar.

"We don't have a choice. You understand that, don't you, K8?"

"Yes, Skip."

The girl's hair was wet at the temples. Her face had become pale and drawn.

"No." Victoria made a cutting motion with her hand. "She's only seventeen, for God's sake. You can't ask her to do this."

Ack-Ack Macaque lit up, and huffed the cigar into life. He took a heavy draw, and blew smoke at the butterflies flittering above his head.

"I don't like it any better than you do. But she hasn't got much choice. The way I see it, that muck in her head's winning. It's going to take her sooner or later, whatever we do. At least this way, she gets to save the world first."

Paul scratched his beard thoughtfully.

"But if she opens herself to the hive," he said, "won't they be able to read her thoughts? Won't they know it's a trick?"

Ack-Ack Macaque curled his lip in irritation. He rolled the fat cigar between his fingers and thumb.

"Okay." He stood over K8. "Can you do anything about that? Send sound and vision only, without the commentary?"

"I can try."

"Good girl."

He went to stand by the veranda's rail, with the darkening November sky at his back. Somewhere far beyond the clouds, the sun had already set. Fuming, Victoria took Lila and Paul to watch from the treeline. K8 sat facing him.

"Ready?" he asked her.

"Yes, Skip." There were tears in her eyes. He straightened his collar and smoothed back the hair on his cheeks and scalp. He had to look convincing to the Gestalt even if, inside, all he wanted was to murder every single last one of the motherfuckers.

How dare they put him in this position.

He bit back the rage, and dropped the half-smoked cigar over the rail.

"Right then, sweetheart," he said gruffly. "Ready when you are."

K8 swallowed.

"Goodbye, Skip."

"Don't say that."

She sniffed.

"What should I say, then?"

For the first time, Ack-Ack Macaque felt a hot lump rise in the back of his throat.

"Be seeing you, kid."

They held each other's gaze for a long moment. They both knew this was it. Then, wiping her cheeks, K8 sat up straight. She closed her eyes. Her posture became stiffer and more formal, and the tension bled from her features. Her lips curled up in the same dreamy, vacant smile that he'd wanted to wipe from Reynold's face.

By the time she reopened her eyes, she looked like a different girl.

The K8 he'd known was almost gone, and he didn't have a lot of time.

Ack-Ack Macaque cleared his throat.

"LADIES AND GENTLEMEN of the Gestalt," he began. "Esteemed colleagues. It is I, your Leader, standing here on my flagship, over London. Apologies for not contacting you directly," he tapped the side of his head, "but my connection has been damaged."

Were they getting this? Did he sound convincing? The Leader had been a wordy bastard with a gob full of corporate waffle. Could he match that?

"I have something important to, um, tell you. And you'd better listen because otherwise I'll... I mean... Look, attacking this world was a mistake." He punched the fist of one hand into the palm of the other. "And the reason I'm speaking to you now is that I require you to stop it. Stop everything. Immediately. Like, *right now*, okay?"

Over by the trees, Paul winced. Victoria shook her head. He was fucking this up, and they knew it. Flustered, he opened his mouth to speak again but, before he could, K8 moaned. Her eyes rolled up in her head, and she fell back, her body as limp as a tossed banana skin.

"Christ!" All pretence forgotten, he hopped forward and took her hand. Her skin felt cold. Before he could do anything else, Victoria marched up and shouldered him aside.

"Get out of the way," she said. She picked K8 from the chair and laid her on the deck, then checked her pulse and breathing.

"Is she going to be okay?" Ack-Ack Macaque asked.

"I don't know." Victoria didn't look up. "I don't even know what's wrong with her. But she's breathing for now, no thanks to you."

"Hey, I—"

Paul's image stepped between them.

"Listen," he said. "The guns have stopped."

Interrupted in mid-protestation, Ack-Ack Macaque cocked his head. All he could hear was the distant rumble of jets. The constant firing from above had ceased.

"Holy shit," he muttered. "They believed me? That speech worked?"

Paul coughed. He ran his tongue around his lips.

"No," he said regretfully. "No, I don't think they did."

Ack-Ack Macaque fixed him with a one-eyed stare.

"What makes you say that?"

Paul swallowed, and raised an arm to point into the trees at the back of the veranda.

"She does."

Another macaque stood in the gloom of the potted forest, squinting at them through a monocle. Two armed Neanderthal bodyguards flanked her. She wore a white business suit with matching gloves and pearls, and carried a furled white umbrella with an ivory handle.

Ack-Ack Macaque curled his lip at her.

"Who the hell are you supposed to be?"

The female removed the monocle from her right eye and smiled, revealing sharp, pointed teeth.

"Me, darling?" She licked her left canine. "Why, I'm the power behind the throne. And I'm here to make you—" she raised her chin, "—an offer."

Ack-Ack Macaque narrowed his eye.

"What kind of offer?"

"A job offer."

"Whoa, lady." He held up his hands. "I think you've got the wrong monkey."

"Please." Her tone was scornful. She blew dust from her monocle, and screwed it back into her eye. "You've just killed my protégé, the least you can do is hear me out." Without taking her eyes from Ack-Ack Macaque, she leant her head towards the Neanderthal on her right, and whispered, "And if any of the humans move, kill them."

Both bodyguards raised their weapons: heavy automatic rifles with long, curved magazines, each capable of hosing all life from the veranda in a couple of sustained bursts.

"Yes, Founder."

# CHAPTER THIRTY-SEVEN
## CORONA OF IRIS

SHE TOOK THEM back to the wrought iron table, and bade them sit.

"You may call me Founder." She walked slowly around the table. As she passed behind each of them, she paused to sniff their hair. "I am the true leader of the Gestalt. The monkey you just killed, the one who liked to call himself the 'Leader', worked for me." Having completed a circuit of the table, she stopped walking and stood between her bodyguards. "I come from a timeline significantly more advanced that this one, and I am significantly older than I look." Resting both hands on the umbrella's pommel, she glared at them through her monocle. "So, I'd appreciate it if you showed me some respect. When I was born, Queen Victoria sat on England's throne."

Paul's image crouched between Ack-Ack Macaque and Lila. He pushed his glasses more firmly onto the bridge of his nose and stammered, "But, but, but that would make you two hundred years old!"

"Two hundred and four, actually."

"How could you still be alive?"

"Technology, dear boy." The Founder straightened up. "I have tiny engines in my blood, which constantly monitor and repair and renew. With their help, I might live to be a thousand years old."

Ack-Ack Macaque stirred uncomfortably.

"Bullshit," he muttered.

The Founder gave a sigh.

"Do you remember my husband's machines, the microscopic ones that turn normal humans into fresh recruits for the Gestalt? The ones you came here to stop? Didn't you ever wonder why they were so much more *advanced* than the rest of his technology? I mean, *airships*?" She rolled her eyes. "Give me a hypersonic scramjet any day."

Victoria Valois had been watching and listening quietly. Now she sat forward, her hands on the table.

"You gave them to him?"

"Precisely." The Founder tapped the tip of her umbrella against the deck. "When I recruited him, he was little more than an escapee from a laboratory." She smiled nostalgically. "I showed him how to move between worlds, and gave him the technology to build an army."

"But why?"

The monkey laughed.

"My dear woman, why ever not?" She swept the umbrella around in a gesture that encompassed all the possible worlds of creation. "You humans are far too irresponsible and squabblesome to be allowed free rein."

"And so you turn us into zombies?" Lila asked indignantly.

The Founder's brow furrowed.

"Think of it as harnessing your potential, child, and turning it to less destructive ends. Sometimes being a grownup means being prepared to take responsibility for yourself, your friends and, if necessary, your entire world."

High above, the grey clouds finally delivered on their promise. Rain beat against the glass panels of the airship's nose. A few drops fell through the holes made by Ack-Ack Macaque's Spitfire, and pattered down onto the uppermost leaves of the trees, dripping from there onto the deck's wooden planks. On the ground below the warship, London lay battered and smoking. Lights flashed as emergency vehicles tried to push through roads choked with abandoned cars. People were cowering in offices and Underground stations, dreading the next bombardment.

Ack-Ack Macaque tapped his fingers on the iron table. He wanted to smoke, but didn't want to risk reaching into his inside pocket for a cigar. He didn't want the Neanderthals to think he was going for a concealed weapon.

"You mentioned a job offer?"

The Founder turned to him.

"Indeed."

"Let me guess." He pushed back in his chair. The metal legs scraped on the timbers. "You want me to join your merry band?"

"Would that be so awful?" She stepped up to him, so that the toes of her shoes almost touched the heels of his outstretched feet. "I know you must have been lonely. Macaques like us, we're not solitary creatures. We need the company of our own kind. We need a place to belong. We need the comfort and security of a troupe."

Ack-Ack Macaque pulled his feet away from her.

He snarled, but he knew she was right. He could feel it as an ache in his chest. And yet—

"You've been alone so long," she said. "But all that's past now."

He could smell her. Somewhere beneath the cotton and pearls, beneath the aromas of shampoo and perfume, lay the scent of a female macaque. The first female of his kind he'd ever met, and maybe the only one he ever would.

His nostrils twitched. Something stirred inside him, and he closed his eye, feeling dizzy.

He could go with her. It would be easy enough to do. He felt the soft fabric of the borrowed suit and tie, and visualised himself at the head of a Zeppelin fleet, with her at his side. He imagined holding her in his arms, and pictured the two of them in heat, mating in a frenzied mutual lust...

"No." The word rolled like molasses from his tongue, and he opened his eye to banish the images playing in his head. "No, you're wrong." He looked around the table, at Victoria and Paul, and K8's unconscious form lying on the deck. They were his friends, his comrades. His family.

"I already have a troupe," he said, and snorted to clear the stink of her from his nostrils. His hands itched, painfully aware of the revolvers in the holsters at his hips.

She gave him a haughty look.

"I could make you a king."

Moving very slowly, he opened his jacket and pulled a cigar and lighter from the silk-lined pocket. He'd made his decision and chosen his side. Now, all he had to do was get her fragrance out of his head, and the only way to do that was to smother everything in a tobacco fug. His hands felt shaky as he bit the end from the cigar and spat it onto the floor.

"Sorry, sweetheart." He paused to light the end of the cigar, and then spoke through clouds of pungent blue smoke. "But I don't want your machines in my head."

The smoke spread warmth in his chest, and he felt his head go deliciously light. *Ah,* he thought, *that's the stuff.*

Looking distinctly unimpressed, the Founder pursed her lips. She reached up and adjusted her monocle.

"Better a few machines in your head than a bullet?"

Their eyes locked.

"That's the deal, huh?"

"I'm afraid so. And if you've got any notions of somehow saving this world, you can forget them right now. The fleet's already begun to dump its cargo. Within hours, the planet will be ours."

Ack-Ack Macaque looked at his friends.

"And what about them?"

"They will join the Gestalt." She peered around at them. "We will be enriched by their bravery."

Ack-Ack Macaque shook his head. He'd already lost K8 to the hive, he'd be damned if he'd let them take Victoria as well.

He looked across at his boss, and noticed her eyes. The pupils had dilated into wide, black pits. Only a thin corona of iris remained and he realised that, while he'd been talking, she'd taken the opportunity to slip into command mode and overclock her system. Her mind must be racing and her heart pounding, ready to fight or flee. All she needed was an opening.

Their eyes met, and an understanding passed between them.

"And as for you," the Founder was saying, oblivious to this byplay, "either you come willingly, or you'll be assimilated right along with them. The process works equally well on monkeys as it does on people."

Ack-Ack Macaque drew himself up in his chair. He sucked in a mouthful of smoke and blew it in her direction.

"Sorry love, but that's not going to happen."

The Founder's gloved hand tried to flap away the cigar fumes.

"And that's your final answer, is it?"

"Not quite." Under his chair, Ack-Ack Macaque pressed his bare feet to the smooth wooden deck, ready to spring. "There's just one more thing."

The female monkey's eyes became suspicious slits.

"And what might that be?"

"Just this." He screamed, and leapt. At the same time, Victoria surged to her feet, sending the heavy iron table flying towards one of the bodyguards.

The machine guns fired.

# CHAPTER THIRTY-EIGHT
## WRECKAGE

CRAWLING ON ALL fours, William Cole worked his way through the shattered remains of the *Tereshkova*'s main gondola. As he moved, he tried to ignore the sounds of battle coming from outside, and the ominous groans and creaks of the superstructure above his head. All he could think of was Marie. Nothing else mattered to him, except to see her safe. He crawled across the carpeted expanse of the main passenger lounge, through piles of broken furniture and shattered fittings, onto the hard steel deck of the corridor that led aft to the infirmary.

"Marie!" he called. "Hold on, I'm coming."

In places, the corridor's ceiling had hinged down to within inches of the floor, and he had to squirm and wriggle his way through sharp-edged gaps that were too small for him. By the time he reached the infirmary, the skin on his arms, shoulders and hips had been scraped raw, and his knees were bruised and battered.

"William?" Her voice sounded weak.

"I'm here," he cried, "I'm here."

Part of a medical trolley had wedged itself in the doorway, and he had to squeeze around it. When he got inside, he saw his worst fears realised. The ceiling had collapsed in the same way as in the rest of the gondola, leaving only a few feet of clearance. Marie, who had been lying on the bed at the time of the crash, now lay pinned to the mattress.

"Marie!"

"William."

Her head was turned towards him, held against the pillow by the steel ceiling panel pressing down from above on her cheek and chest. The foot of the bed was a tangle of wreckage, and he couldn't see her legs.

"Oh, crap. Marie." He knelt beside the bed and reached in to touch her face. "Don't worry, honey. Don't try to move. I'll get you out."

Bracing his back against the fallen ceiling, he tried to heave upwards, pushing until sweat broke out on his forehead and his temples felt ready to burst.

"No." Her voice was a whisper, but it stopped him.

"What do you mean?"

Marie licked her lips.

"No, you're not getting me out."

William felt panic surge up inside.

"But, I—"

"No." Marie swallowed. "It's too late. I'm sorry."

William stopped pressing against the ceiling and dropped to his knees. He reached for her, and brushed a curl of auburn hair away from her eyes.

"I'm not leaving you."

"I'm afraid you'll have to, my love."

He ran his hand back along the bed, past her shoulders and down, following the curve of her body beneath the blanket. He got as far as her hip before he found something blocking the way. His fingers hit metal where there should have been flesh. A girder had broken through from above, driving the ceiling down into the mattress. Her abdomen and legs were crushed. Her torso stopped in a mess of torn blankets, slathered in something warm and sticky.

Fighting back a cry of anguish, he jerked back his hand and, without looking at the blood on his fingers, wiped it on the sheet.

"No," he said. There had to have been some sort of mistake...

Marie closed her eyes.

"I'm sorry," she said again.

William wanted to cry. He wanted to curl into a ball and block his ears, and make it all go away.

"It's not fair," he said.

Marie looked at him with liquid eyes.

"You haven't lost me," she whispered. "I'm still out there somewhere, on another parallel close to this one."

"I'm not leaving you. Not like this." William's mind raced. There had to be some way to save her, some way he could get her out.

Overhead, the wreck quivered. Something in the corridor collapsed with a metallic crash.

"You have to go now. Lila needs you."

William blinked.

"Lila?"

"I'm going to need you to look after her now."

"I can't." Misery threatened to envelop him. "I can barely look after myself."

"Of course you can. Look at you. You risked your life crawling in here. I need you to be just as strong for her."

"But I don't know anything about being a father."

"You know enough." She winced in pain, and tried to adjust her position beneath the weight pressing down on her. "Besides, you're all she's got. I need you to be strong for her, William. Can you promise me that?"

"I don't want to leave you."

"Promise me."

He reached out and touched her cheek. Her skin felt clammy. Her bright eyes implored him.

"Okay," he said. "Okay, I promise."

Marie let her eyes fall shut.

"Then go find her. Go now."

"But what about you?"

Marie kept her eyes closed. Above her, the ceiling pinged and popped as it struggled to support the weight of the collapsing structure above it.

"We both know what's going to happen to me, and it's not going to be pretty. I don't want you here when it happens. You have to get out." She opened her eyes and fixed him with a brittle stare. "You have to get out. You're all she's got."

William looked down at the gun in his hands. He pictured his daughter's face, and his fingers squeezed the grip. Marie was right. It didn't matter how many white suits were outside waiting for him; he knew what he had to do. Lila was out there somewhere, and he had to protect her.

He was her father.

He touched his wife's face for the final time.

"Don't worry," he said. "I'll find her."

Marie smiled.

"Thank you, my love."

# CHAPTER THIRTY-NINE
## PROTECT THE TROUPE

TEETH BARED AND fingers grasping, Ack-Ack Macaque lunged towards the Founder, only to find that she'd anticipated his attack. As they came together, she grasped the lapels of his jacket and fell back. She rolled away from him, using his momentum to throw him over her head, onto the deck. He landed on his back with a smack that drove most of the wind from his body.

As he lay gasping, the Founder sprang to her feet and fled into the jungle.

He heard gunshots and shouting, and his hands went to the holsters at his sides. One of the Neanderthals was down, toes crushed by the edge of the iron table. Victoria had been upon him before he could fight through the pain and bring his gun to bear. Unfortunately, she hadn't been quite fast enough. The second bodyguard had seen her move and fired. He was too late to save his colleague—in fact, he'd caught the other caveman with a couple of stray shots—but he'd managed to hit her as well, and now she lay on her side a few feet from her victim, in a spreading pool of blood.

Ack-Ack Macaque struggled to his feet, wheezing for breath. Wide-eyed, the surviving Neanderthal swung the machine gun at him. For half a second, Ack-Ack Macaque stared into the black eye of its muzzle.

Then a shot rang out.

Ack-Ack Macaque winced, but it was the Neanderthal who fell.

Still seated in her chair, Lila held a smoking pistol in her lap.

"Go," she said.

Ack-Ack Macaque hesitated, looking at Victoria. The former journalist moaned, and tried feebly to move. Her feet scraped the deck as if trying to gain purchase. Clearly distressed, Paul's hologram image bent over her, calling her name.

"Go on," Lila said. "We'll take care of her."

Ack-Ack Macaque lingered for another moment. He looked from Victoria to where K8 lay, on the other side of the veranda. His two best friends were both down, and both fighting for their lives. He holstered his guns, dropped onto all fours and, with a snarl of fury, plunged headlong into the trees.

THE FOUNDER COULD run, but she couldn't hide her scent. It itched in his nose, maddening him as he pursued it through the potted forest and out, through the brass door, into the corridor beyond.

Half a dozen white-suited men and women marched towards him. He rose to his feet and drew his guns. Without breaking stride, he shot the first two, and ducked into the alcove housing the companionway that led upwards to the roof. Ahead, on the curving staircase, he could hear the tap, tap, tap of the Founder's shoes.

He went up two steps at a time, hauling himself along with one hand on the banister. Having stepped over their fallen comrades, the remaining Gestalt followed him, but couldn't keep up. By the time he got to the top, they were far behind. His chest burned with the effort, but he knew he was only moments behind her.

The remains of the *Tereshkova* loomed over him in the rain. The hull looked broken and sad, like a partially collapsed party balloon, and the gondolas had been smashed almost flat. An engine nacelle stuck out like a broken limb, water dripping from its bent and broken blades.

The Founder stood in front the wreck, brandishing her umbrella. As he emerged from the stairwell, she tugged, and the handle came away from the rest of the brolly, revealing a wicked-looking steel blade. She dropped the canopy, and took up a fencing stance. The wind blew her skirt and flapped her jacket.

"Get back," she said.

Ack-Ack Macaque still held one of the Leader's pistols in his hands. It wasn't one of his trusted Colts, but it would do.

Overhead, Commonwealth fighter jets rumbled in the overcast.

"Stop it," he said.

She glared at him, and swiped the umbrella handle sword.

"Stop what, sweetie?"

"Stop the plague. The machines. Whatever the fuck they are."

"Why should I?"

He waggled the gun.

"Because if you don't, I'll shoot you."

She brought the sword up, and held it over her head, with the tip pointing at him. She looked like a scorpion, ready to strike.

"Then you'll just have to shoot, my dear."

She started to back away, one step at a time. With a curse he took a pace forward. Her arm whipped down, and the sword flew out like a thrown knife. It caught him in the left thigh. With a howl, he fell to the deck and the pistol fell away. Before he could reach for it, she was there before him, grasping the handle of the sword. He screeched again as she pulled it out of his leg. He used both hands to try to cover the wound and staunch the spurt of blood.

"Shit," he wailed. The airship's armour plates were wet beneath him. Rain fell against his face. "Shit, that hurts."

Above him, the Founder laughed.

"Face it, flyboy, you've lost."

Still gripping his leg, he snarled at her with such vehemence that her monocle fell out. She stepped back, out of reach, waving the sword's slick point at him.

"There's nothing you can do," she crowed. The rain stuck her hair to her face and scalp. "This world's mine now. Or soon will be. And when it is, I'll simply move on to another world, and find another monkey somewhere else. One with more vision." She shook her head, spraying drops in all directions. "And hope he's a darned sight more cooperative than you."

Ack-Ack Macaque thought of his fallen friends, and felt rage boil up inside, blotting out the pain.

"Yeah, well. I ain't finished yet, lady."

Teeth clenched, he clambered to his feet. He could feel blood running down his leg, soaking into his white trousers, mixing with the rain. He ignored it. Every instinct in his body told him to protect his troupe, wreak bloody vengeance against this interloper, and drive her from his territory.

"Oh, please." The Founder raised her sword. "Don't you ever give up?"

Ack-Ack Macaque shrugged. He gave her a defiant grin.

"Let's find out."

He took a step towards her, clawed hands stretching for her throat. At the same time, she pulled her arm back, ready to run him through with the blade. He knew he couldn't win, but figured that, even if she skewered him, he could still probably choke her to death before he died.

For an instant, their eyes locked. They stood poised, ready to strike.

And then the bomb on the *Tereshkova* exploded.


BOWLED OVER BY the blast, they tumbled together, rolling off the armoured section of the hull and onto the sloping glass of the airship's nose. Faster and faster they slid. Behind them, the remnants of the *Tereshkova* burned. Ahead lay the point of the bow, with nothing beyond it save sky and death. In a panic, they scrabbled at each other, still fighting. Leathery hands squeaked against toughened glass, trying in vain to slow their descent.

And then they were there.

The edge rushed at them, and they felt themselves going over. In desperation, Ack-Ack Macaque flung out his hand and caught something. At the same time, the Founder grabbed his foot. They jerked to a halt, their combined weight almost enough to tear his fingers from their precarious hold, and his shoulder from its socket.

Swearing at the agony in his arm, he looked up. A communications antennae stuck out from the glass point of the airship's bow, and it was from this that they now hung, swaying, a couple of thousand feet above the muddy waters of the Thames. The Founder's skirt flapped in the wind. A patch of it was on fire. Her feet pawed at emptiness.

"Please," she said. "Please, don't drop me."

Wincing with pain and effort, Ack-Ack Macaque reached up with his other arm and caught hold of the mast.

"Stop thrashing about then," he said with a grunt, "or we're both going to fall."

Beneath them in the gathering darkness, the wind chopped the surface of the river into little waves. Rain fell on the burning wreckage of the Commonwealth Parliament.

Heaving upwards, he managed to hook an elbow over the metal pole that formed the mast.

He could kick her off. She'd hurt his friends, attacked his world, and unleashed all kinds of hell. And now he had her at his mercy. She clung to his ankle with only one hand. All it would take to kill her would be a simple jerk of his leg.

She deserved it, and yet, he couldn't bring himself to do it. Twice he tensed, ready to shake her off—but each time, he relented.

He swore under his breath.

Try as he might, he just couldn't kill her in cold blood. She was the only intelligent female monkey he'd ever met; and the only one who could call off the invasion.

He looked down at her and their eyes met.

"Okay," he said.

The Founder started to climb. Her hands worked their way up his legs, tearing cloth and stretching skin. She touched the wound in his thigh and he growled.

"Wait, for fuck's sake."

She stopped moving, eyes wide, and monocle long gone.

"What?"

"I'll let you up on one condition. Contact the hive. Tell them that I'm the new Leader."

She grimaced.

"No."

"Listen, lady, I've got nothing to lose, okay? I don't want to live in a world of drones. So do it, and do it now, or I'll let go of this pole, and drop us both. Do you understand?"

She looked him in the eye again, but it wasn't a challenge. Their faces were almost touching, and he could smell her breath.

"I'd rather die."

"Yeah?" He showed her his teeth, and took one of his hands from the mast. "I can arrange that."

He now held the weight of both of them on one arm.

"All I have to do is let go," he said. He could already feel his fingers slipping.

"You wouldn't."

"Try me."

For a long, agonising moment, they remained frozen, locked together high over the river. A squall of rain hit them, drenching them further. Ack-Ack Macaque's arms felt as if they were being dragged from their sockets.

"No."

"Fine."

He let go.

For half a second, they were falling. The Founder screamed. And they jerked to a halt.

Ack-Ack Macaque had his tail wrapped around the mast.

Swinging from it, he put a hand to her forehead, ready to push her away. "Last chance, lady."

Hair wet and bedraggled, dress torn, the Founder looked up at him. Her eyes blazed. Then she dropped her chin and sighed.

"All right," she said. "I'll do it."

"And tell them to stop spreading that fucking plague."

The Founder closed her eyes and hugged him tight.

"Okay," she said.

The wind battered them, and he saw smouldering fragments of the *Tereshkova* blowing down towards the distant, darkened roofs of the city.

After what seemed like an eternity, she reopened her eyes.

"All done."

"No tricks?"

She shook her head. The fight had gone out of her. She'd stopped struggling, and now just hung there, holding on to him as the weather howled around them in the night.

"All activity ceased." She spoke so quietly he could barely hear her. "They await your orders."

He looked up. The Gestalt drones on top of the airship had lowered their guns. They stood in the rain and wind, staring impassively ahead.

"And you?"

She looked down at the city beneath her shoes. Her hands were slippery and red with blood from his thigh.

"Please," she whispered, "just get me out of here."

Above, William Cole shouldered his way between the passive drones. He held a gun in one hand, and a coil of rope in the other.

"Here," he called. "Catch this."

# CHAPTER FORTY
## AN INFINITE NUMBER OF MONKEYS

THE RAIN STOPPED during the night. As the sun rose, Ack-Ack Macaque sat on the wooden veranda with his legs dangling over the edge. His leg had been cleaned and dressed by a Gestalt nurse, and he'd been given a fresh white suit, over which he'd squeezed the remains of his leather flying jacket. Now, he was smoking the last of his cigars.

Below, in the streets of London, he could see the blue lights of emergency vehicles and the dull khaki of troop lorries and armoured cars. This morning, the city looked like a disturbed ants nest. Fires still burned in parts of Whitehall. News choppers wheeled around like flies. Columns of refugees were heading outwards, choking the arterial roads, desperate to escape the destruction and contagion of the inner city.

Behind him, he heard the big brass door open, and the whine of a small electric motor approaching through the trees. Paul's car zipped up beside him, the lenses of its camera and projectors bristling.

"Hey Ack-ster, how are you doing?" The dead man's image shimmered into apparent solidity beside him. This morning, Paul had opted for a dark suit and sombre tie.

"Just smoking." He looked down at the tangle of wires and servers beneath the balcony. If he was right, they formed an important node in the Gestalt's wireless network: a router to bounce their thoughts from mind to mind. If he turned it off, he might be able to free some of them. Or possibly kill them. With K8's neck on the line, he wasn't about to try messing around until he was damn sure how the machinery worked.

"Did the 'Founder' give you any trouble?" he asked.

Paul's image lowered itself until it appeared to be sitting next to him.

"A little," he said. "But there's a brig in the stern that's shielded against transmissions. Once we got her in there, and she realised she couldn't talk to the rest of the hive, she quietened down."

"She's an interesting woman."

"If you say so."

Ack-Ack Macaque cleared his throat. His cheeks felt hot. He decided to change the subject.

"How's the boss?"

"She's fine." Paul scratched his bristled chin. "Or, at least, she's going to be fine. In fact, Lila's bringing her up here now."

"They sent you on ahead, did they?"

Paul gave a guilty smile.

"They thought it prudent to see what sort of mood you were in."

Ack-Ack Macaque stretched. He felt like he'd been pulled through a jet engine's air intake, and then spat out the back. Every muscle ached and there was hardly a patch of skin without some sort of scratch or bruise. But the painkillers he'd been given by the

Gestalt were remarkably effective, and he actually felt kind of good, despite everything.

"I'm okay," he said, kicking his feet. "Why shouldn't I be? After all, we saved the world."

"Again."

He looked down at the roofs below. "How are things down there?"

Paul's face grew serious.

"Reports coming out of San Francisco aren't good. The city took a pasting, and the airship above it managed to release its entire cargo before it received the abort command. Also, Madrid and Singapore report heavy casualties. Some places have been using flamethrowers and napalm to destroy areas suspected of infestation, and infected people are being herded into hospitals and quarantine camps."

"So, it's all a bit of a mess?"

"That's putting it mildly."

"But the nano-whatsits have been stopped?"

"Mostly, yes."

"Then I call that a win." He took a deep drag on the cigar, and blew smoke from his nose.

The brass door opened again, and Lila appeared through the trees, pushing Victoria in a wheelchair. Victoria had her left arm in a sling, and bandages across her ribs and stomach. Behind them, William Cole walked with his back straight and shoulders thrown back.

Ack-Ack Macaque stood to meet them.

"Hi, boss."

Victoria didn't return his salute.

"I'm not your boss anymore, monkey man. I'm not even a captain. I lost my ship."

Ack-Ack Macaque huffed. The *Tereshkova* had been the only real home either of them had known.

"Yeah," he said, "that was a shame. She was a real lady, and I'll miss her."

"How's K8?"

He shrugged. "They tell me she's part of the hive now."

"But she's alive?"

"Oh yes." He couldn't help a rueful smile. "And kicking up hell in there, from what I can gather."

They looked at each other for a moment: two old soldiers comparing losses. Then William Cole stepped forward to put a protective arm around his daughter's shoulders.

"So," he said, "what happens now?"

Ack-Ack Macaque gave him a wary squint.

"How do you mean?"

The writer smoothed his unruly hair with his free hand. He had his own share of scrapes and grazes, but they didn't seem to bother him. "I mean, where are you going to go?" he said. "What are you going to do?"

Ack-Ack Macaque rubbed his leather eye patch. The empty socket beneath itched.

"If there's any way to pull K8 out of the hive, I'll find it."

"And beyond that?"

The monkey turned to look at the pall of smoke above London.

"Well, this place has gone all to shit." Cigar clamped in his teeth, he rubbed his hands together. "Perhaps it's time to move on?"

"Actually," Victoria said, "I spoke to Merovech.

He thinks the shock of this attack might be good for us. He thinks it'll bring the fractured politics of this world into a new unity, now that the nations know there are bigger threats out there."

Ack-Ack Macaque made a farting noise with his lips.

"Pffft. Let's see how long *that* lasts."

"You could help them," Lila said. "You're the leader of the Gestalt. You have an army. You can help them rebuild."

Ack-Ack Macaque shook his head.

"Sorry, sweetheart, not really my style."

"Then, what?" Cole asked.

Ack-Ack Macaque fingered his chin.

"I'll tell the Gestalt to surrender," he decided. "There are thousands of them, in all those airships. They can help clear up the mess they've made."

"And what about you?"

Ack-Ack Macaque turned to Paul.

"Hey, Paulie," he said. "Do you think you can fly this thing?"

Paul put a hand to the back of his neck and puffed out his cheeks.

"The ironclad? Sheesh, I don't know. I'd need to take a look at the computers they're using. But, in principle, I guess it's possible."

"Would you like to?"

Victoria raised an eyebrow.

"Are you suggesting we keep this ship?" she asked.

Ack-Ack Macaque showed his teeth.

"Why not? Fair's fair. They wrecked ours."

"But it's a battleship," she said. "It doesn't carry cargo or passengers. Where will we go? What will we do with it?"

He tapped the side of his nose.

"Last night, the Founder said something about moving on and finding another monkey. I reckon we do the same."

Paul gaped at him. "You mean, travel between worlds?"

"Fuck yeah." He threw a reckless smile. "There's not a whole lot to keep us here. And there must be other monkeys out there. Hundreds, maybe thousands of them."

Lila let go of the handles of Victoria's chair.

"All your alternate selves?"

"Yeah. We can find them, and tell them—" He licked his suddenly dry lips. "Tell them they don't have to be alone anymore." He glanced at Victoria. "What do you think?"

Victoria Valois ran a hand back over the smooth skin of her scalp, and shrugged.

"What the hell, I'm in."

"Excellent. Paul?"

The hologram looked at the lady in the wheelchair.

"I go where she goes."

"How about you, Cole? You've been writing about these parallel worlds all these years. Maybe you could help us navigate?"

"To Mendelblatt's world?" Cole frowned. "I don't know about that." He gave Lila a squeeze, and straightened his posture. "But there must be other Maries out there. If you need a couple of crew, then sure, I guess. We're with you."

"Okay, then. It's settled." Ack-Ack Macaque clasped his hands together. "Paul, go and see if you can hook yourself into the navigation software. The rest of you are welcome to stay here, or join me on the bridge."

Lila looked incredulous.

"You want to leave *right now*?"

Ack-Ack Macaque turned to her.

"Can you think of a better fucking time?"

Straightening his tie, he walked through the potted jungle, heading for the airship's command deck. For the past year, he'd been casting around, wondering what to do with his life. Now, he had a mission and a purpose... and an army. He'd moved from the game world to the real one—and now a million other worlds were out there, just waiting for him. His tiredness had gone, burned away like morning mist, and all he could see ahead were possibilities.

AND IF YOU want a picture of the future, try to imagine a hundred thousand talking monkeys, gathered from a hundred thousand worlds, their numbers ever-swelling, swarming across the worlds of men—forever.

# THE END

# ACK-ACKNOWLEDGEMENTS

As I SAID in a recent article on Tor.com, there's something strangely compelling about primates in human clothes. Crowds used to gather at London Zoo to watch the chimpanzees having a tea party. The PG Tips ads became instant classics. When creating Ack-Ack Macaque, I felt as if I'd tapped into some sort of archetype. I made him surly and rude, and unconscionably violent, and people responded. They seemed to connect with him on a primal level. I don't know what it is about him. He has his own Twitter account [@AckAckMacaque] and people love talking to him. Ladies flirt with him. Men tell jokes and post links to funny monkey pictures. He seems to have struck a chord—and I think it's because he represents a certain freedom that we, as supposedly civilised human beings, have lost. He can smoke and drink and blow shit up, and not care. The normal rules don't apply to him. He doesn't have to bite his lip or bide his time. He's a wild animal. Put him in clothes and he looks comical, but also dangerous. He's us, but not us. The Hyde to our Jekyll. Our inner child. And you lot can't seem to get enough of him.

This is the first novel-length sequel I've ever written, and I'd like to thank the team at Solaris for their hard work and support, especially Jonathan Oliver, Ben Smith, David Moore, and Michael Molcher. Also my family, for their unflagging belief and constant encouragement, especially my mother, who taught me to read and bought me my first typewriter. Jake Murray, for another excellent and inspiring cover illustration. My friend, Su Hadrell, and my sister, Rebecca Powell, for their invaluable feedback on the first draft. My agent, John Jarrold, for his support. And my wife, Becky, who gave the first draft a thorough line-by-line edit, and whose belief, love and support make all this possible.

Lastly, I'd also like to express my gratitude to everybody who bought, read, recommended or reviewed *Ack-Ack Macaque*, and say a big thank you to all his followers on Twitter and Facebook. Without your enthusiasm, this sequel might never have happened.

My thanks to you all.

US ISBN: 978-1-78108-060-3 • $8.99 // UK ISBN: 978-1-78108-059-7 • £7.99

ACK-ACK
MACAQUE

'Fizzes with wild ideas... A ripping yarn about murder,
mayhem and monkeys' *Philip Reeve, author of Mortal Engines*

**GARETH L. POWELL**

In 1944, as waves of German ninjas parachute into Kent, Britain's best hopes for victory
lie with a Spitfire pilot codenamed 'Ack-Ack Macaque.' The trouble is, Ack-Ack Macaque
is a cynical, one-eyed, cigar-chomping monkey, and he's starting to doubt everything,
including his own existence.

A century later, in a world where France and Great Britain merged in the late 1950s and
nuclear-powered Zeppelins circle the globe, ex-journalist Victoria Valois finds herself
drawn into a deadly game of cat and mouse with the man who butchered her husband
and stole her electronic soul. In Paris, after taking part in an illegal break-in at a research
laboratory, the heir to the British throne goes on the run. And all the while, the doomsday
clock ticks towards Armageddon...

 **WWW.SOLARISBOOKS.COM**

US ISBN: 978-1-907519-98-7 • $7.99 // UK ISBN: 978-1-907519-99-4 • £7.99

When his brother disappears into a bizarre gateway on a London Underground escalator, failed artist Ed Rico and his brother's wife Alice have to put aside their feelings for each other to go and find him. Their quest through the 'arches' will send them hurtling through time, to new and terrifying alien worlds.

Four hundred years in the future, Katherine Abdulov must travel to a remote planet in order to regain the trust of her influential family. The only person standing in her way is her former lover, Victor Luciano, the ruthless employee of a rival trading firm.

Hard choices lie ahead as lives and centuries clash and, in the unforgiving depths of space, an ancient evil stirs...

Gareth L. Powell's epic new science-fiction novel delivers a story of galaxy-spanning scope by a writer of astounding vision.

**WWW.SOLARISBOOKS.COM**

*Follow us on Twitter! www.twitter.com/solarisbooks*